*His Royal Highness,
King Easton Carradigne of Korosol,
requests your presence during his secret search
for a new heir to his throne.*

*Please join the King and his regal entourage
as they journey to the United States on the quest
to name a successor. First stop: the city of Manhattan,
where three American princesses are about to get
a surprise of royal proportions.*

Don't miss any of these exciting tales from

THE CARRADIGNES: AMERICAN ROYALTY

The Improperly Pregnant Princess
by Jacqueline Diamond
March 2002

The Unlawfully Wedded Princess
by Kara Lennox
April 2002

The Simply Scandalous Princess
by Michele Dunaway
May 2002

And don't miss the special Harlequin Intrigue tie-in:

The Duke's Covert Mission
by Julie Miller
June 2002

Dear Reader,

March roars in like a lion this month with Harlequin American Romance's four guaranteed-to-please reads.

We start with a bang by introducing you to a new in-line continuity series, THE CARRADIGNES: AMERICAN ROYALTY. The search for a royal heir leads to some scandalous surprises for three princesses, beginning with *The Improperly Pregnant Princess* by Jacqueline Diamond. CeCe Carradigne is set to become queen of a wealthy European country, until she winds up pregnant by her uncommonly handsome business rival. Talk about a shotgun wedding of royal proportions! Watch for more royals next month.

Karen Toller Whittenburgh's series, BILLION-DOLLAR BRADDOCKS, continues this month with *The Playboy's Office Romance* as middle brother Bryce Braddock meets his match in his feisty new employee. Also back this month is another installment of Charlotte Maclay's popular series, MEN OF STATION SIX. Things are heating up between a sexy firefighter and a very pregnant single lady from his past—don't miss the igniting passion in *With Courage and Commitment*. And rounding out the month is *A Question of Love* by Elizabeth Sinclair, a warm and wonderful reunion story.

Here's hoping you enjoy all that Harlequin American Romance has to offer you—this month, and all the months to come!

Best,

Melissa Jeglinski
Associate Senior Editor
Harlequin American Romance

THE IMPROPERLY PREGNANT PRINCESS

Jacqueline Diamond

TORONTO • NEW YORK • LONDON
AMSTERDAM • PARIS • SYDNEY • HAMBURG
STOCKHOLM • ATHENS • TOKYO • MILAN • MADRID
PRAGUE • WARSAW • BUDAPEST • AUCKLAND

Special thanks and acknowledgment are given
to Jacqueline Diamond for her contribution to
THE CARRADIGNES: AMERICAN ROYALTY series.

For Ari and Hunter
who are both princes in their mother's eyes.

ISBN 0-373-16913-2

THE IMPROPERLY PREGNANT PRINCESS

ABOUT THE AUTHOR

Jacqueline Diamond, who has published more than fifty novels, is a former Associated Press reporter. When she isn't taking care of her husband, two sons and two cats, she enjoys growing vegetables and flowers. A native of Texas, Jackie grew up in Nashville, Tennessee, and currently makes her home in Southern California. You can write to her at P.O. Box 1315, Brea, CA 92822.

Books by Jacqueline Diamond

HARLEQUIN AMERICAN ROMANCE

Don't miss any of our special offers. Write to us at the following address for information on our newest releases.

Harlequin Reader Service
U.S.: 3010 Walden Ave., P.O. Box 1325, Buffalo, NY 14269
Canadian: P.O. Box 609, Fort Erie, Ont. L2A 5X3

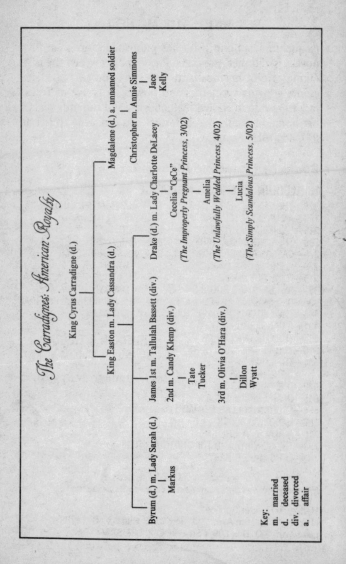

The Carradignes: American Royalty

King Cyrus Carradigne (d.)

King Easton m. Lady Cassandra (d.)

- **Byrum (d.) m. Lady Sarah (d.)**
  - Markus

- **James 1st m. Tallulah Bassett (div.)**
  - Tate
  - Tucker
  - 2nd m. Candy Klemp (div.)
  - 3rd m. Olivia O'Hara (div.)
    - Dillon
    - Wyatt

- **Drake (d.) m. Lady Charlotte DeLacey**
  - Cecelia "CeCe"
    (The Improperly Pregnant Princess, 3/02)
  - Amelia
    (The Unlawfully Wedded Princess, 4/02)
  - Lucia
    (The Simply Scandalous Princess, 5/02)

- **Magdalene (d.) a. unnamed soldier**
  - Christopher m. Annie Simmons
    - Jace
    - Kelly

Key:
m.   married
d.   deceased
div.   divorced
a.   affair

Prologue

King Easton Carradigne clicked off the phone with a sense of relief. He had just set in motion events that should secure the future of the tiny kingdom of Korosol.

He gazed fondly around the high-ceilinged, tapestry-hung office on the second floor of his palace. Perhaps his successor, after she was crowned, would allow him to occupy this room a little longer...but no. When he handed over the reins of power, he must do so completely.

Feeling restless, the seventy-eight-year-old monarch sprang to his feet and strode to the high, multipaned window. From here, his gaze swept the beloved scene he was about to hand over to a virtual stranger.

Although it was evening, the king could fully appreciate the sweep and splendor of the landscaped grounds, having long ago memorized every inch of the gardens and ponds. Even in February, they were free of snow because of the mild, Mediterranean climate.

To his right, the royal-blue-and-silver flag of his homeland flapped as a groundsman lowered it for the night. A semitame deer raised its head at the sound. Seeing nothing to fear, it resumed grazing.

There was nowhere else in the world quite like Korosol, Easton thought. Tourists flocked to this refuge, which sloped from the mountains to the sea between France and

Spain. They prized the beaches and mountain hot springs, the good weather and the rare wines.

He knew that his people credited him with much of Korosol's affluence and stability. Easton, who had performed his duty for over fifty years to his hundred thousand subjects out of love, only hoped his successor would do as well.

Until last year, the obvious heir had been his eldest son, Byrum. Then, while on safari in Africa, Byrum and his wife, Sarah, had died when their Jeep exploded.

Although by tradition Easton's choice should have fallen to their son, Markus, terrible rumors had reached him. A few of his grandson's acquaintances believed Markus was somehow involved in the death of his parents. Even if they were mistaken, Markus's drinking and dark moods made him unsuited to ruling.

Grieving for Byrum, Easton had let the matter slide until this month, when his intermittent weak spells had intensified to the point that they alarmed his physician. The doctor had sent him to Paris for secret medical tests.

The verdict: Easton suffered from a rare blood disease of unknown origin. The doctors said he would grow frailer over the coming months and had at most a year to live.

The need to choose an heir became urgent. While it was true that, in its eight-hundred-year history, Korosol had rarely been ruled by anyone not in a direct line of father-to-eldest-surviving-child descent, the law allowed the king to name his own successor.

That was what he planned to do.

A discreet knock at the door heralded the entrance of General Harrison Montcalm, Easton's royal adviser. A thoughtful man with erect military bearing, Sir Harrison stood six feet tall, the same height as the monarch.

At age forty-five, however, the retired general was considerably more muscular. A good man to lean on in a crisis, in more ways than one, the king reflected.

"Is everything set, Your Majesty?" asked his adviser.

"The royal jet can leave first thing in the morning, as we discussed," Easton said. "My daughter-in-law was most receptive to my plans, although I suppose she'd have been happier with more than a day's notice."

"You *are* springing quite a surprise on her," Sir Harrison said.

"She doesn't know the half of it yet." Easton smiled, picturing stylish Charlotte DeLacey Carradigne. He hadn't seen her in—how many years? Twenty? Amazing.

The last time they'd met had been after his youngest son, Drake, died in a plane crash, leaving a wife and three daughters in New York. Busy running her family's DeLacey Shipping Co., Charlotte hadn't traveled to Korosol since the funeral, and, Easton had to admit, he'd sorely neglected his granddaughters.

Time passed so quickly. Much too quickly, he could see now.

"You didn't mention your purpose?" Sir Harrison asked. Like his monarch, he chose to speak in English in preparation for their trip. In addition to French, the nation's first language, almost all Korosolans spoke fluent English and Spanish.

"I did not." Easton hoped he was doing the right thing by keeping his illness and his plans secret. "I want to see my granddaughters as they really are. The less preparation they have, the better. Especially Cecelia."

"You haven't reconsidered Prince James?" Only Sir Harrison would dare to ask such a question. It was, indeed, his duty to make sure the king weighed all aspects of this crucial decision.

"Out of the question," Easton said sadly. "I wish it were otherwise, believe me."

His middle son had turned out wild. Thrice divorced and a heavy drinker, James worked as something called a "wildcatter" in Wyoming. Easton believed his job had something to do with oil wells, although he wouldn't put it past his renegade son to hunt mountain lions for a living, either.

James had a variety of children by an assortment of unsuitable wives. It seemed unlikely any of them would be prepared to assume the mantle of monarchy.

No, Charlotte's daughters were his best bet, the king mused. Their mother, a debutante from a well-connected family, met Easton's high standards, and her daughters were the toast of New York society.

Her eldest daughter, Cecelia, had earned an MBA and served as executive vice president of DeLacey Shipping. At twenty-nine, she appeared well qualified to run a country.

There were two younger daughters as well. While he assumed they had also been raised with a sense of propriety, Easton knew little about them.

The only other younger member of the royal family was the king's nephew, Christopher, a married father of two, who lived in California. Unfortunately, Christopher was the illegitimate son of Easton's deceased sister, Magdalene, and therefore not really considered part of the royal family.

"As you requested, we're taking only a small staff," Sir Harrison said. "I believe we can keep our presence out of the press."

"I certainly hope so. The people of Korosol should learn of their new ruler from me, not from some scandal sheet," the king said. "Ellie's agreed to go, has she?" Eleanor Standish, a young woman of good family who had been his wife's goddaughter, served as his personal secretary.

"Certainly. She's devoted to you."

"Glad to hear it." Lively Ellie lifted the king's spirits and saw to his comfort whenever they were away from the palace.

"We'll take six bodyguards, two per eight-hour shift," the adviser continued. "The captain of the Royal Guard will accompany us, of course."

Sir Harrison made no reference to the fact that Captain Devon Montcalm was his son. The young man, a fine military officer who had been knighted two years ago, was not close to his father.

"The Duke of Raleigh is coming also, is he not?" Easton demanded. "It was my personal request that he be assigned to the embassy in New York."

"Of course," said Sir Harrison. "He understands the delicate nature of his assignment."

The duke, Cadence St. John, was to serve as acting ambassador. In reality, as a commander in the Korosol Special Operatives, Cade was under orders to watch for any threat to the three New York princesses.

If Markus had indeed arranged the deaths of his parents to promote his own succession to the throne, he wouldn't stop at frightening or even killing one of his cousins. The king wanted Cade St. John to keep an ear to the ground.

"Since we're leaving in the morning," the adviser said, "perhaps Your Majesty should get some rest."

"I'm not decrepit yet." Easton's doctors had assured him that he could make this trip safely if he didn't over-exert himself.

"I was implying no such thing."

"You're my adviser, not my nursemaid," the king added for emphasis. He didn't want his staff members fussing over him, however noble their motives. "In any case, with luck, it will be a short trip. I will inform Lady Charlotte's family of my intentions and spend a few days observing Princess Cecelia. Then we can all fly back here."

"I hope the princess is everything you expect," said Sir Harrison.

"She will be." Easton stifled a yawn. After his protestation, he didn't want his adviser to see how sleepy he suddenly felt. "The girl has royal blood and a proper up-bringing. What could possibly go wrong?"

"Nothing, Your Majesty," said the general.

"That's right. Nothing!" said the king. "Don't you need to go to bed?"

"Me?" said Sir Harrison.

"You look tired," he said. "Go on with you."

"Yes, Your Majesty." The royal adviser bowed and withdrew.

King Easton waited a couple of minutes to make sure the man had cleared the corridor, then took himself off to his chamber. He was already dreaming, before his head hit the pillow, of what a perfect choice his granddaughter would turn out to be.

Chapter One

"Congratulations," the doctor said. "You're pregnant."

"I'm what?" Sitting on the edge of the examining table, CeCe Carradigne wished that, by some miracle, she would suddenly see that another woman had slipped in to the examining room and was now hearing the happy news.

A married woman. A woman who wanted children.

There was, however, no one else in the well-appointed examining room. Just unmarried CeCe, who didn't have a maternal instinct in her body, and Dr. Elizabeth Loesser, known to her patients as Dr. Beth.

"I take it this pregnancy wasn't planned," the doctor said.

"That's an understatement." CeCe struggled to maintain her composure. It was no use. "How did this happen?" she wailed. "Wait. Don't answer that."

Dr. Beth smiled. "I'm sure you know the facts of life, Miss Carradigne...or should I call you Princess?"

"I wish people would forget about that royalty business," CeCe said. "I haven't felt like a princess since my father died."

"A pregnancy is something to be welcomed, especially when the mother is in good health, as you are," her physician continued. "Of course, if you want to consider adoption, I'd be happy to make a referral."

A Carradigne, give up a baby for adoption? The tabloids would splash the story across every newsstand in America. Royal Baby to Be Given Away.

The paparazzi were the bane of CeCe's life. Even without an adoption to ignite their interest, she shuddered to think what they would do if they learned of her out-of-wedlock condition. "Princess Pregnant, But Where's the Prince?" they'd trumpet.

Not to mention the snide remarks that would pass among the executives who reported to her at DeLacey Shipping. They'd already nicknamed her "the barracuda" after she reorganized their departments to increase efficiency.

"I'm afraid adoption is unacceptable," she said. "Just give me the vitamins and the prenatal pamphlets."

"I'll send in the nurse with some information," said the doctor. "You don't have to go through this alone, you know. I'm sure the father will take responsibility."

"The father?" CeCe repeated. Oh, heavens. She'd been so stunned by the news that until this moment she hadn't given any thought to Shane O'Connell. "As far as I'm concerned, he's out of the picture."

"Oh, dear." Judging by Dr. Beth's expression, she assumed the man was married.

"'Oh, dear' is right." CeCe decided there was no need to fill in the blanks.

Blast Shane O'Connell! How like that ruffian to try to stamp a claim on her.

Well, she had nothing in common with the other women he dated, judging by their descriptions in Krissy Katwell's *Manhattan Chronicle* gossip column. CeCe Carradigne didn't hang on anyone's arm or gaze adoringly into any man's eyes.

No, all she'd done was to jump impulsively into bed with that dark-haired, dark-eyed stallion, she thought sarcastically.

It had been an amazing experience, though. The memory of Shane's lean hips and probing mouth stirred flames deep within CeCe.

Annoyed at herself, she finished the conversation with the doctor, only half paying attention. All she could think was, What am I going to do?

After meeting with the nurse and scheduling her next appointment, CeCe called to summon her driver from a nearby parking garage. Her briefcase stuffed with vitamins and pamphlets, she marched out through the waiting room with the sense of running a gauntlet.

Heads turned as the waiting patients followed her progress, and she could hear the buzz of conversation even before the door closed. "Isn't that Cecelia Carradigne?" "She really does look like a princess, doesn't she?" "It isn't fair to be so rich *and* so..."

It wasn't fair, all right. It wasn't fair that CeCe Carradigne, who never quite lived up to her mother's expectations, should find herself in this mess.

Pregnant! And by Shane O'Connell, of all men!

It had been CeCe's idea to forge an alliance between his package delivery service and DeLacey Shipping, to better compete for international shipping contracts. Although their business interests dovetailed, the negotiations had proved tempestuous.

Both of them were hard-driving, no-holds-barred people, she supposed. Whenever they found themselves in the same room, they clashed. Except for one night.

She and Shane had agreed to meet at his apartment, which was more private than the two-story penthouse unit she shared with her mother, one of her sisters and assorted staff. CeCe hadn't even considered the implications of spending an evening alone with a man at his place, because she didn't think of Shane O'Connell as a man. He was more of an unavoidable irritant.

They'd talked business, quarreling as usual while sharing a few drinks. Suddenly, they were all over each other. What on earth had happened?

They'd both been hideously embarrassed afterward. At least, she had. She'd fled with the briefest of goodbyes.

When she realized they'd forgotten to use contraception, CeCe had persuaded herself that nothing would result from a single encounter. Half of New York was pursuing infertility treatments, it seemed. Why should she be any different?

When her period failed to arrive on time, she'd rationalized. Hard work and excuses had kept her fears at bay for a few weeks. Then she'd made this doctor's appointment.

There was no more room for doubt. She was carrying Shane O'Connell's child.

CeCe descended in the elevator, uncomfortably aware that people were staring at her here, too. The problem with standing five foot eight and having blond hair and green eyes was that people immediately noticed you, and it didn't take long for them to connect you to the photographs that ran far too often in the newspapers.

CeCe wished she were an anonymous shipping executive whose problems concerned no one but herself. She also wished, more than anything, that she hadn't spent that night at Shane's apartment.

Outside, traffic jammed the street and pedestrians scurried by, bundled against the February chill. Cold nipped at CeCe's legs through the front opening in her long coat.

She would have preferred to wear pantsuits in winter, but her mother insisted that skirts were more ladylike. And what Charlotte wanted, Charlotte got.

From a nearby vendor's stand, CeCe caught the scent of hot dogs roasting. She was starved. Absolutely ravenous.

She didn't understand why, because normally she kept

so focused on work that she often forgot to eat. It must be the hormones.

Were hot dogs bad for babies? She didn't have time to read the pamphlets before making a decision about lunch, so CeCe bought one. As she finished paying, the Mercedes stopped at the curb. She had to rush and fold herself inside, briefcase, wiener and all.

"Where to, Miss Carradigne?" asked Paulo, the family's chauffeur.

"The office, please." CeCe checked her watch. It was after one o'clock, and she had a one-thirty meeting with Shane. "I'm afraid I'm running late."

Paulo zipped through tiny openings in traffic with a race-car driver's skill. If anyone could get her to work on time, it would be him.

Shane had no patience for being kept waiting. The last thing CeCe wanted was to arrive late and find herself already at a disadvantage.

They'd concluded arrangements for their alliance a week after that indiscreet evening. Since then, the pair of them had maintained contact by fax and e-mail. However, now that they planned to seek a joint shipping contract with a Chinese toy company, they were meeting to discuss strategy.

Should she tell him about the pregnancy? CeCe supposed Shane had a right to know. Yet she couldn't see herself blurting out the bald fact of impending parenthood to the intense, self-made millionaire.

Shane's meteoric rise had put him on Top Ten lists at *Forbes, Fortune* and *Newsweek*. His rough-hewn good looks and reputation for dating around had put him on some very different Top Ten lists at *Cosmopolitan* and *Redbook*.

Darn it, CeCe was not going to let the man intimidate her. As far as she was concerned, this was her baby, not his.

After finishing the hot dog, she started to stuff the wrappings into a rubbish container, then realized her mother would notice them later. She stuck them in her briefcase instead, even though she knew her papers would smell like wiener for days. That was preferable to a lecture from Charlotte about nutrition.

The thought of lectures from Charlotte inspired a question: Was there one for unplanned pregnancies? If so, CeCe wondered how long it lasted and whether she could arrange to have her secretary page her with an urgent call in the middle of it.

At 1:29 p.m., they reached the nineteen-story DeLacey Shipping building on Broad Street, near the East River and, of course, the DeLacey Shipping terminal. CeCe scurried out of the car, thanked Paulo and raced for the lobby.

Employees scattered from her path. A couple of clerical workers, whose medical benefits and holiday bonuses CeCe had increased last year, offered smiles and greetings. Several executives, having been threatened with demotions after she audited their departments, glowered.

On the nineteenth floor, CeCe burst through double glass doors labeled Executive Vice President. Her secretary, Linzy Lamar, jumped up from the computer. A pleasant-looking divorceée in her thirties, she blended seamlessly into her role.

"Mr. O'Connell is waiting in your office," she said. "Also, your mother stopped by."

That was hardly big news, since Charlotte's even larger office suite lay at the opposite end of the corridor. "Did she say why?"

"No, Miss Carradigne." The secretary, although a reserved woman, talked fast because she'd learned that otherwise she'd never get to finish her spiel. "She said she'll drop by again when she has time. I put the new traffic study on your desk." That was a compilation of data by

DeLacey executives regarding potential problem areas, including trade routes and competitors.

"Thank you," CeCe said as she breezed past.

She flung open the broad, polished-wood door into her office. Even in February, light flooded the expansive room overlooking the harbor.

A large silhouette blocked one window. "I'll get back to you," Shane said into his cell phone, and clicked off. Frowning, he turned to face CeCe.

Time stopped. Even the adrenaline rushing through her arteries slammed to a halt as their gazes met.

The man's fierce brown eyes pinned her with such force that CeCe could hardly breathe. In the two months since they'd seen each other, she'd forgotten the impact of Shane's presence.

His husky build and broad shoulders made most other men look scrawny. Even more impressive was the masculine confidence that showed in every movement.

He tapped his watch. "You're five minutes late. I have a busy schedule."

She rejected the idea of blaming her tardiness on traffic. "I was unavoidably delayed," she said, and clapped her briefcase onto her broad desk.

That was a mistake, because it forced out some air. Shane caught a whiff. "You stopped for lunch, I gather."

"I didn't stop. I ate on the run." CeCe grabbed the hot dog wrappers and dumped them in a wastebasket.

"You'll get indigestion."

I'm going to have indigestion for about seven more months, so what the heck? No, she scolded herself, that was not the best way to break her earth-shattering news. "That's my problem."

Shane gave her a crooked grin, revealing a devastating dent in one cheek that sent heat flooding through CeCe's body. Annoyed with herself, she unbuttoned her coat and tossed it onto a chair.

"If you don't want to discuss your eating habits, let's get down to work." He set his laptop computer on her conference table and flipped it open. "To date, Wuhan Novelty has cobbled together a variety of carriers to transport toys down the Yangtze River, across the Pacific and on to warehouses and stores. Add the fact that they've also begun selling directly on-line, and you've got a complicated mess."

"Which we can uncomplicate," CeCe said.

"Absolutely." Swiftly, he outlined his plan for combining DeLacey's shipping capacity with his fleet of trucks and planes to provide door-to-door service to North America.

Sitting beside him at the conference table, CeCe felt the energy pulsing through Shane as he talked. If there were a bed in her office, she might be tempted to fall into it.

Hadn't she learned anything?

"Your eyes are glazing over," he said. "Am I boring you?"

"Not at all," CeCe said. "It's a brilliant plan."

What she needed, she realized abruptly, was a brilliant plan of her own. Not to win the contract with Wuhan, but to introduce the subject of children.

"Do you have anything to add?" Shane asked.

"Toys!" she said.

"Excuse me?"

"They make toys." It was the perfect lead-in.

"I'm aware of that," he said.

As usual when CeCe's mind was racing a mile a minute, an idea popped into it. "We're going to do more than transport their product," she said. "We're going to give them free publicity and get some for ourselves."

"How do you propose to do that?" From the glint in his eye and the way he leaned forward, it was clear she'd engaged Shane's interest.

"As you know, if we get the contract, DeLacey will be

buying a couple of new container ships,'' CeCe said. ''We'll paint them—what are Wuhan's corporate colors?''

''Yellow and red,'' Shane said.

She should have known that, CeCe thought, hating to be caught short in even the smallest detail. ''Great. Also, we'll put their logo alongside ours and fly their flag right below ours. We'll paint some of your planes and trucks, too. We want everybody to notice that DeLacey and O'Connell are bringing them toys.''

''Like Santa Claus,'' he suggested.

''Yes!'' The more she expanded on it, the more CeCe loved her idea. ''We'll design an ad campaign. Not just for trade publications, but TV commercials and billboards.''

''We don't ship for the general public. We only serve corporate customers,'' Shane pointed out.

''Corporations are run by people who have children,'' CeCe said. ''We'll make them love us. When we pitch them our services, it'll give us an edge over our competitors.''

''It could work,'' Shane agreed. ''Personality is one thing most freight companies lack.''

''Speaking of children,'' CeCe said, and stopped, unable to figure out how to finish the sentence.

''Yes?'' His face, close to hers, was manly. A strong jaw. An expressive mouth...

''Do you like them?'' she asked.

''Do I like kids?'' he echoed. ''I'm not sure I follow your point.''

''You might...act as a spokesman. In the ads,'' she improvised. ''You could talk about how having children humanizes corporate executives. About how you can't wait to have children yourself.''

''Me?'' he said.

''Who better?'' CeCe asked. ''I mean, I'm a woman,

so it wouldn't make people sit up and pay attention if they heard me talking about children.'' *Unless they knew me, of course.* "But if you said a few words about how much fatherhood meant—or might mean—to you, or was something you looked forward to…''

He leaned back, disconnecting. "Sorry, CeCe, but I'm not the type.''

"What type is that?'' She hoped her sinking feelings didn't show on her face.

"I'm not cut out to have kids.'' Shane's voice had a tight quality that hadn't been there before. "I don't have the time or the interest. I don't even like them.''

"We're talking theoretically,'' CeCe said. "About how you might feel someday, not right now.''

"Children make me feel trapped,'' he said. "My childhood was pretty miserable. Not that I use that as an excuse for anything. The whole family thing just doesn't work for me.''

"That's so—so—1980s of you!'' she flared, hopping up because she couldn't bear to sit next to this man for another instant. "You've heard of the 'me generation'? We're supposed to be past that! Men today march in picket lines for fathers' rights. How'd you get stuck in the past?''

"Wait a minute.'' Shane, too, got to his feet, apparently unwilling to have CeCe tower over him. In this position, his six-feet-one-inch frame would have dwarfed hers had she not been wearing three-inch heels. "We're talking about an ad campaign, for heaven's sake. Don't take it personally.''

"It's a great ad campaign!'' CeCe could hear her tone rising. "Or it was until you loused it up!''

"I never claimed to be an actor.'' He regarded her thoughtfully. "What's going on?''

"Nothing! Everything! Isn't it obvious?''

"I guess we should talk about what happened between us," Shane said.

"Nothing happened," CeCe said. "Didn't we agree on that?"

"If nothing happened," came her mother's voice, "why are you shouting about it?"

Shocked, CeCe came to a dead stop. How much had Charlotte heard?

The president of DeLacey Shipping glided into the room. The Duchess of Avion—who had received the title upon her marriage, although no one called her that outside of Krissy Katwell's gossip column in the *Manhattan Chronicle*—moved with natural grace.

"Good to see you, Shane," she said.

"It's a pleasure, Lady Charlotte." As they shook hands, Shane's manner became subtly more polite and restrained. Like everyone in New York except Charlotte's own daughters, he was a little in awe of her.

She could do things that nobody else got away with. Take, for instance, her short hair, which had turned completely white as she approached her fiftieth birthday. The unfashionable hue looked so attractive that a lot of people assumed she'd bleached it, and hairdressers had hurried to follow the trend.

As for her clothing and grooming, they were always immaculate and perfect for the occasion. Today she wore a blue wool jacket that brought out the color of her eyes, over a gray silk blouse and winter-white skirt.

"Discussing the Wuhan account?" Charlotte asked. "What have you decided?"

She didn't sit down, so Shane and CeCe kept their recital brief. The company president nodded approval when they finished. "Let me know when you've finalized the presentation."

"Before we submit anything formally, a trade representative has invited CeCe and me for brunch day after tomorrow," Shane said. "He seems thrilled at the idea of meeting a princess."

"Good. She'll be there." Charlotte didn't bother to ask CeCe whether the engagement fit her schedule. "Now, if you'll excuse us?"

"Of course." Shane closed his laptop. CeCe felt his gaze linger on her as he said goodbye.

After closing the door behind him, Charlotte said briskly, "Well, well. That man likes you."

"Excuse me?"

"You're not his type, of course," her mother continued with maddening certainty. "A man like him needs a lady who builds her life around him. Someone compliant, which no one has ever accused you of being."

Although she didn't consider Shane O'Connell to be her type, either, CeCe bristled at her mother's words. She knew better than to say anything, though. Revealing one's feelings to Charlotte meant turning them over for inspection and rearrangement.

"Linzy said you dropped by earlier. What's going on?" she asked.

"Your grandfather is coming to visit," said Charlotte. "How's that for a bombshell? Arriving tomorrow, no less. I suppose it's a royal prerogative not to give much advance notice."

To CeCe, who hadn't seen King Easton of Korosol since she was nine, the king was both a stranger and a legendary figure. A thrill of excitement ran through her.

"Why?" she asked. "He never travels this far."

"He refused to say anything except that the trip is secret," Charlotte said. "He'll be staying with us. The rest of his staff will reside at the embassy, except for the bodyguards. As it turns out, the apartment below ours is vacant, so they'll be housed there."

CeCe's head spun. She wasn't sure she could deal with

a royal visit while her personal life was in such an uproar. Still, what choice was there? "What can I do to help?"

"He's expressed a desire to spend time with you," said her mother. "You'll accommodate anything he requests. The king expects to get his way, and he shall."

"But my work—"

"If you need to take time off, then do it," her mother said. "You'll attend that brunch with Shane. There's nothing like a princess to impress the customers. Otherwise, I've run this business since your father died and I can handle it without you just fine."

Her words hit CeCe like a slap in the face. Since earning her master's degree in business five years earlier, she had worked long hours to reorganize and modernize DeLacey Shipping's corporate structure. It appeared none of that meant anything to her mother.

She had to speak up on her own behalf. She didn't, however, want to sound like a little girl whining to an all-powerful parent, so CeCe chose her words carefully. "I'm sorry you don't value my contributions more than that."

"Don't get all worked up over nothing." Charlotte waved her hand dismissively. "You're a big help, most of the time. Now, remember, the king is arriving tomorrow afternoon, so you'll need to leave the office early. We'll discuss the rest of the arrangements at home."

Then she was gone, leaving CeCe steaming. Sometimes it was hard to tell who infuriated her most, Shane or her mother.

A roiling sensation in her stomach brought her back to reality. The delicate matter of her pregnancy would have to be kept secret, even within the family, until the king departed.

Thank goodness she hadn't told Shane. No one must know and there must be no risk of scandal in front of King Easton, or CeCe would never be able to face her mother again.

Chapter Two

Shane had his cell phone clamped to one ear as the cab halted in front of his Madison Avenue office building. O'Connell Industries occupied an entire floor of the sleek high-rise.

"We'll see you Thursday morning," he confirmed to the Chinese trade representative. They had already agreed to eat at a French restaurant near Central Park, convenient to CeCe's apartment. "The princess looks forward to meeting you."

The cab driver turned and gave him a hurry-up look. On the sidewalk, a man tugged at the door and called, "You getting out or what?"

Mindful of the Chinese sensitivity to protocol, Shane said a polite goodbye into the phone while paying the driver. After hanging up, he pocketed the phone, collected his laptop and hurried across the sidewalk into the lobby.

Other people jostled him as Shane bolted for the elevator and wedged himself inside. The first thing he would do when he owned his own building was to designate a private elevator, he vowed.

On the thirty-first floor, Shane stepped into the East Coast headquarters of O'Connell Industries. He always relished passing through the vast outer office filled with desks and ringing phones. What a contrast to the shabby hole-in-the-wall where he'd begun his career!

"Mr. O'Connell? Ferguson is here," said Tawny Magruder, Shane's secretary, when he reached his office suite. A tall, dark-skinned woman who took no guff from anyone, she nodded toward the man sitting outside Shane's office.

His personal assistant and valet, Ed Ferguson, rarely came to the headquarters. His domain included Shane's apartments on both coasts, his vacation cottage, his yacht and his corporate jet.

Today, Ferguson's purpose was evident from the tuxedo, encased in a plastic cleaner's bag, draped over his arm. "I thought you might not get home in time to change for tonight," he said.

"What would I do without you?" Shane asked. Ed, a former foster child with whom he'd shared a group home, had been first a friend, then his devoted employee. Slight of build and modest of manner, the man might appear colorless to others, but Shane valued his steadfastness and honesty.

"You sure do need him. Don't anybody ask *me* to fetch their dry cleaning," said Tawny.

"I wouldn't dare," Shane said.

His secretary smiled. Like him and Ed, Tawny had had a difficult past, including a stint as a welfare mother. She'd turned out to be a real tiger, quick to defend her boss and untiring in her work.

Her loyalty, like Ferguson's, was intense. Shane's willingness to hire people with troubled backgrounds—as long as they adhered to his high standards—was, he believed, one of his company's strengths.

"You're expected at the Foster Children's College Fund dinner at six-thirty," Ferguson reminded him.

"He knows that," Tawny said. "I entered it into his organizer."

"A busy man has other things to do than look up lists," the personal assistant retorted stiffly.

"I never leave the office without making sure Mr. O'Connell knows his plans for the evening," snapped the secretary.

Shane grinned at them both. "I appreciate your concern, you two."

"If you need help dressing, I can return," Ferguson said.

"Look, if the man needs..." Tawny stopped in mid-sentence. "Okay, if he wants somebody to zip his pants, I'll let you do it."

"I can zip my own pants, thank you very much," Shane said. "Ed, I appreciate your bringing the tux."

"Also, there were a couple of messages." The aide handed him an answering-machine tape. "Of a personal nature."

"Thanks."

"You could have left that with me," Tawny said. "Mr. O'Connell, I told him earlier there was no need to wait."

"It was my pleasure to wait," Ferguson said. "Good day, Mr. O'Connell, Miss Magruder." His back straight, the aide withdrew.

"I'm going to start calling him Jeeves," muttered Tawny, and returned her attention to her computer.

Inside his private office, Shane dealt with his e-mail and returned business calls. As he talked, he propped his feet on the broad desk.

He loved this office, and the one at his West Coast headquarters in Long Beach, California. CeCe Carradigne might take her surroundings for granted, but Shane never did.

CeCe Carradigne. He pictured her tall, slim figure striding across her office to greet him this afternoon. Her blond bangs and slightly angular bone structure emphasized the size of those green eyes, and he relished the fullness of her lips.

Today, he'd watched for any sign of the warmth they'd shared that night they spent together. Surely at some point, he'd believed, she would relax and joke with him. Touch his cheek. Move suggestively closer...

It hadn't happened. She must be made of ice, as people said. Or else that night simply hadn't meant anything to her.

Shane wished he didn't find the woman so fascinating. He had relished discovering the feminine side underneath her tough exterior. And he loved the quick way her mind worked.

They were too much alike, though. If he ever did settle down with a woman, she wouldn't be someone who worked as hard as he did and fought every battle to the bitter end.

Besides, Shane had gradually come to accept, as one relationship after another failed, that he wasn't suited to long-term intimacy. Maybe it was because his private life always came second to business. Or because, as an orphan, he'd learned that emotional safety lay in depending exclusively on himself.

That didn't mean he'd lost interest in women, only that he was realistic about the terms of endearment. Reminded of the tape Ferguson had left, he inserted it into the answering machine.

"Shane! Darling!" It was Amy, a recently divorced stockbroker who'd flirted with him at a cocktail party. "I've just been handed tickets to the most fabulous musical for Saturday night, and of course I immediately thought of you."

The next message came from Janet, an attorney he'd met at a charity event. She had sharp, lively features, he recalled, and had recently separated from her husband.

"I'm throwing a little dinner party for a few friends on

Saturday," she said. "I'd be so pleased if you could attend."

Their interest flattered Shane. Both were attractive, successful women.

He didn't want to start anything, however. Especially when, pointless as it seemed, he couldn't get CeCe out of his mind.

Why had she gotten so miffed today because he'd refused to hawk the joys of fatherhood? It must have been pique because he'd spoiled her brilliant public relations idea. Well, she'd picked the wrong guy for the assignment.

Shane had no interest in children. And he certainly wouldn't consider having one himself. It was too painful. When he happened to look into one of those little faces, he saw himself as he'd once been, vulnerable and helpless.

At eight, his father had died in an industrial accident. His mother, Annie, had had to work two jobs, in day care and as a waitress, so most days Shane had come home alone from school, fixed his own dinner and put himself to bed.

When he was twelve, Annie stumbled into a gang fight outside the restaurant where she worked. She was in the wrong place at the wrong time, the police had said.

Desperately missing his mother, Shane had hated both of his foster homes. He'd run away repeatedly, until he was placed in a group home.

There he saw the other boys picking on shy Ed and sprang to his defense. From then on, Shane stuck around to protect his friend.

Why was he dragging up memories that he'd sworn to leave untouched? he wondered. It must have been CeCe's mention of children.

Still, he was sorry to have left their conversation unfinished. After making his excuses to Amy and Janet, Shane turned to his computer.

His office and DeLacey Shipping had recently installed equipment to allow videoconferencing. It was time to put it to good use.

KING EASTON DOZED DURING the nine-hour flight from Korosol to New York. He was grateful for the comforts of a private jet, although there was a lot to say for the old days when luxury liners were the transatlantic transport of choice.

He and his bride, Cassandra, had traveled to America by ship a few years after the death of Easton's father, King Cyrus. They'd combined business of state with their honeymoon.

Although Cassandra claimed to feel awkward in public, she became a darling of the press with her fashionable figure and ready wit. Easton had enjoyed his meeting with President Truman and had retained a fondness for the United States ever since.

He missed Cassandra terribly. Wise and well educated, she'd been his closest friend and adviser. Had she been born a generation later, she would surely have pursued a career of her own.

Her death six years ago had devastated the king, although in a way it came as a blessing after a series of strokes. If he could have spared her any suffering by taking it on himself, he would have.

He'd have given his life to save either of his dead sons, as well. Twenty years ago, he'd shared his grief with Cassandra when Drake died in the crash of a private plane. It had also killed Drake's father-in-law and seriously injured his nephew Markus, who'd been in America on holiday.

Easton remembered how Byrum and Sarah had posted a vigil by their son's hospital bed, and how joyfully they'd brought the fifteen-year-old home to Korosol. It was almost beyond belief that their beloved son had had a hand in their deaths, yet Easton couldn't discount the rumors.

Troubled, he gave up trying to sleep and called for a meal. A short time later, the flight arrived in New York.

While Harrison Montcalm and Cadence St. John went directly to the embassy, two helicopters fetched Easton, his bodyguards and his secretary to the roof of an apartment building overlooking Central Park. He was impressed all over again by the vast stretch of greenery marking the heart of the metropolis.

"All cities should have a refuge like this," Cassandra had declared. Easton wished, achingly, that she was with him now.

"We're so high up!" Ellie Standish said as the helicopter's motor fell silent.

"Do you think we should build skyscrapers in Korosol la Vella?" teased the king. His country's capital city had its share of modern buildings, but none this tall.

"Absolutely not!" Ellie pushed her glasses up on her nose and smoothed out her skirt. "I wouldn't change a single thing about my home."

At twenty-six, the young woman had all the makings of a knockout, with her bright blue eyes and long, curly brown hair, but she hid beneath frumpy clothes. That suited Easton fine. Otherwise, some young fellow was likely to fall in love with his secretary and snatch her away.

"Please stay here, Your Majesty, while we secure the area," said Devon Montcalm, the captain of the Royal Guard.

"Certainly," Easton said.

Since his daughter-in-law's two-story penthouse apartment was already guarded, it took only a few minutes for Devon to make contact with her security chief and reassure himself as to the arrangements. Then he and the other guards escorted the king across the roof and down a private elevator.

Easton declined Devon's offer of his arm for support. The king had no intention of appearing as an invalid.

He found his heart beating faster as the elevator halted. It was exciting to meet the granddaughters he hadn't seen since they were children. Especially the one who, he hoped, held the future of his kingdom in her hands.

The doors opened on a marbled foyer. What an elegant place, Easton thought, noting the two-story-high ceiling and the curving staircase to his right.

"Your Majesty!" He would have recognized Charlotte DeLacey Carradigne anywhere. The tall, slim woman in the designer suit had hardly aged in twenty years.

She curtseyed gracefully. Easton caught her hand and pulled her up. "My dear, you look splendid," he said. "I wish I hadn't waited so long to pay you this visit."

"You're as handsome as ever. So much like Drake." She flashed him a smile tinged with sadness. After so many years, he could see that she still mourned her husband. "You look a little pale. Was it a long flight?"

"Long enough," he said. "And a colder winter than usual in Korosol. Charlotte, let me introduce my secretary, Eleanor Standish. She's not staying here, but she'll make sure my room's settled the way I like it."

"Of course."

The housekeeper appeared as if by magic and whisked Ellie away. "Have the guards bring the suitcases to suite A," he heard her say, and then he was alone with his daughter-in-law.

"Where are the girls?" Easton asked.

"Waiting in the Grand Room, right across the gallery." Charlotte clasped her hands together. "That is, Amelia and Lucia are here, and CeCe's on her way."

The king felt a twinge of irritation at this tardiness. "Cecelia isn't waiting for me?"

"She's monitoring a severe storm in the Pacific that could impact a couple of our ships," Charlotte explained. "Your granddaughter takes her duties very seriously."

"That's a good sign," Easton said, his annoyance soothed, as they crossed a long corridor hung with paintings and large photographs.

"A good sign?" asked his daughter-in-law.

"We'll get to that," the king said.

COMMUNICATIONS FROM DeLacey's ships in the storm area had been disrupted. Despite all their satellites, international weather sources couldn't pinpoint the storm's latest activity.

"What good is all this technology, anyway?" CeCe moaned, leaning back in her chair. Since she was alone in her office, no one answered.

The morning had been filled with one frustration after another. Her mother had called twice to urge her to get home before the king arrived. And, in truth, there was little CeCe could do to help her valiant captains, other than validate any decisions they made.

Still, she felt obligated to stick it out. At least this way, if a decision was made that derailed scheduling and angered a client, CeCe would take the blame on herself. It seemed only fair.

A beep from the computer startled her. For a moment, she couldn't remember what that meant.

Puzzled, she minimized the maritime weather page so it disappeared from the screen. Instantly, it was replaced by the grinning face of Shane O'Connell.

"You can see me, but I can't see you," he said. "Turn your video on!"

CeCe had made so little use of the videoconferencing program that she'd almost forgotten it was installed. Annoyed and intrigued at the same time, she straightened in her chair and finger-combed her bangs. Then she clicked on Send Video.

Shane's grin broadened. "Hey, you look pretty darn good for a digital image."

"What's going on?" There must be a new development in the Wuhan negotiations. "I thought everything was set."

"For the ad campaign?" Shane's dark eyes narrowed. "Whoa, lady."

"I meant for brunch tomorrow," CeCe said. "Forget the ad campaign."

"You seemed pretty keen on it yesterday." His expression shifted into confusion, or maybe that was the effect of the pixels. They sometimes rearranged themselves jerkily, giving the impression that she was watching stop-action animation instead of a real person.

Except that Shane was very, very real. His voice had a fierce vibrancy even through the computer speakers, and CeCe got the shivery sense that he was right here in the room with her.

Close enough to touch, yet out of reach. Just like in life.

"I've got a lot on my mind." She couldn't tell him about her grandfather's visit, so she explained, "We're having some bad weather at sea. What's this call about, Shane?"

"Us," he said.

Her heart nearly stopped. Surely she'd misheard him. "I beg your pardon?"

"When your mother came in, we were on the verge of talking about what happened that night at my apartment," he said. "It's time to finish the conversation."

Not now! CeCe thought. Not with her mother's silent nagging pulling at her mind, and worry about the storm making her feel guilty about taking even a moment for herself. "Forget that night. It doesn't matter."

"It doesn't matter?" Shane repeated. "Does that mean I can expect you to drop by my place again, say, tonight?"

CeCe stared at him, trying to make sense of his comment. "What are you talking about?"

"You say that what happened doesn't matter. So it won't matter if we get together again, will it?" he replied, his eyes daring her to argue. Or maybe that was once again, the effect of digital imperfections. "We're both consenting adults and whether you want to admit it or not, we enjoyed ourselves."

"Life isn't about having fun," CeCe snapped, although it was difficult not to be amused by Shane's outrageous remarks. Something about the man appealed to her even when he infuriated her.

"Lighten up," he said. "Let me bring out the best in you. Or the worst. Whatever. Shall we say, seven o'clock, my place?"

"I have plans," she said.

"So do I," he admitted. "I didn't figure you'd agree."

"You louse!" CeCe couldn't help laughing. "You have a lot of nerve!"

"So are we past it?" he asked.

"Past what?"

"That circling-each-other-and-snarling business," Shane said. "What happened, happened. We're both consenting adults and we both enjoyed it. No harm done."

"Well…" CeCe swallowed. It seemed awfully abrupt to break the news about her pregnancy over the Internet. Besides, the connection might not be secure.

Then there was the matter of her grandfather's visit. She couldn't tell Shane yet, even if she wanted to.

A tap at her office door was followed by Linzy's entrance. "Miss Carradigne? Did you see the latest weather bulletin?"

"No. What's it say?" CeCe reached instinctively for her mouse.

"Don't you dare minimize me!" Shane said.

Linzy frowned. "Is there someone on the speaker-phone?"

"I'm videoconferencing with Mr. O'Connell," CeCe said. "What's the news?"

"The storm's veered. The worst of it is expected to miss the shipping lanes," said her secretary.

"Thank heaven." CeCe checked her watch. "Oh, my goodness." At last report, her grandfather was expected to land right about now. Even if she hurried, she'd be late to greet him. "I've got to go."

Linzy withdrew discreetly. "What's so important?" Shane asked.

"Family business," CeCe said.

"So when it comes to our little escapade, it's forgive, if not forget?" he pressed.

"Don't worry about it," she said, and clicked off.

She didn't want to keep the king of Korosol waiting any longer than she had to. Especially not for the impudent Shane O'Connell.

THE GRAND ROOM LIVED UP to its name, the king saw as he entered. Large enough to serve as a ballroom, it soared a full two stories. Fabric wall paneling in shades of beige and light blue set off the antique furnishings, and the windows opened onto a covered lanai.

Two young women sprang to their feet as Easton entered and dipped in slightly shaky curtseys. They were lovely women, both tall and blond.

Amelia, who wore a tailored dress, gave him a concil-iatory smile. "I'm sure CeCe will be here any minute."

Lucia, a shade taller and slimmer, wore a swirly, bo-hemian dress and large, bright earrings. She was, the king recalled from one of Charlotte's letters, a jewelry designer, so she'd probably made them herself. "I'm so glad to meet you," she murmured. "I mean, to see you again."

She'd been six, and her sister seven, the last time he met them. It seemed like another lifetime.

"Come give your grandfather a big hug, both of you," Easton said.

They embraced him shyly. Close up, they smelled of springtime.

"They're beautiful girls," he told Charlotte. "You've done well."

"I must apologize again for Cecelia," she said. "She has a computer in her suite upstairs. I told her she ought to keep track from here until…"

Across the hall, the elevator doors opened and Easton heard high heels click across the marble floor. Such an impatient sound, and an oddly familiar one.

His chest tightened. His wife's steps used to sound exactly like that when she was in a hurry.

"With all those weather satellites, you'd think we could get some accurate information sooner about…" A tall, loose-limbed young woman, hair straggling across her face, stumbled to a halt in the doorway. "Oh, he's here! I mean, you're here. Welcome to New York, Your Majesty."

As she dipped in a curtsey, he distinctly heard her knees crack. Then she straightened and King Easton forgot everything as he got a good look at her face.

It was his Cassandra, come back to life in her eldest granddaughter.

CECE FIGURED SHE'D BLOWN IT this time. Everyone was staring at her, especially her grandfather.

He was tall and erect, although thinner than she'd expected, and looked in his early sixties rather than his late seventies. His gray hair might be thinning, but there was nothing faded about his green gaze.

She hoped he wasn't going to scold her. The chauffeur had set a crosstown speed record getting her here, which had done nothing to ease her churning stomach.

And she wished she hadn't been quite so abrupt in ending the call with Shane. When he wasn't scowling and trying to drive a hard bargain, the man could be downright charming. Dangerously so, as she'd learned.

"Please accept my apology for the delay," CeCe said. "I hope my mother told you about the storm."

"She did indeed." Never taking his eyes off her, King Easton crossed the room and caught CeCe's hands in his strong ones. "Your devotion to duty does you credit." He spoke with a charming French accent.

Charlotte, who had opened her mouth to intervene in what she obviously expected to be a difficult moment, clamped it shut again. Amelia looked relieved, and Lucia amused.

Nothing had prepared CeCe for her grandfather's absorption in her. As he stood directly in front of her, his stare seemed to bore into her.

Until this moment, he had been a remote figure with little impact on her life. Now, suddenly, a connection sprang to life between them.

She knew she ought to make polite conversation, to ask about his journey or offer him some refreshment. CeCe couldn't find the words.

"You look exactly like your grandmother," he said.

"That's quite an honor. We have a portrait of her, you know." Several people had pointed out a resemblance that escaped CeCe.

Her coloring was lighter than Cassandra's, and she was taller. Hester Vanderling, the family's former nanny and current housekeeper, attributed the similarity to the independent set of their chins.

The king blinked as if emerging from a daze, and released her hands. "Sit down, everyone. We need to talk."

"I'll have one of the maids bring coffee," Charlotte said.

"It's a bit late in the day for caffeine," the king reproved. "Herbal tea and biscuits—cookies, you call them, I believe."

"Right away." On the intercom, Charlotte summoned the kitchen staff. Soon an ornate silver tray was wheeled in, with a handcrafted teapot and cups on top and two levels of cookies and small cakes.

Charlotte reached for the teapot, then stopped. "CeCe, as the eldest daughter, you should pour."

Not since she'd had to defend her master's thesis in front of a faculty panel had CeCe experienced such a jolt of alarm. Her tea-pouring ability was only one level above abysmal.

"Of course," she said, doing her best to hide her dismay. Princess Bluster, that's what her college classmates had nicknamed CeCe after she brazenly answered a teacher's questions about a textbook chapter she'd neglected to read, and got away with it. "It would be my pleasure."

Her sisters regarded her with varying degrees of surprise and concern. When CeCe reached for the teapot, Amelia leaned forward as if trying to help with body language.

King Easton regarded her quizzically. "You're left-handed?"

"I'm afraid so." Living in a right-handed world contributed to CeCe's clumsiness, although Charlotte had never considered that an excuse.

"So was your grandmother," said the king. "She used to complain that servingware was designed for right-handed women. We had several teapots made especially for her."

"I'm afraid I left mine at the office," CeCe said.

"You left your what at the office?" asked Charlotte.

"My left-handed teapot," she said.

There was a moment's pause, and then King Easton burst out laughing. "My granddaughter is joking! How delightful."

CeCe's sisters released a few giggles. Charlotte smiled cautiously.

"Would you like me to pour?" asked Amelia.

"She's very good at it," said Lucia.

"And I'm not," CeCe concluded.

The king beamed at them. "I appreciate your frankness, and I'm glad to see that your sisters have kind hearts. Lady Charlotte, they're a tribute to their upbringing."

Their mother basked in his praise. For once, CeCe was glad to see, the three of them had won her approval.

Amelia proceeded to serve the tea without spilling a drop. Charlotte herself couldn't have done better.

When they were all settled, the king said, "I want to tell you why I've come."

"You don't need a reason," said his daughter-in-law.

"That's true. Yet there is one."

Since her mother's announcement the previous day, CeCe had turned the matter over in her mind. Now she figured she had a pretty good idea what to expect.

Three years ago, there'd been talk that King Easton would retire on his seventy-fifth birthday. However, after his eldest son decided he wanted a few more years of relative freedom, the retirement was postponed.

Now that a year of mourning for Byrum had ended, her grandfather must have decided to hand the reins of power to Markus. Her cousin had made no secret of his eagerness to assume the role.

She wasn't sure why Easton wanted to announce the transition to his granddaughters in person. The most likely explanation was that he sought the family's support for the new king, along with their attendance at the corona-tion.

Of course they would go. CeCe only hoped her pregnancy wouldn't be too obvious by that point.

"I've decided to step down from the throne," Easton said.

CeCe nodded. It was what she'd assumed.

"We're sorry to hear it," Charlotte said.

"Don't be. As long as I can hand Korosol to a strong, benevolent monarch, we should all rejoice."

"When is the coronation to take place?" CeCe asked.

"That depends on you."

"On us?"

"On you personally." Easton studied her closely. "You see, Princess Cecelia, I've decided that you are to be my successor."

Chapter Three

In the stunned silence that followed King Easton's announcement, CeCe became acutely aware of the ticking of an antique clock. Of the swirl of dust motes down long shafts of light. Of the swift thumping of her heart.

Was he joking? One look at his face told her otherwise.

Her mother and sisters sat frozen. If anyone had dared to light a bomb under Charlotte's chair, she wouldn't have stirred.

Queen of Korosol? Such a thought had never entered CeCe's mind, even in those childhood days when she and her sisters used to play at being princesses for real.

Of course, they *were* princesses for real. Living in New York, however, those titles meant little beyond the interest they stirred among the status-conscious.

"I don't even know Korosol," she said, then realized how ungracious that sounded. "I mean, I don't deserve this honor. I haven't visited the country since I was nine."

"I'm aware of that." Her grandfather sank back on the couch, looking weary. "I blame myself for not insisting that you girls spend a month each summer with me. However, a businesswoman with your credentials should be able to familiarize yourself with Korosol's needs rather quickly."

Charlotte coughed before managing to speak. "Your Majesty, I'm astounded. We're all incredibly grateful—"

The king lifted one hand to halt the flow of words. "It's a lifelong commitment. Since my granddaughter hasn't been prepared for it the way I was, I won't try to force it on her."

"Naturally, my daughter will do anything you ask," Charlotte assured him.

CeCe couldn't begin to absorb the ramifications of becoming a queen. Moreover, her grandfather's decision puzzled her.

"Although I realize the law doesn't require it, I always assumed Markus was next in line," she said.

Her cousin, who was half a dozen years older than CeCe, maintained an apartment in New York and a playboy lifestyle. Having seen him often over the years, she found him charming at times and manipulative at others.

Thin frown lines puckered Easton's forehead. "I have reason to believe my grandson may not be, well, quite right for the job. That's all I care to say on the matter."

Perhaps it was Markus's occasional heavy drinking that bothered their grandfather, CeCe thought. She couldn't help feeling sorry for her cousin, who'd mentioned several times how much he looked forward to assuming the throne.

"I think CeCe will make a wonderful queen," Amelia said, fulfilling her accustomed role of peacekeeper.

"She'll be terrific, if it's what she really wants to do," said Lucia.

Queen Cecelia of Korosol. CeCe was sophisticated enough to know how the world would trumpet the storybook elevation of a New York executive into such a romantic position.

Romantic to others, perhaps. She doubted Shane would be impressed. He'd made it clear he admired people for their accomplishments, not for what was simply handed to them.

That was one of the reasons that his respect meant so much to her. Until that embarrassing night they'd spent together, she'd secretly looked forward to their negotiations. The flare of approval on his face when she raised a point that he hadn't considered, even when it came at his own expense, thrilled her.

She'd missed Shane these past few months. Even though he sometimes annoyed her, she came alive during their verbal battles.

Becoming queen meant CeCe would never again walk into her office and see him standing there. She would never be able to call him on the phone and ask his advice or outline her latest idea.

Of course, she wasn't queen yet. Under the circumstances, she reminded herself, she probably never would be. Could she possibly have timed her pregnancy worse?

CeCe knew she ought to say something now, but she couldn't bear to blurt out the truth and see the disgust on her grandfather's face. Not to mention that Charlotte would squawk loud enough to set off car alarms for blocks.

Despite lacking a course of action, she still needed to give her grandfather a response. "It's a tremendous opportunity," she said. "One I'm not sure I'm ready to handle. Would it be all right if I think it over?"

"There's nothing to think about!" snapped her mother. "If your father were here—"

"If Drake were here, he'd be pleased that she takes the matter so seriously," said the king. "I'm glad you don't grab at the chance to glorify yourself, Cecelia. You understand, as you should, that saying yes will change not only your life but the lives of thousands of people."

It was a solemn responsibility to have all those people counting on her. CeCe had never shrunk from taking charge, and she wasn't about to start now—if it turned out her grandfather still intended to give her the chance, once she figured out how to break her news to him.

"We'll get to know each other over the next few days," the king said. "That will give you a chance to weigh the matter, and me an opportunity to make sure you're the right person to rule my land."

"I'm looking forward to it," she said.

The monarch rose stiffly to his feet. The four women jumped up also. "I want to make sure my room is arranged to my liking before Ellie leaves. I shall see you all at dinner."

"Let me show you the way." Charlotte accompanied him from the room.

The young women sat in stunned silence for a few minutes. Then Lucia said, "I'm glad he picked you and not me!"

"I can just imagine you turning the royal palace into an artists' loft like the one you live in," Amelia teased.

"Well, I *am* an artist, and I can't live my life to please other people," replied their younger sister.

"You're the one who'd make a good queen, Amelia," CeCe said. "You could still work with the International Children's Foundation. I'm sure they'd love to have a queen as a figurehead."

"I'm not a figurehead!" Amelia answered in a rare display of temper.

"Of course not. I didn't mean it that way."

Although CeCe didn't know the details of her sister's work, she couldn't help noticing that Amelia vanished from the apartment for weeks at a time. Often, she suspected, to travel to war-torn lands.

The ICF, a nonprofit relief organization, rescued orphans overseas and found them good homes. Because of the risk of being kidnapped if anyone discovered her identity, Amelia worked and traveled under an assumed name.

"You shouldn't feel obligated to take the job just because grandfather and mother want you to," Lucia told CeCe. "Once you become a queen, you won't have a moment to yourself. Forget about finding the right man, not that it's so easy for the rest of us."

Three years earlier, Lucia had been duped by a gold-digging fiancé. Ever since, she'd avoided entanglements to concentrate on her design business.

Charlotte sailed through the door. "Don't you dare try to talk your sister out of this! Being offered the throne is a dream come true."

"Or a nightmare," retorted Lucia.

"I don't understand why you contradict me at every turn." Charlotte's tongue made a disapproving click. "Isn't it bad enough that you live in SoHo and hang out with all those artsy types?"

CeCe was in no mood to hear old arguments rehashed. "I hope grandfather understands that I'm not going to be entirely at his beck and call these next few days."

"His secretary mentioned he's got some business at the embassy tomorrow morning, so you can keep your appointment with Shane," Charlotte said. "Now, pipe down, all three of you. I have something to say."

"Uh-oh," muttered Lucia. Amelia shook her head at her sister.

CeCe perched on the arm of a sofa. The way her stomach felt, piping down was more difficult than her mother might guess. "Go ahead."

Charlotte eyed the dessert cart longingly. "Before we start, there's no point in letting these go to waste, I suppose."

To keep her figure trim, she rarely indulged. Now she helped herself to a slice of mousse cake, taking dainty bites with a small silver fork. She must, CeCe mused, have expended a great deal of energy in worrying about the king's arrival to have worked up such an appetite.

Her daughters needed no encouragement. Soon th
were all sitting around, eating and waiting on th
mother's pronouncement.

At last the final bite of cake disappeared. It was typi
of Charlotte not to begin speaking while she might ha
even a crumb of food left in her mouth.

"Now, listen closely," she told her daughters. "I'm
sure when we'll have another moment alone."

"We're listening," Lucia said.

The dessert plate issued a refined pinging noise
Charlotte set it on the coffee table. "You know how h
I've worked all these years at the shipping company.
wasn't entirely by choice, I assure you."

"We know it was for our welfare," Amelia said.

"After my husband and my father died, the busin
was in turmoil," Charlotte said. "Twenty years ago,
world wasn't as accepting of women executives as it
today."

CeCe could sympathize with what her mother m
have endured. She'd met with her share of patronizi
remarks from competitors and potential clients, and fou
them infuriating.

"Although you were safe in Hester's hands, I wisl
could have spent more time with the three of you," th
mother continued. "I know I wasn't always there for t
moments when you needed someone to talk to."

A break in her voice revealed a rare vulnerable side
Charlotte. However, despite the sacrifices, CeCe kn
that her mother wouldn't have had things any other w
Fierce pride had motivated her to seize the helm of t
company when she might have sold it or looked to l
father's family for assistance.

"Most of all, I regret not raising you with a grea
appreciation of your father's heritage," she said. "It is
entirely the king's fault that we drifted apart. I take so
of the blame on myself."

"I'm not sure how much more we could appreciate it without living there full-time," Lucia said. "We're Americans, after all."

"You have dual citizenship and don't forget it!" said her mother. "If I'd had any inkling that this day would ever come…well, I can only hope that CeCe will rise to the occasion. If she doesn't, you two other girls must keep yourselves available. I won't tolerate excuses. Do I make myself clear?"

CeCe's cheeks flamed at the suggestion that she might be found lacking. Despite her pregnancy, she couldn't tolerate the thought of failing her family, especially her mother.

She'd always felt a duty to assist her mother, even if Charlotte rarely seemed to notice. As a teenager, CeCe had fussed with pretty dresses and social occasions only when her mother required it. Mostly, she'd devoted herself to her studies and to working part-time at the shipping company, learning the business from the ground up.

Now she was ready to take on the monarchy. The fact that she might not be allowed to, that she might bring disgrace on herself and her family just when everyone's hopes were riding on her, made CeCe want to cry.

Well, she wouldn't cry. She never cried, or hardly ever. Somehow, she was going to find a way to save face and pull this whole thing off.

SHANE WISHED HE COULD READ CeCe's thoughts. Something must be buzzing through her mind, he'd concluded during brunch. Fortunately, the Chinese trade representative, Mr. Wong, hadn't appeared to notice anything amiss.

To someone who knew her well, CeCe's attention seemed scattered. At the same time, she'd changed in a subtle way that made her coloring more vivid and her manner less brisk. Shane couldn't stop looking at her.

When they left the restaurant, he was glad to find that

the sun had come out. Despite the winter chill, across the street women were pushing baby carriages through Central Park while college-age skateboarders whizzed past.

"Let's take a walk," he said after Mr. Wong departed in a taxi.

CeCe regarded him suspiciously. "A walk?"

"I'll escort you to your apartment building, if you like," Shane said. "Or are you heading to the office?"

"The apartment." She pushed a wing of blond hair off her temple and started to step off the curb against the light.

He grabbed her arm. "What's wrong with you today?"

"I'm a little distracted," CeCe said.

"Tell me it's the effect of my boyish charm," Shane teased.

"Sorry, but it isn't."

The light changed and they crossed in a swarm of people. For no logical reason, he found himself wanting to protect her against jostling passersby.

"What's wrong?" he asked again. "Anything I can help you with?"

CeCe's eyes widened. "You want to help me?"

"If I can." He wondered if she was surprised by the idea that a woman in her lofty position might need anything from a man who'd had to claw his way up in the world. No, he thought, CeCe had never struck him as a snob. "What's going on?"

"It's…personal," she said.

Personal. That might mean she was seeing another guy. Shane disliked that notion thoroughly.

They veered onto a park path. Most of the other strollers were elderly people or mothers with young children. A couple of students, book bags at their feet, sat on a park bench, smooching.

On the lake, a few brave souls were ice skating. One

tiny ballerina spun around three times and then, losing her balance, plopped onto her rear end.

"So is he in the shipping business, too?" Shane asked.

"Is who in the shipping business?"

"This personal problem," he said.

CeCe burst out laughing. "I don't believe you said that!"

She thought he was jealous, Shane realized. Of course he wasn't. "Not that I care," he added.

"It's my family," CeCe said. "I'm sorry, I can't tell you any more than that. They're very strict about privacy."

Not having had a family since he was twelve, Shane had no idea what sort of matters families kept to themselves. He didn't enjoy feeling like an outsider. "We're practically partners. Your business is my business."

"This isn't business," CeCe corrected him. The cold air stung her cheeks and brightened her eyes, or perhaps the sunlight merely highlighted the changes Shane had noticed in the restaurant.

He decided not to pursue the subject. Instead, he made conversation about Mr. Wong and how their meeting had gone.

CeCe relaxed. Any minute, he thought, she'd let slip whatever was bothering her and then he could help her fix it.

SHE OUGHT TO TELL SHANE about the pregnancy, CeCe thought. But if she did, she would have to mention the repercussions involving her grandfather's visit and his offer to make her queen, both of which were state secrets.

It wasn't as if Shane was eager to be a father, she reminded herself. He'd made it clear how much he disliked children.

Also, from working in a mostly male environment, CeCe knew that most men's reaction to a problem was to leap in with an instant solution. That worked all right in business situations. When it came to personal matters, however, she would find it highhanded and infuriating.

She didn't want to get irritated with Shane today. His presence comforted her, even though she couldn't confide in him.

Central Park was a different place when she was with him. Usually, she walked through it mentally reviewing reports and formulating plans for DeLacey Shipping.

Today, she didn't want to concentrate on anything but Shane. The pattern of light and shadow falling across his face fascinated her. So did the vulnerable twist of his mouth.

Despite his protestations, what kind of father would he make? CeCe watched a mittened toddler tossing a ball with his father and tried to picture Shane in the man's stead. She couldn't make the stretch.

At least his company was peaceful. So peaceful that it wasn't quite normal.

"I know what's missing," she said.

"What?"

"Your cell phone's not ringing."

"Neither is yours," he said.

"I turned it off during brunch. So did you, I guess." When he nodded, CeCe said, "Maybe we should both turn them on."

"Maybe we shouldn't."

He moved closer. Despite their coats, she could feel heat radiating from his body. It made her itch to slide her hands inside his clothing and stroke his chest.

If she became queen, she would have to choose a husband who could reign alongside her, presumably someone from European nobility. CeCe hoped it was possible for her to get this excited about being close to another man. If she couldn't, well, she supposed that was the price a queen had to pay.

But right now, she had Shane to herself. There were so many details of his life that she wondered about, and it might be her last chance to ask him.

"Do you mind if I ask you something personal?" she said.

"Go ahead."

"I've heard the stories about your being an orphan." Seeing nothing in his expression to indicate she was trespassing on forbidden territory, she continued, "I've read that you built a struggling air-freight company into a major contender by carving out your own niche in the package-delivery business."

"You left out the part about my dogged work ethic and brilliant flashes of insight," Shane joked. "Otherwise, you got it right."

"What I never understood was how you got your hands on an air-freight company in the first place," CeCe said.

"CPR," he replied cryptically.

She tried to place the initials. "Is that a venture capitalist firm?"

"It stands for cardiopulmonary resuscitation."

"Oh, that kind of CPR," CeCe said.

"They taught it to us at the group home. Part of our health-and-safety training." Shane moved her gently aside as a messenger's bicycle whizzed past, its bell ringing. "Probably they figured we ruffians might give the counselor a heart attack."

"What's the connection to air freight?" she asked as they strode with their long legs in sync.

"While I was in high school, I got a part-time job at an air-freight company at Long Beach Airport," Shane said. "The owner, Morris O'Day, suffered a heart attack my third day on the job. While everyone else was waiting for the paramedics, I administered CPR."

"You saved his life?" CeCe asked.

"So Morris believed," Shane said. "Once he recovered, he took me under his wing and taught me the business."

"You must have impressed him in a lot of ways. He wouldn't have wasted his time on you otherwise." The teenage Shane, although no doubt slighter of build and less polished, must still have been a force to reckon with.

"We became friends," he said quietly. "Morris took the place of the father I'd scarcely known. My mentor, that's how I describe him to people, but he meant much more to me than that."

"You're speaking in the past tense," CeCe said. "Did he die?"

"Five years later, when I was twenty-two, he suffered another heart attack." Shane's pace slowed. "That time, I couldn't save him. Later, I was astonished to learn that he'd willed me the company. The assets were mortgaged and the planes were outdated, but it gave me a start."

"He didn't have any family?" CeCe couldn't imagine such isolation. "How sad that he didn't have a wife or a child. He worked so hard and then he had no heir."

"He did have an heir—me," Shane said crisply.

CeCe saw that she'd offended him. "Of course. You meant a lot to him."

"I've had to blaze my own trail. So did Morris," Shane snapped. "I guess that's hard for you to understand."

"What do you mean? I've had to..." She stopped herself in midsentence.

She'd intended to say that she'd had to work hard, but so what? There was no denying that her path had been paved. Much as CeCe hated to admit it, she would never have become executive veep at twenty-nine if she weren't the owner's daughter.

She knew that, with her drive and organizational abilities, she'd have made a success of herself one way or another. Not on the scale that Shane had, however, or at least not as rapidly. For one thing, she couldn't get by on five hours' sleep a night, as he was reputed to do.

They reached the west side of the park and headed for her apartment building a block away. CeCe wished she could undo the offense she'd given by her thoughtless remark about Morris.

Making truces came so easily to her sister Amelia. If only CeCe could borrow a pinch of her kind nature before it was too late.

"I didn't put things very well," she said, by way of preamble.

"You said what you meant. There's no need to apologize for the fact that you and I look at the world from very different perspectives." Shane spoke in an even, impersonal tone. "We're about as different as two people can be. I don't hold that against you, and I hope you don't hold it against me, either."

"It doesn't sound like you're leaving much room for us to meet in the middle," CeCe said.

"Was there ever any hope of that?"

She had to be honest with him, and herself. "I guess not."

In front of her building, they shook hands formally. "I'll keep in touch about the negotiations with Wuhan Novelty," Shane said, and walked away.

CeCe drank in the sight of his broad shoulders as he cut through the slow-moving tide of pedestrians. Her palm tingled where it had touched his moments before.

If her grandfather still wanted her to be queen after he learned of her pregnancy, she might not be handling the Wuhan negotiations, CeCe realized with a start. That meant there was a scary chance that she might never see Shane O'Connell again.

When she glanced back at the street, he'd disappeared.

Chapter Four

On her way up to the apartment, CeCe noticed that the royal guards weren't patrolling with Charlotte's regular staff. That meant her grandfather must still be at the embassy, thank goodness.

She needed time to sort out the turmoil in her mind. There were so many decisions to make, and despite her reputation as a take-charge executive, she had no idea how to make them.

Against her better judgment, she yearned to bring Shane into the picture. He'd just made it clear, however, that he saw no common ground between them, outside of their business alliance.

This would be the right time for most women to ask their mothers for advice. Unfortunately, CeCe knew exactly what Charlotte would say: (a) The man isn't right for you, (b) Of course you'll be queen, and (c) You're what?

Under the circumstances, she was glad to learn from Hester Vanderling that Charlotte had gone to the office. According to the housekeeper, Amelia was in her room, working on her computer, and otherwise the vast apartment was practically empty.

"The cook and her assistant have to work late tonight

to prepare a special dinner for your grandfather, so your mother gave them the morning off,'' explained Hester.

The housekeeper and her husband, Quincy, the Carradigne's butler, occupied private quarters. Since they lived on the premises, they were usually around although, like now, not necessarily on duty.

"Could we talk?" CeCe asked.

"I'd like that." Hester gave her a pleased but slightly puzzled smile.

Although she'd confided in Hester a lot in her younger years, CeCe rarely turned to her these days, believing she ought to handle her own problems. However, Hester, with her gentle nature, loyalty to her native land of Korosol and devotion to the Carradigne girls, might have exactly the perspective CeCe needed.

They went into the kitchen for coffee. From the broad terrace came a scuffling noise.

"What on earth?" said Hester.

"Got you, you skulking scumbag!" roared the voice of Quincy Vanderling.

"Oh, dear!" Hester pressed a wall button to summon security. "We'd better find out what's happening."

"It sounds like Quincy caught an intruder." No one had ever penetrated Charlotte's guards before. Or had the butler taken one too many nips of kitchen sherry and tried to tackle a pigeon? Quincy had his vices, but a better butler couldn't be found.

CeCe hurried into the breakfast nook. Through the wide-open French doors, she saw the husky butler wrestling a darkly tanned man with short brown hair. In his forties, the intruder was thin but muscular and easily held his own.

"He was in the kitchen!" Quincy panted when he spotted the women. "I chased him out here and caught him!"

The fellow stopped struggling and turned toward CeCe. "Hello, princess," he said with oily familiarity. "Why don't you call off this old geezer before he injures himself?''

Winston Rademacher. CeCe hadn't seen him in several years, but it was hard to mistake that creepy smile and those shifty eyes that always seemed to be squinting.

From the other side of the terrace, two guards raced toward the pair. "Hold on," CeCe called, stepping outside. "It's my cousin Markus's adviser."

Quincy dropped the fellow's arm. "You work for Markus Carradigne? Why didn't you say so?"

"No one gave me a chance." Rademacher tugged on his wrinkled coat sleeve.

"What are you doing here?" CeCe demanded.

His gaze met hers, then veered away. "Looking for the king. I'm in New York on Markus's business while he's tending to his affairs in Korosol."

"He was snooping, is more like it," retorted Hester. "I'm sorry, Miss CeCe. I shouldn't have said that, I suppose. Now, come inside, Quincy. It's cold out there."

"Call off your dogs, will you?" Rademacher sneered at the guards and strode toward CeCe.

On the few previous occasions when she'd met him, he'd struck CeCe as a dangerous type. She hoped Markus had researched the man's background.

Right now, his attitude offended her, and he'd had no business bypassing security on his way up. Still, it would give unnecessary offense to her cousin if her guards bodily ejected his confidant.

"You may go. Please check the locks on the back and side stairs," she told the two men.

That was probably how he'd broken in. In addition to connecting the apartment's two floors, the staircases served as emergency escape routes down through the building, although the heavy intervening doors could only be opened from the Carradigne side. "Quincy, you were very brave. Thank you for defending us."

"It was completely unnecessary." Rademacher oozed past CeCe into the kitchen.

"Mr. Rademacher." Her sharp tone halted him as he headed for the coffee carafe. "Your behavior is unacceptable."

"Is it indeed, princess?" Despite the supercilious tone, he hesitated.

"You had no business sneaking into this apartment without announcing yourself to the guards. The king is not here. I suggest you look for him at the embassy, and I suggest you do it now," CeCe said.

Resentment flashed across his face, and was instantly replaced by obsequiousness. "Whatever you wish, princess."

"I'll show you out," said Hester. Quincy accompanied her, watching Rademacher's every move.

A short time later, Hester returned alone. "We put him on the elevator," she said. "What an unpleasant man."

"Is your husband all right?" CeCe was fond of Quincy, a former handyman whose devotion to his wife and to the Carradignes was beyond question.

"He's better than all right. A scuffle like that makes him feel young again." Hester smiled. "Now, let's have that coffee."

They took their mugs to the breakfast table and sat facing each other. Outside, boxed evergreens on the landscaped terrace blocked the cityscape.

Memories from years past drifted comfortably over the scene. There'd been summer days when blooms transformed the terrace into a lush paradise, and rainy days when the nanny entertained the three girls with hot chocolate and Korosol folktales.

"What's on your mind?" asked the housekeeper.

CeCe released a long breath. She had to tell someone her news, and the longer she waited, the harder it would get. "Oh, Hester, I'm pregnant."

Her old friend blinked in surprise. "Well! I don't know what... You know, it might be the best thing for you."

"What?" CeCe had never expected this reaction.

"It's time you figured out you're a woman. You've been denying your feminine instincts ever since your father died," Hester said.

"I have not!" she flared.

"It was as if you thought you had to be the man of the family," said her friend, undeterred by the outburst. "For a while, you refused to wear anything but pants. It nearly gave your mother fits."

"I remember that." CeCe had assumed her behavior must have represented a typical preteen phase. Perhaps, though, there was some truth in the housekeeper's observation. "But, Hester, this isn't the right way to rediscover my feminine instincts, as you call them, even if I wanted to. It's a disaster!"

"That depends on who the father is." The nanny rose and brought back the coffee carafe. "I think we're going to need all of this. Want some pastries?"

"I don't know. I'll be big as a house soon enough as it is." CeCe moaned. "As for the father, he doesn't want children."

"Is he married?" On the table, the housekeeper set a crystal plate piled with lemon and apple Danishes.

"Of course not! He's out of the picture, though, believe me." Restlessly, CeCe picked a piece of apple off one of the pastries and popped it in her mouth.

"That's too bad," Hester said. "I was hoping you'd found someone special."

"I could claim I was artificially inseminated," CeCe mused. "Mother would never believe it, but the media might. Oh, who am I kidding? They'll raise a fuss whether I did it the old-fashioned way or not."

"Honesty is usually the best policy." Hester selected a lemon Danish.

"I've always believed that. Now I'm not so sure," CeCe admitted, picking away at her selection. "I've had these crazy ideas, like what if I start wearing caftans and hide the whole thing? I read about an old-time movie star who had a baby secretly out of wedlock, then spirited it off to an orphans' home. A while later, she adopted it."

"There are a few problems with that scenario." From long experience, Hester clearly knew that CeCe's racing mind would fill in the blanks.

It did. "Caftans would never escape my mother's eagle eye," CeCe conceded. "Plus, with today's open birth records, the media would catch on to that one in a second. It's hopeless. I don't know how to handle this."

"Are you asking whether I'll take care of the baby? Of course I will," Hester said. "If that's what you really want."

"That would be wonderful, but you'd have to come back to Korosol with me. Mother would throw a fit."

"Korosol?" asked her former nanny. "Why are you going there?"

The king's decision to name an heir apparently hadn't been disclosed to the staff. Although CeCe knew Hester would learn of it before long, it wasn't her place to break the news. "Lady Charlotte will explain about that soon enough. Oh, Hester, you can't believe what a problem this pregnancy is!"

"Getting back to the father," the housekeeper said. "Sooner or later, he's going to find out that you're expecting. I doubt any man you got involved with would walk away whistling."

"You don't know Shane." The name flew out of her mouth. Dismayed, CeCe wished she could call it back. Too late.

"Shane O'Connell is the father of your child?" Hester asked. "I thought you two quarreled all the time."

"Not *all* the time, I'm afraid." CeCe caught her breath

as she heard a rustling noise from the staircase. "What's that?"

"If it's termites, they're getting bigger every year." Hester went to investigate. After opening the door adjacent to the pantry, she peered down. "Nothing here."

"You don't suppose...?" CeCe's throat constricted, cutting off the words.

"I don't suppose anything," said the housekeeper. "You've always been one to worry, Miss CeCe. Right now you need to put your mind on your own health. Have you seen a doctor?"

"Of course."

"Did you get nutritional information?"

"It's in my rooms." CeCe's quarters lay directly above Hester's. "On the kitchenette counter, I think."

"I'll make sure Cook gets the information about your new diet. There's no need to tell her why," Hester said. "Take my advice and inform the father before he learns the truth from someone else."

"I don't see how he could. I haven't told anyone but you," CeCe said. "Not even Mom." She rarely referred to Charlotte by that childhood endearment.

"Don't delay." Hester might have said more, but just then the door to the back staircase opened.

Amelia stepped out. "Oh, good, there's something tasty to eat. I'm starved." Her upstairs suite, which was smaller than CeCe's, lacked its own kitchen facilities.

That must have been her poking around a few minutes ago, CeCe thought. She wondered how much her sister had overheard, and knew that, in any case, she could count on Amelia's silence.

Soon the king returned from the embassy along with his secretary and royal adviser, and Charlotte arrived at almost the same time. The day and evening passed in a blur, and CeCe never did find time to call Shane and set up an appointment to meet with him.

ON FRIDAY MORNING, Shane awoke at 5:00 a.m., as usual. After showering and dressing, he got on the Internet in his home office and checked business news around the world.

Everything that happened affected the shipping industry. Natural disasters, unstable governments, the weather, the economy and tariffs all had an impact on routes, insurance and expenses.

He noted changes in the port regulations in Genoa and that a twenty-year reconstruction project to deepen Shanghai's harbor was proceeding on schedule. Shane was pleased that he'd allied himself with a major player like DeLacey Shipping. It was exactly the complement he needed to his fleet of planes and trucks.

His new venture wasn't the only reason he was glad for the alliance. It had brought him together with CeCe. Shane still relished the lingering traces of her essence in his apartment, although perhaps that was his imaginiation.

Regretfully, he reviewed yesterday's conversation with her. He hadn't meant to push her away, yet that's exactly what he'd done. Why had he made it sound as if there was no hope of them getting together?

He'd been nettled by that comment she'd made about Morris not having a family. A man didn't need to marry and have children in order to care about people and enrich their lives.

Her remark had reminded him that he and Princess Cecelia Carradigne came from opposite and incompatible worlds. She couldn't begin to understand what it was like to be an orphaned teenager, unwanted, unloved and unvalued, or how precious the ties were that he'd forged with people like Ed and Morris. They *were* his family, even if their relationship didn't meet other people's narrow-minded definition of that term.

Nevertheless, Shane didn't understand why he'd lashed out so tactlessly. For some reason, it had angered him to

be reminded of the chasm stretching between him a
CeCe. Well, they'd run into each other again before lo
and the matter could be smoothed over then.

At 6:30 a.m., he heard Ferguson clattering around
the kitchen. Shane let his friend set his own schedule, a
Ed, who lived downstairs in a smaller unit, preferred h
ing free time in the middle of the day.

When the smell of turkey bacon reached him, Sh
logged off and went to eat. "This is great," he told
aide.

He knew how hard his assistant worked at keeping I
healthy. The man studied books on nutrition, and h
with his employer's permission, installed workout equ
ment in the spare room. Shane used it frequently, as mu
to make Ferguson happy as to keep himself in shape.

"Thank you, sir. I'm glad you like it." The assista
being by nature precise and detail-oriented, had train
himself to speak formally despite his rough-and-tum
upbringing. Although he occasionally dated, none of
women put up with his fussiness for long.

Next to Shane's plate lay today's newspapers. Od
Ed had set the *Manhattan Chronicle* atop the *Wall Str*
Journal. Even more oddly, he'd folded it open to Kri
Katwell's gossip column on page seven.

Shane occasionally read the column to keep up w
New York society. Many of the people featured in it w
potential business contacts.

He was in no mood for idle chitchat first thing in
morning, however, so he tucked the *Chronicle* beneath
Wall Street Journal and turned to the stock market repo
O'Connell Industries was up slightly, even in a down m
ket.

Ferguson, who preferred to eat his breakfast stand
at the counter, coughed discreetly. Shane ignored him

Despite his proper reserve, the aide loved coming i
personal contact with the rich and famous, and follow

their activities with keen interest. The man was apparently projecting his own love of gossip onto Shane. Whatever item had attracted his interest could wait.

Shane flipped to the front page of the *Journal* and read up on the situation in China and Russia. After finishing his nutritionally balanced meal—egg substitute, nonfat cottage cheese and fruit, along with the turkey bacon—he tucked the newspapers into his briefcase, bid his assistant farewell and set out for work.

When he got there, the elevator of his building was jammed, as usual. To his annoyance, Shane caught several people staring at him. It felt like an invasion of privacy, and besides, it made him wonder if there was a smear of something on his chin.

On the thirty-first floor, he went into the men's room and regarded himself in the mirror. Nothing was stuck to his face or tie.

Although his stylishly trimmed hair was getting a bit shaggy, it didn't look bad, he noted. Tawny had probably already scheduled him for a haircut next week. If not, Ferguson would remind her.

His scrutiny completed, Shane entered the sprawling front office of O'Connell Industries. As always, he treasured the music of telephones ringing, faxes beeping and voices taking orders and scheduling pickups.

Today, though, the noise seemed to diminish the moment he stepped inside. Faces turned in his direction, then were quickly averted.

Had he missed an important item of news? It seemed unlikely. If one of his planes had crashed or some other catastrophe occurred, he'd have been notified at once.

Maybe the staff was planning a surprise party. No, his birthday was in September, not February.

Shane entered his outer office and saw a woman from another department conversing in animated fashion with

Tawny. When she spotted Shane, the other woman said a quick "Good morning, Mr. O'Connell" and hurried out.

"You're looking sharp today," said his secretary. "Sleep well?" She gave the word *sleep* extra emphasis.

"I'm fine. Is today some kind of holiday?" Shane asked.

"Not for most of us." Tawny gave him a big grin. "It's a little early for Father's Day."

"What's that supposed to mean?"

"Don't tell me Ferguson didn't fill you in," she crowed. "I can't believe he let you walk out the door spit-ignorant."

Uneasily, Shane remembered the copy of the *Chronicle* folded open to Krissy Katwell's column. Evidently he'd been mentioned.

He searched his brain for anything he might have said or done this week that the pushy gossip writer could distort for her readers' amusement. Shane drew a blank.

"Don't bother to tell me," he said. "I'll find out for myself."

"I'm sure you will," said his secretary. "By the way, if you don't want the flowers, can I take them home?"

"What flowers?" said Shane.

"You'll see."

He went into his private suite. On a low table bristled an enormous arrangement of white lilies, pink roses, white baby's breath and blue carnations, tied with pink and blue ribbons.

Shane opened the card. "Congratulations! I knew you had it in you." It was signed by his office manager on behalf of the staff.

Sinking onto the couch, Shane opened his briefcase and took out the newspapers. The *Chronicle* was still open to page seven.

Looking at it, he couldn't imagine how he'd missed the headline before. In huge type, it read, Princess Royally Knocked Up.

Chapter Five

Ordinarily, the Carradigne women read the newspaper over breakfast. With King Easton as their guest, however, that seemed impolite, so Charlotte set the *Chronicle* and the *Times* aside to peruse later.

The cook, Bernice Styles, a red-cheeked, rotund woman in her sixties, provided a breakfast buffet. The selections ranged far beyond the family's usual cereal, eggs, orange juice and coffee.

CeCe supposed the small, salty fish and couscous must be traditional cuisine in Korosol, since she vaguely remembered eating them when her father was alive. She preferred to indulge herself with eggs and bacon, and added a bowl of oatmeal because it was on her doctor's recommended list.

Lucia joined them, having taken the subway from the SoHo district. "I'm sorry I had to work on some orders yesterday," she said. "Did I miss anything exciting?"

"We had a lovely dinner." The king sat straight in his chair, although to CeCe he looked a bit drawn. Traveling so far must be hard on a man of his years.

"What else did I miss?" Lucia asked.

"We caught Winston Rademacher sneaking around," CeCe said.

Charlotte nearly choked on a bite of pancakes. "You never mentioned that!"

"I figured it would be in the security report." The truth was that CeCe had been so preoccupied with thinking about her pregnancy that she'd forgotten about the incident until now.

"I haven't read it yet," her mother admitted. Every morning, the guards turned in a log of incidents during the past twenty-four hours.

"The man got by the guards?" Easton's hands formed fists on the edge of the table. "Did he threaten you?"

"Nothing so dramatic," CeCe said. "He was sneaking around when Quincy caught him. That's our butler."

"Is there some reason for concern?" Charlotte asked the king.

He frowned. "I hope not."

"Rademacher said Markus asked him to pay his respects to you," CeCe said. "I tried to be diplomatic, Grandfather, but I don't trust the man and I ordered him out."

Easton nodded approvingly. "You did the right thing. Very brave of you."

"Quincy's the one who was brave," she said.

"It speaks well of you to give credit to others." Her grandfather smiled at her approvingly.

He'd been doing that a lot. The previous evening, while they were dining and conversing with a few carefully chosen guests, CeCe had felt him watching her. As far as she could tell, she was meeting his standards.

Today, she must break the news about her baby. First, she'd decided, she would take Charlotte aside and admit the truth. Together, they could explain matters to the king and await his decision.

Last night, as she drifted off to sleep, CeCe had pictured an inquisitive baby gazing into her face. A chubby

toddler pelting through the palace gardens. A shy pre-
schooler holding her hand on the way to church.

She must have a few mothering instincts, although they
were only in the formative stages. With luck, King Easton
would turn out to have great-grandfatherly instincts and
forgive her indiscretion.

The fact that Shane didn't want to be involved could
be a benefit, CeCe mused as the breakfast-table chatter
swirled around her. Since there was no question of his
becoming her royal consort, they didn't have to worry
about his acceptability to the people of Korosol.

Only about whether the citizens would accept an out-
of-wedlock child. But who could resist a royal baby? she
wondered.

If Hester couldn't relocate, she'd find a Korosol
nanny. Under her care, the child would grow up secure
and comfortable during the hours that CeCe focused her
attention on running the country.

Relaxing a little, she sipped her orange juice. For the
first time since she'd received the doctor's news on Tuesday, her spirits rose.

Crisp footsteps marched toward them along the gallery
and the captain of the king's guard appeared. After a bow
to Easton, he said, "Excuse me, Your Majesty. Princess
Cecelia has a visitor."

"She usually doesn't receive guests during breakfast,"
Charlotte said.

"He's very insistent," said the captain. "He says he's
your business associate. A Mr. Shane O'Connell."

"Oh!" Charlotte's expression cleared. "Please show
him in."

"Very good, my lady." The captain withdrew.

CeCe's pulse sped at the realization that Shane was
here. Why had he come? It must have taken something
urgent to bring him here in person, when he could easily
have phoned.

"Should we let him see grandfather?" Amelia asked. "I thought his visit was a secret."

"Thank you for your concern, my dear, but I don't plan to skulk in back alleys," the king said. "It's only the press I'm avoiding."

CeCe patted her mouth with her napkin and wished she'd worn something more flattering than a simple blouse and skirt. Oh, well, at least she wasn't sitting here in her pajamas.

She heard the men approaching down the gallery and considered going to meet them. Since this was business, there was no need to subject Shane to a lot of social introductions.

A quelling glance from Charlotte nailed CeCe to her seat. Apparently their new partner had been chosen to receive the royal treatment.

The captain preceded him. "Your Majesty and ladies, Mr. Shane O'Connell." At a nod from the king, he departed.

Shane's presence filled the room. From CeCe's seated position, he looked even taller than usual.

"Your Majesty?" Shane repeated, studying the king in astonishment. "I didn't realize I was interrupting such an important occasion."

Charlotte rose graciously. "Your Majesty, may I present Mr. Shane O'Connell? His company and DeLacey Shipping recently formed an alliance. Mr. O'Connell, King Easton of Korosol."

"I've read about you." The king extended his hand. Still looking a bit stunned, Shane shook it, and nodded politely to Amelia and Lucia when they were introduced in turn.

He had a newspaper tucked under one arm, CeCe noticed. She wondered if he'd come to confer about some late-breaking development that affected their companies.

"Please join us," Charlotte said as she resumed her seat.

"Thank you. I already ate." Shane's jaw worked as if he had too many things to say and they were all trying to crowd out at once.

CeCe couldn't stay silent any longer. "Are you here on business?"

"Not exactly. I was hoping you'd have an explanation for this," he said, and set the newspaper on the table.

It was folded open to Krissy Katwell's column. When CeCe saw the headline, she wondered why no one had had the sense to install a floor that could open up and swallow her.

ON THE CAB RIDE from his office, Shane had rehearsed a list of questions to throw at CeCe. Was she carrying his child? If she was, why hadn't she told him before she blabbed to someone else?

He knew she wasn't foolish enough to have told the columnist herself. Obviously, however, she must have told somebody. The first person she should have confided in was Shane.

While cooling his heels downstairs waiting for Security to clear him, he'd grown angrier. How dare they treat him like a beggar? It seemed arrogant of the princess and her mother to surround themselves with guards decked out in military-style uniforms.

Discovering the presence of the monarch took the wind out of his sails. The precautions were justified, he conceded.

Since Shane had never heard CeCe mention her grandfather, he'd formed the impression that contact between the New York Carradignes and those of Korosol was almost nonexistent. He wondered what His Majesty was doing here, and wished his visit hadn't coincided with this scandalous bit of gossip in the newspaper.

Shane wasn't thrilled about airing his personal business in front of all these people. Since it had just been aired in front of a few hundred thousand readers, however, he didn't see that it made much difference.

For once, CeCe had nothing to say. She sat at the table wearing a horrified expression and avoiding everyone's eyes.

It was clear from her reaction that she hadn't told her family. Perhaps an employee at her doctor's office had betrayed patient confidentiality to earn a few bucks. Shane wouldn't put bribery past Krissy Katwell.

Charlotte was the first to speak. "This is nonsense. How dare that woman invent a story like this to smear my family?"

"She also smeared Mr. O'Connell," pointed out one of the sisters. He thought it was Lucia.

"Is it true?" the king asked quietly.

"It can't possibly be," Charlotte said. "My daughter and Mr. O'Connell are nothing but business associates."

CeCe's face went white. Shane hoped she wasn't going to faint.

The last of his anger evaporated. Seeing her reaction, he wished he could shield her from everyone else. Except, of course, himself.

"I don't see how…" CeCe stared at the newspaper so intently that Shane wouldn't have been surprised to see it burst into flames. "How did she…?"

"There can't be any truth to it." Charlotte sounded less sure of herself.

"Is there?" Shane asked.

"What do you mean, is there?" Charlotte's tone verged on shrillness. "There can't be any question in your mind, Shane—" she'd stopped addressing him as Mr. O'Connell, he noted "—unless you and CeCe, unless the two of you, well, you know."

"Cecelia?" the king asked gravely.

There was nothing of the kick-butt executive about her now. Tears glimmered in her green eyes and her lower lip trembled. She looked about fifteen years old.

"Yes," she said in a small voice.

"You're pregnant?" Shane said. "Why didn't you tell me?"

He focused on his sense of betrayal, because he couldn't immediately absorb the implications of impending fatherhood. It still seemed, as it had when he first read the gossip item, like something concerning a stranger.

"You said you didn't want children," she answered.

"I was speaking theoretically!" Well, not exactly, Shane had to admit, but he was in no mood to split hairs. Or heirs. "You asked me about appearing in a TV commercial, for Pete's sake."

"You mean the two of you…and then you found out you were…and you didn't breathe a word to me, your own mother?" Charlotte sputtered.

"She should have told him first, not you," Lucia said.

"Please, everyone," Amelia said in a placating tone, "it doesn't matter, anyway. The cat's out of the bag one way or the other."

"I'm sorry, Grandfather," CeCe said. "I know I've failed you."

Why was she apologizing to the king? This whole family was a bit off-center in its priorities, as far as Shane was concerned. "With due respect to Your Majesty," he said, "this is a matter between the princess and me."

"I'm afraid it's not that simple." Gripping the edge of the table, Easton stood up. "Young man, we need to discuss this matter outside."

For a disoriented moment, Shane pictured the king whipping out a sword and challenging him to a duel. Or, more likely, sending that muscular captain of the guard to do the deed. He'd never before regretted the fact that his education didn't include fencing lessons.

Charlotte fluttered to her feet. "I'll get your coat, Your Majesty. Or perhaps you'd prefer to use the family room? It's right through this door."

"It appears that in this apartment, the walls may have ears." The king glanced meaningfully at the newspaper.

"I'm sure nobody here had anything to do with it! But by all means use the lanai if you wish," said his daughter-in-law.

Summoned, the housekeeper brought coats for Shane and King Easton. The two men stepped onto a long covered porch, which, Shane reflected, must be a beautiful place in the summer. Even now, the surrounding terrace overflowed with potted evergreens.

His attention was fixed on the man beside him. King Easton, whom he'd read about and respected as a shrewd business and political leader, was tall and a bit thin, and possessed a piercing gaze.

Mercifully, there was no sign of a sword.

"I need to know your motives, young man." Easton's voice rang the length of the lanai.

"I'll admit to being irritated that my entire staff knew of my paternity before I did, but I'm not vindictive," he said. "Frankly, I don't know what I expected to happen once I got here."

The king stared across the greenery. "You wouldn't be the first self-made man to try to legitimize himself in society by taking a wife with royal blood."

"Excuse me, what?" Shane said. "You think I got your granddaughter pregnant on purpose?"

"It takes two to tango."

He struggled to rein in his temper. "I had no intention of getting her pregnant or using her to increase my social standing. As for CeCe, in case you haven't noticed, she has a mind of her own. I doubt she would even consider marrying me."

Shane couldn't believe he was standing here discussing

the possibility of marriage, and doing so with the King of Korosol. The world was turned upside down.

"I'm sure my granddaughter would never have gone to bed with you if she weren't interested in marriage," the king said.

"We're friends," Shane said. "What happened was unplanned. Until I read the newspaper this morning, I had no reason to think our relationship was going to develop any further."

"I must know your feelings about my granddaughter," said the king. "Do you love her?"

Shane couldn't answer that question because he had no idea what love felt like. It had died inside him the day he learned of his mother's death. "I wish her happiness," he said.

"What will make my granddaughter happy," the king said, "is to be spared a scandal by getting respectably married."

Married? If only the king knew how little happiness that was likely to bring his granddaughter!

Happiness was the one thing Shane couldn't promise anyone. Especially not CeCe, who, despite her reputation as a barracuda, was deeply sensitive.

He was too focused on self-preservation and success. Too selfish, perhaps. He couldn't see himself ever becoming the sort of reliable, domesticated husband who dandled children on his knee and opened his heart to his wife.

"There already is a scandal," Shane pointed out. "It's too late to prevent one."

"Not if you announce that you've been secretly engaged." Easton clasped his hands behind his back and paced along the lanai. Shane walked alongside. "You can be married before the birth, which is what matters."

"Not to everyone," Shane said.

"Pregnant brides were common and accepted throughout history, even royal history, despite the way our Victorian ancestors tried to hide that fact,'' the monarch replied. ''Children born out of wedlock are a different matter to my people.''

Shane couldn't believe the king was pressing him, an orphan and former runaway from the streets of Los Angeles, to marry a princess. In any case, it was CeCe who needed to make this decision. Did she want to get married?

And what kind of marriage could he offer her? And a baby! Shane already knew that he couldn't bear to see his childhood self reflected back at him, dredging up the long-buried sense of loss.

He'd done his best to leave that miserable part of his past behind him. When the memories came haunting, he threw himself harder into his work. One of the advantages of compressing his rest hours, he'd learned, was that he slept so soundly that he almost never remembered his dreams.

He didn't want to remember them. He didn't want to relive his childhood and he believed a marriage to CeCe would make both of them miserable.

''Your Majesty,'' he said, ''I know your granddaughter pretty well and I think you're mistaken about what she wants for her future. As far as it concerns me, that is.''

''You think she enjoys scandalizing decent society?'' Easton glared at him.

Scandalizing decent society? Did anybody still think in those terms? Shane wondered. Well, obviously the king did, and he was the one whose opinion mattered to the Carradigne family.

''What I meant was, I don't think she wants to get married just for the sake of propriety,'' he said. ''Why should a beautiful woman like her settle for a marriage of convenience?''

''I'll tell you why,'' said the king. ''So she can be queen of Korosol.''

He might as well have suggested that CeCe wanted to plant cabbages on the moon. "I beg your pardon?"

"This is a state secret, which I'm only revealing to you because of the unusual circumstances," Easton said. "Do I have your word that you'll breathe nothing of it to anyone?"

"You have my promise."

"I plan to retire soon, and I've chosen Cecelia as my successor," the king said.

Shane could hardly breathe. CeCe was going to be a queen? The guy wasn't kidding! "Has she agreed?"

"Of course. It's a tremendous honor and she has all the right qualifications." Easton reached the end of the lanai and turned back. Shane stayed by his side, his mind racing.

Although he knew of CeCe's royal connection, it had never meant anything to him. People with even the slightest claim to nobility traded on it in New York society. They didn't suddenly find themselves ruling European kingdoms, however.

"Naturally, she can't assume the throne while she's under a cloud," the king continued. "It would reflect badly on my people. Korosol isn't only a country, it's also a business entity. Tourism and exports are affected by the way other nations view us."

"I don't doubt it."

"Well?" said the king. "Are you a man or a cad?"

Shane visualized CeCe's face as she'd looked a few minutes ago at the breakfast table. The tears in her eyes. The slumping shoulders. The crushed expression.

He'd never meant to hurt her. Only yesterday, he'd been trying to get closer to her as they walked in the park, until she accidentally touched a nerve.

Why not marry her, if it would save her from public humiliation and grant her dream at the same time? That didn't mean they had to become a conventional couple.

They didn't have to live together, he supposed. Still, he hoped there would be occasional splendid interludes like the one at his apartment.

"Would you expect me to live in Korosol?" Shane asked.

"That's for you and the princess to decide," Easton said. "With your business in America, you could spend as much time here as you like. You'd be expected to make appearances in Korosol on state occasions, that's all."

"You really are talking about a marriage of convenience," Shane said.

"Naturally, you'd have to keep that fact to yourself," the king said. "We don't want the whole world knowing the details of your relationship."

Shane had never expected to marry, not with the hours he kept. But this wouldn't be a real marriage, so he wouldn't be making a sacrifice. As for the baby, he'd have to maintain some contact, but since he wouldn't be around much, he could avoid the daily pain of reliving his own childhood.

Shane was sorry, for his child's sake, that they must remain virtual strangers, but he knew his own limits. Besides, the child would have King Easton's fatherly presence.

"I'll be glad to marry CeCe, if she'll have me," he said.

"Good. Now you won't have to face a Korosolan firing squad." The king smiled. "I won't insult you by asking if you expect any financial advantages."

"I'd prefer that there weren't," Shane said. "I don't want anyone to think I'm marrying CeCe for money. I'm very fond of her and I want to do what's right."

"Good." Easton's approval warmed him. There was a quality of gruff kindness about the monarch that reminded Shane of his mentor. "Shall we go inside?"

"Certainly," he said, and opened the door for the king.

Chapter Six

The moment the men left the breakfast room, CeCe braced herself for an onslaught. It wasn't long in coming.

"Well!" said her mother. "What did you think you were doing?"

"I've known the facts of life for quite some time," CeCe said, purposely misunderstanding her mother's point.

"That's not what I meant!"

"You mean, going to bed with Shane?" Now that the king wasn't watching her every move, she no longer felt so constrained. "It was late at night and we got carried away. Are you telling me you've never looked at another man since Dad died?"

"Never!" Charlotte said. "Well, maybe I've looked, but that's as far as it goes. Besides, this has nothing to do with me."

"The best defense is a good offense," Lucia teased. "My sister knows the rules of battle."

"We need to focus on the matter at hand," Amelia said. "CeCe can't undo the past, even if she wants to, so there's no point in scolding her."

Charlotte wasn't going to let the matter drop that easily. "When I asked what you thought you were doing, CeCe, I was referring to contraception."

"Hester told me what I needed to know when I was thirteen," CeCe said. "She discouraged me from having sex, of course."

"Thirteen?" Charlotte's hand flew to her throat. "I had no idea she was filling your head with such ideas."

"They taught us all that stuff at school, too," Lucia said. "Get with the times, Mom."

"I can see what 'getting with the times' has done for your sister," Charlotte retorted.

"There's nothing new about an unwed mother," Amelia pointed out.

"In this case, there is," snapped their mother. "Your grandfather had chosen you as his successor, CeCe. Now heaven knows what he'll decide."

"What do you suppose Shane is going to do?" Lucia asked. "He sure is handsome, CeCe. I just hope he's not a jerk like...never mind."

Three years earlier, Lucia's fiancé had turned out to be a social-climbing liar. Since then, she'd kept men at arm's length.

CeCe didn't know what to expect from Shane. Just because he was a decent, honest guy didn't mean he was suddenly going to change his mind about children. "He rarely thinks about anything but work."

"Oh, really?" said her mother. "I'd say he thought about something else at least once."

"All men think about *that*," Lucia said.

"Becoming a father might change him," Amelia added. "Some men really dote on children."

CeCe shook her head. "He told me himself he doesn't like kids and has no interest in having any."

"He said he was speaking theoretically," Amelia pointed out.

"I don't care what he wants," Charlotte said. "He'd better shape up or I'll make his life miserable."

"Mother!" CeCe said. "It's my life, too, and it would

be pretty darn miserable being married to a man who doesn't love me.''

''You'll do it, anyway,'' her mother said.

CeCe folded her arms. ''No,'' she said. ''I won't. And he isn't going to ask me, anyway.''

The door from the lanai scraped open. Cold air blasted past them as the men hurried inside and shrugged off their coats.

Quincy appeared from the hallway to assist them. CeCe's cheeks burned to realize that some of the servants must have overheard enough of this conversation to know what was going on. Then she remembered that they'd all probably read Krissy Katwell's column before they came to work, and she blushed even harder.

King Easton was smiling. Shane gave CeCe a reassuring nod. Somehow she didn't feel reassured.

''I'm glad to say that you've chosen a sensible young man,'' her grandfather told her as he chafed his hands together.

She hadn't chosen Shane, CeCe thought. At best, her raging hormones had chosen him. She knew better than to say so, however.

''Lady Charlotte,'' the king said, ''you will please arrange for your public relations consultant to issue a press release. I presume you have a PR person?''

''Of course,'' she said. ''We keep a firm on retainer.''

''Have them announce the engagement of my granddaughter to Mr. Shane O'Connell,'' he said. CeCe's jaw dropped, and she barely summoned the presence of mind to close it. ''We will make clear that the engagement has been of some months' standing and is being publicized only because of the breach of privacy caused by a certain newspaper article.''

Charlotte clapped her hands together. ''I knew it! They're getting married.''

Did they actually believe she would agree to an arranged marriage? CeCe wondered in shock. True, she'd fallen into bed with Shane of her own free will, but people these days didn't feel compelled to marry just because they'd made a mistake.

"Grandfather—"

He cut her off. "The marriage will take place immediately."

"What do you mean, immediately?" Charlotte said.

"Within a few days."

"I'm sorry, Your Majesty, but I won't have them rushing to some judge's chambers to sign papers!" It was amazing to see her stand up to her father-in-law, probably for the first time ever. "I've dreamed all my life about my oldest daughter's wedding. My other daughters', too, of course, but this is the first one. Besides, the future queen of Korosol ought to get married in style!"

"The future queen of Korosol isn't going to—" Again, CeCe didn't get a chance to finish.

"You're right, my dear. It won't do for her to sneak off as if she had something to hide," the king said. "We'll announce the wedding for two weeks from tomorrow."

"Two weeks?" Charlotte shrieked. "That isn't even enough time to get out the invitations!"

"My secretary will help you," Easton said. "She's a marvel."

"We'll all help," Amelia said. "Mom, with your social secretary and your PR firm, we can do it."

"I don't know," Lucia said. "Big weddings are kind of stuffy, don't you think? They might want to get married on our yacht."

CeCe thought of reminding them that she got seasick on the yacht. That wasn't the point, though. "Listen, everybody—"

"I'll call my favorite designer," Charlotte said. "She'll turn her entire salon over to us. She had some fabulous wedding gowns in her last collection. Thank goodness the baby isn't showing yet! We'll need two bridesmaid's gowns, and of course I have to be properly turned out.''

"Reality check!" called CeCe. "I haven't said yes. Did anybody notice?"

"I did," Shane said.

"The two of you must talk." King Easton studied them meaningfully. "There's an important decision to be made."

"There's nothing to decide." Charlotte's face took on the brook-no-arguments look that CeCe had learned to dread. Until now, she'd never defied it. "My daughter will do what I tell her to."

This was different. If there was one thing Charlotte could not command, it was CeCe's marriage. "Wait a minute," she said. "It's my life and I'll do what I want with it."

"Not if you expect to be queen of Korosol," said her mother. An implied threat hung in the air. *The king will choose one of your sisters.*

Two days ago, when her grandfather first mentioned the possibility, CeCe hadn't seriously entertained the idea of becoming queen. She'd only held off giving a response out of respect.

Yet during the tumultuous past day and a half, her acceptance had begun to seem inevitable. There was so much good she could do, with her organizational and business skills.

CeCe didn't relish the prospect of mastering the arts of diplomacy and politics. She hated to leave the shipping company after all the work she'd put into it, too. Yet it went against the grain to tuck her tail between her legs and flee from the challenge her grandfather had presented.

Especially, she hated to have her decision forced by a snoopy gossip columnist and by wagging tongues. But CeCe couldn't marry Shane. Even though her grandfather had persuaded him to go through with it, that didn't mean he loved her.

Or that she loved him. In fact, she wasn't sure how she felt about him.

"It's time for CeCe and me to have a private discussion," Shane said.

"This is a matter of state!" Charlotte protested. "We're all involved."

King Easton made a quieting gesture with his hands. "My dear, I can tell you that what goes on inside the palace walls involves fallible human beings, not figureheads. Princess Cecelia must agree to this match of her own free will. My people don't want a quarreling royal couple, let alone a divorce. Once the knot is tied, it stays tied."

Shane paled slightly. Or perhaps CeCe imagined it, because his voice was steady when he said, "Is there somewhere private that isn't freezing cold?"

"My place." She opened the door to the backstairs. "This way."

SHANE HAD NEVER BEEN in an apartment as enormous as this one. In fact, he'd seen few houses as spacious.

They emerged on the upper level. To one side, a railing separated them from the two-story grandeur of an immense salon. On the other side, he glimpsed an office. "That's the guest suite where my grandfather's staying," CeCe explained. "The office used to be my father's. His portrait hangs over the desk."

Shane glanced inside. The painting showed a handsome man with green eyes like CeCe's. He looked startlingly young, and Shane remembered that the prince had been only in his thirties when he died.

They went into the central hall, which extended for quite a distance to their left. "What's down there?"

"Amelia's suite and two guest bedrooms," CeCe said.

"At the end is the exercise room and sauna." Turning right, she led him through a home theater equipped with the latest in big-screen technology. From what he could see, the sound system would have done credit to a commercial theater.

Through a far door, they entered a self-contained suite. CeCe even had her own kitchen, Shane noticed, although some coffee remaining in a carafe was the only sign of recent use.

Skirting the dining counter, they entered the living room. Unlike the huge formal salon, this room had a cozy air, with brightly colored cushions scattered across several armchairs and a couch. French doors led onto a balcony.

"Nice place," he said.

"Want some coffee?" A wisp of blond hair fall across CeCe's face, making her look shy. "I can reheat it in the microwave."

"No, thanks." As he sank into one of the armchairs, Shane noticed a photograph of boats with many-hued sails. "I like your taste in decorating."

"This is the one place I can be myself." CeCe walked to the counter and leaned against it. With her long legs and slender neck, she was pure Thoroughbred.

Shane remembered the exhilarating sensation of having those legs wrapped around his hips. When she made love, CeCe threw her entire body into it, and what a body it was.

He fought the impulse to go over and unbutton that red silk blouse. He'd like to lift her tailored skirt to reveal the lacy panties he knew she wore underneath. He would, of course, do nothing of the sort.

"My parents used to live in this suite when I was little," CeCe explained. "After my father died, my mother moved downstairs. When I started college, I didn't ask permission—I just took over. Mom never objected, so here I stay."

"Until you move to the palace," Shane said.

Restlessly, CeCe perched half on and half off a stool. "Isn't it weird? Grandfather sprang the whole business on me two days ago."

"Out of the blue?"

"Completely." Her eyes widened expressively. "Can you picture me in a tiara?"

"I think you should wear one at our wedding," Shane said.

"About that," CeCe said. "You can't be serious."

"Far be it from me to separate a queen from her throne." He kept his tone light.

"Is this your idea of making a sacrifice for my sake?" She regarded him suspiciously. "Exactly what did my grandfather tell you?"

Any implication that his offer of marriage was charity, and CeCe would undoubtedly refuse. The Carradignes had been raised to give to others, not to take for themselves. Shane wondered if they realized that sometimes other people wanted to give to them.

He'd meant it when he said he desired CeCe's happiness. It was going to take a lot of careful phrasing to persuade her to accept, however.

"Your grandfather didn't have to talk me into anything," Shane said. "I may have grown up poor, but I have my pride. A man doesn't abandon his child."

"You don't need to worry. This baby will have everything a child could want." Idly, she swiveled her stool a few times.

"You mean money?" Shane said. "You've always had money. Does that mean you had everything you wanted?"

"I didn't have my Dad," she conceded.

"That's my point."

"You can be a father without being my husband," she said.

The woman was too smart for her own good, he

thought. "Okay, I admit it, I wasn't primarily concerned for our baby."

"Now we're getting down to it." CeCe popped off the stool and straightened some magazines on a table. "He talked you into rescuing me, didn't he? Save poor Princess Cecelia from the evil gossipmongers!"

"No. I'm doing this because I like you." To Shane, his words sounded incredibly tepid. "Scratch that. I want to marry you because there's something between us. I'm beginning to realize that we're a lot alike."

"In some ways." She twisted a strand of hair around her forefinger, then released it and squared her shoulders. "That's even more reason for us to keep our distance."

He needed more arguments but, in truth, Shane didn't know why he'd decided to marry CeCe, except that it felt right. "I don't want to marry anybody else," he said. "Ever."

"You mean I win by default?" Her smile quickly frayed around the edges.

"Neither of us is the romantic type," he said. "This marriage makes perfect sense, and that's a good enough reason for it."

For one vulnerable moment, CeCe looked as if she'd been hoping for the champagne-and-roses, down-on-his-knees approach. Then her chin came up. "Why does it make perfect sense? Explain it to me logically."

"We both know we're physically compatible," Shane said. "We can talk to each other. And you're pregnant. Those are important elements, so why not marry? I won't be living in Korosol, but everyone will be a winner. You get the throne, our child has two parents even if one of them isn't around much, and I get a wife I admire and find incredibly attractive."

CeCe drew in a long, shaky breath. "So attractive that you don't plan to stick around?"

"You wouldn't want me hanging out in the palace, trying to run your life, would you?'' Shane teased. ''Remember how much alike we are. Both bossy, for one thing.''

''It's just not—I mean, when I think about marriage, I picture what my parents had,'' CeCe admitted. ''They were so much in love. Mom got into a flutter every time Dad came home from work.''

''I can't imagine you getting into a flutter,'' Shane said.

She started pacing. ''I'm not the kind of person to find my identity in a man, that's for sure. But I have these pictures in my mind of what a marriage ought to be. I guess they're childish.''

''You can't be a queen and have the kind of marriage your mother did,'' Shane said gently. ''From what I've heard, she was a socialite with very few responsibilities until your father died. When she took over DeLacey Shipping, people thought she'd make a mess of it.''

''She wasn't prepared,'' CeCe agreed. ''I'm not so sure I am, either.'' She perched on the arm of a chair. ''Can you visualize me as a queen? What if I trip over the carpet during royal audiences? And I can't pour tea worth a darn.''

''Queens don't have to pour their own tea,'' Shane said. ''Although I'll admit I hadn't given much thought to how you'll manage state occasions.'' He grinned at the image of coltish CeCe trying to transform herself into a regal figure. ''I'm sure you'll grow into the job.''

''You know, maybe marrying you isn't such a bad idea,'' she said.

''What changed your mind?''

''The fact that you have no illusions,'' CeCe said. ''You already know what a klutz I can be. If I married some European prince, he'd have me pigeonholed as this paragon of virtue. The real me would be a letdown.''

''No guy in his right mind would feel let down when he got to know you,'' Shane said.

"That's sweet." She tapped her fingers on the back of the chair. "Let me clarify this. When you said we were physically compatible, you meant that our marriage would include...I mean, it wouldn't be completely platonic."

Was she kidding? Shane wanted to get unplatonic right now, and five minutes from now, and five minutes after that. "There's no sense in leaving out the fun part."

The corners of her mouth twitched with suppressed humor. "I see."

"Come on, deny that you had a good time! I want to hear you tell a whopper," he teased.

"I refuse to dignify that remark with a response," CeCe said. "But I agree that a marriage ought to include at least the possibility of, well, having more children. If we're going to get married, that is."

"Our marriage is going to include the possibility of making a whole lot of whoopee, as people used to say in my grandparents' day," Shane replied. "We agree on that."

She didn't give him an argument. Instead, she said, "I need to think. Would you mind going downstairs for a few minutes?"

"No problem." Shane stood and laid a reassuring hand on her arm. The woman had an appealing scent, sophisticated and unpretentious at the same time, and, up close, her eyes gleamed at him with green clarity. "I'll be waiting."

He ached to gather her in his arms, and knew he would only make her uncomfortable if he tried. Firmly, he took himself out the door and left the princess to make her decision.

CECE MISSED SHANE the moment he disappeared. At the same time, it was a relief to be alone. She hadn't had a moment to think since she learned about Krissy Katwell's column.

She walked to the French doors and stood staring over the balcony toward Seventy-seventh Street. Traffic noises drifted upward. CeCe tried to remember what sounds floated through the palace in Korosol. Not traffic, that was for sure.

When she'd first learned that she might become queen, she recalled thinking that it would mean never seeing Shane again. Now, it appeared, she could have him and the crown, too.

Not really have him, of course. He hadn't mentioned love, only sex.

Why not? she wondered. Hadn't their night together meant more than that to him? On the other hand, what exactly had it meant to her?

A self-protective instinct made her want to push him away. She felt too vulnerable around the man, too much in danger of losing her self-control.

When Shane had touched her arm a moment ago, she'd yearned for him to hold her close. But he hadn't, and it was for the best.

CeCe didn't want to give in to her weakness. She never wanted to depend on a man and risk suffering the way her mother had when, one way or the other, she lost him. Why on earth had she said she wanted a marriage like her parents'?

Her grandfather and Shane had the right idea. Make it a marriage of convenience, save everyone's honor and allow her to give Korosol the single-mindedness its people deserved from their ruler.

CeCe went into the bedroom. From among a group of stuffed animals on a seat, she lifted a well-worn toy owl.

Staring into its black eyes, she remembered the day her father had brought the owl back from a trip to Montreal. One of her sisters had eagerly seized a fuzzy stuffed moose, and the other hugged her white bunny with a cry of glee.

Drake had knelt and placed the owl in CeCe's arms. "The minute I saw this guy, he reminded me of you," he'd said. "While I'm gone, I get the feeling you're watching over things until I return."

"Somebody has to," CeCe recalled saying. She'd been about eight years old at the time.

"You're the steady one," her father had said. "I know I can rely on you."

I know I can rely on you. Those words had echoed through her mind all these years, guiding her. As they guided her now.

Korosol, her father's heritage, was counting on CeCe. Who needed a man to love and cherish when she had a kingdom to take care of?

With a sense of surrendering to fate, she returned the toy owl to its place and went to announce her decision.

Chapter Seven

Watching Shane, King Easton thought, *he's in love with her and doesn't know it.*

The young man had joined the others in the family room a few minutes before, explaining that CeCe wanted time alone to think. He'd been peering anxiously toward the door every thirty seconds since.

No one else appeared to notice Shane's fixation, not with the fuss Charlotte was making. She kept taking out her cell phone and then putting it away. "I want to start setting the wedding plans in motion," she said. "Why doesn't my daughter get it over with?"

"There might not be anything to set in motion," Lucia cautioned. The girl had spirit, Easton thought, although her sharp edges could use a little buffing.

Charlotte ignored the comment. "I don't think we should have the wedding here. Too many people traipsing through the apartment. We'd never be able to maintain security."

"A hotel would be too public," cautioned Amelia. The girl showed good sense, her grandfather decided.

"Definitely not a hotel," Charlotte agreed. "Amelia, do you remember Sandra Abernathy's wedding last year? They rented an old mansion on the Upper East Side. It was beautiful, and private, too."

Her daughter nodded. "There was a courtyard, and the couple left in a horse-drawn carriage like in a scene from Cinderella. It was great."

Charlotte made a note in her pocket organizer. She'd been jotting things down every few seconds, or so it seemed to the king. "I'll have my secretary see if it's available. The mansion *and* the carriage."

"For enough money, anything is available," Lucia observed dryly.

"What do you think, Shane?" asked Amelia.

He glanced up, startled. "About...? Oh, renting a mansion. That's an excellent idea. It'll be easier to keep the press out."

"It's going to be wonderful!" Charlotte said. "Absolutely perfect. Now, why doesn't that girl come down here so we can get started?"

The king was looking forward to the wedding, too. He enjoyed the pomp and circumstance of his position, although he was careful not to waste the public's money. In this case, his very wealthy daughter-in-law would be spending the ample DeLacey funds, and she would indeed spare no expense.

He and Cassandra had been married at the palace, in a lavish ceremony attended by royalty from throughout Europe and the Middle East. To the groom, the festivities had flown by in a blur.

What remained sharply in memory was his bride, the descendant of French nobility, looking fresh and angelic as she stood beneath a rose-covered trellis. When she gazed at him, her eyes shone with happiness.

They'd had no idea of the tragedies that lay ahead. Or the joys, either. They'd been lost in their love for each other, a love that had sustained them through a half century of married life.

"Remember the wedding designer who staged Phyllis

Talley's affair?'' Charlotte asked her daughters. "I'll challenge him to come up with a special theme.''

"A fairy-tale wedding!'' Amelia said. "What else could it be?''

"Oh, there she is,'' Charlotte said. "Finally!''

Easton caught his breath as a figure appeared in the doorway. It was Cecelia, looking gloriously like Cassandra.

"I'm sorry to have kept you all waiting.'' To Shane, she said, "I'll be happy to marry you.''

He hurried to take her hands. "It's the right decision.''

"We…we agree that I'll be living in Korosol and you'll be free to pursue your business interests, right?'' she said. "Do we need to sign any papers?''

"A prenuptial agreement?'' Charlotte said. "I'm sure that isn't necessary!''

"It isn't,'' Shane said. "CeCe, we understand each other. If there are any rough patches, we'll talk things out.''

"Okay.'' Tension visibly eased from her shoulders and jaw. "What's next?''

"We need to pick a ring,'' said the groom.

"Your dress comes first!'' insisted her mother.

"What are the bridesmaids going to wear?'' asked Amelia.

"I'll make you a special piece of jewelry,'' said Lucia. "I can't wait to get started.''

Easton took out his cell phone and called Ellie. For the next two weeks, this family was going to need all the help it could get.

THE PRESS RELEASE was issued Sunday night, too late for the TV news, on the advice of Charlotte's press agent. The woman suggested they would have more control over what was stated, and less of a media circus, if the announcement came out first in the morning newspapers instead of on television.

She had underestimated the press's interest, Shane discovered when he arrived at work Monday morning.

Camera crews from a local station, a network and a European news service had staked out the sidewalk in front of his office building. In addition, there was no missing the predatory figure of Krissy Katwell, her jet-black hair flying in the breeze and her dark eyes snapping with impatience.

Shane broke his stride when he saw what awaited him. For one wild moment, he considered fleeing, then rejected the idea as unworthy.

Might as well get it over with. Besides, he'd been spotted.

The fortyish gossip columnist outshoved her rivals in the race toward him, and then halted, blocking his path. Although she was short, Krissy's fierce determination gave her an edge over her rivals.

"Shane!" Although they'd never been introduced, she addressed him as if he were a pal. "Was it my column that forced your hand?"

"No one forced anything," he said. "CeCe and I have been engaged for months."

"Oh, really?" Krissy returned. "You were seen in Tiffany's on Saturday, buying a diamond ring. If you've been engaged for so long, why wait until now?"

"We wanted to keep it secret," he said. "If CeCe had showed up wearing an engagement ring, that wouldn't have been very discreet, would it?"

"Is the princess really pregnant?" asked a reporter.

"I'm happy to say we're expecting our first child in September." Shane had rehearsed his lines carefully. His normal off-the-cuff manner was too perilous for a situation like this.

"What does her grandfather, the king, think of this situation?" said a woman from the European news service.

Here was a touchy point. There must be no mention of Easton's presence in New York, or of CeCe's future as queen of Korosol. Those matters would be revealed later, when it suited the king.

"I understand he's delighted," Shane said. "We have his blessing. Now, if you'll excuse me, I've got work to do."

Krissy remained planted directly on front of him. "I'd like to know whether the princess became pregnant before or after you negotiated your business alliance with De-Lacey Shipping."

"Somewhere in the middle," Shane couldn't resist saying. The other reporters laughed.

He was starting to think he'd have to move Krissy bodily out of his way when Tawny Magruder trotted out of the building. Despite a killer pair of high heels and a straight skirt, his secretary made top speed as she barreled at Krissy. Alarm flared through the columnist's beady eyes, and she sidestepped at the last minute.

"You've got an urgent call, Mr. O'Connell," Tawny said, although he guessed it was merely an excuse for an interruption. "You're needed upstairs at once."

"Thanks. She's a great assistant," he told the press, and followed her into the building.

"How're you holding up?" she asked when they were in the elevator.

"Getting tired of being polite," he admitted. "If you hadn't rescued me, I might have spoiled my suave image."

"Yeah, real suave." Tawny plucked a stray scrap of paper from his hair. "You should check yourself in a mirror when there's this much wind."

Shane made a mental note to avoid watching himself on television that night.

YUKI YAMAZAKI, CHARLOTTE'S favorite dress designer, rescheduled her Tuesday appointments so the Carradigne women could descend on her showroom undisturbed. "I'm thrilled to be doing the wedding," she said when they arrived. "We'll get everything ready on time, I promise."

The designer ushered them into a private salon furnished with couches and armchairs. An aide offered coffee, tea and white wine.

Eleanor Standish, who was assisting the king's family at his request, peered around the salon in confusion. "I don't see any clothes," she murmured to CeCe.

"They'll bring them out later," she answered. "Let's order something for you to wear, too."

The secretary ducked her head. "No, thanks. I brought a gown with me."

CeCe wondered if it was as unflattering as the baggy clothes Ellie usually wore. The young woman obviously didn't like to put herself on display, though, and if the king had no objection to her manner of dressing, it was no one else's business.

Normally, CeCe spent as little time as possible on her own wardrobe, although she'd been named on someone's Best Dressed list last year. Familiar with her tastes, Yuki would send over sketches of new designs from her seasonal collections, along with suggested swatches of fabric.

CeCe would make her choices, and after the clothes were sewn to her measurements, she went in for a final fitting. Other than that, she did as little shopping as possible. There were too many more important matters occupying her mind.

Her interest sparked, however, as models entered the salon in the latest bridal designs. Yuki's gift for drama showed in one explosion of lace and satin, which was followed by a tightly wrapped, strapless length of silk that appeared suspended around the chest by sheer willpower.

"How does that thing stay up?" Ellie asked.

"Must be Velcro," Lucia said.

"I'll bet the groom can't wait to unwrap her," said Amelia, and then blushed furiously.

"Something a bit more traditional, I think," Charlotte said.

CeCe agreed. A few minutes later, her heart leaped as a model appeared wearing an antique-style gown with a high collar, Empire waist and long, cuffed sleeves. Unexpectedly sheer fabric across the upper chest, back and arms created a sensual effect.

"It's a bit revealing," Charlotte said.

"I love it." On CeCe's mental movie screen, Shane's dark eyes deepened with passion as he gazed at her from the altar.

She pulled herself up short. There was no point in fantasizing about a man who was only marrying her because of the circumstances.

At Tiffany's last Saturday, Shane's manner had been courteous but distant. During dinner on Sunday, when he'd joined her family, he'd spent most of his time talking to the king about the European economy.

She longed for his touch and for some kind of reassurance. He'd offered nothing of the kind.

"If you like it, we'll buy it," Charlotte said. It took a moment for CeCe to remember that her mother was referring to the wedding dress.

"Excellent choice," Yuki said. "That's the one I thought would suit Princess Cecelia. Now for a veil…"

"I'd prefer a tiara," CeCe said.

Everyone gazed at her in surprise. Charlotte recovered first. "That's a wonderful idea."

"I'll make some sketches," Yuki promised. "Now, let's look at gowns for the bridesmaids."

"The wedding colors are royal blue and silver," Ellie told her. "Like the flag of Korosol."

The designer smiled. "How appropriate. Don't worry—anything in my collection can be made up in whatever fabrics you like."

"Oh," Ellie said in a small voice.

Predictably, Lucia and Amelia made different choices. Lucia's pick was a striped, form-fitting gown that suited her dramatic nature. Amelia preferred a softer, flowing design with a scooped neck.

"We can coordinate the fabric so they form a pleasing picture," Yuki said.

"You're saying they don't have to match?" Charlotte quirked an eyebrow.

"Certainly not," the designer assured her. "They'll make a much more interesting statement this way."

Once Charlotte selected her own suit—a long skirt with a soft silk blouse and Edwardian jacket, all in shades of peach—the women indulged in an orgy of buying accessories: gloves, stockings, slippers, hats and more.

It was like the days before their father's death when the sisters had relished the idea of being princesses. They'd enjoyed nothing more than plowing through their mother's castoffs on a rainy day, layering themselves with finery.

The only thing missing, CeCe thought, was the prince she used to dream about. The prince whose heart melted whenever she came close. The prince who vowed on bended knee that he would love her forever.

BY FRIDAY AFTERNOON, CeCe had to give her mother and security guards the slip. Although it might be foolish to go around New York unprotected when she was the object of so much frenzied attention, she felt ready to scream if she didn't escape for a little while.

After spending the morning at her office, CeCe caught a cab downtown. En route, she donned a designer scarf and some owlish glasses that her secretary had picked up at her request. Traveling incognito made her feel high-spirited, like Audrey Hepburn in *Roman Holiday*.

She told the cab driver to drop her anywhere on Madison Avenue. All she wanted to do was window-shop and eavesdrop on normal people living normal lives.

Not until after the cab dropped her off did CeCe realize she'd chosen a location around the corner from Shane's office. Oh, well, not much likelihood of bumping into him while he was working, she told herself.

Her tension evaporated as she poked through one shop after another. No one recognized her, although some people studied her with interest, perhaps because of her height or the dark glasses. CeCe made a point of not meeting anyone's gaze.

As she emerged from an antique store, a man passed by, and she caught her breath at his resemblance to Shane, although she couldn't see his face from this angle. The same broad shoulders and muscular build filled out his coat, and the confidence in the stride set her tingling with excitement.

Sheer physical longing for her husband-to-be caught CeCe off guard. Although they'd agreed that sex would be part of their marriage, surely she shouldn't feel this intense about a man who was only marrying her for practical reasons.

Then, at a sandwich shop, the passerby stopped and turned to hold the door for an exiting diner. In the split second before he went inside, she glimpsed his face.

It was Shane. CeCe's heart hammered.

He stepped away, then swung back abruptly. His eyes met hers. "Am I imagining things?" he called.

"You caught me." CeCe hurried toward him. "I sneaked out for a little freedom."

"Join me?" Shane cocked his head invitingly. "I'll treat."

Nobody had to treat the wealthy Carradigne princesses,

as he well knew, which made his offer all the more light-hearted. "I don't know. Will it compromise my virtue?" CeCe joked.

"For a pastrami?" he shot back. "I certainly hope not."

By luck, they found a booth away from prying eyes. Shane fetched their bountiful deli sandwiches at a counter and brought them to the table.

CeCe removed her glasses and tucked them into her purse. "This smells wonderful. A person can only take so much gourmet cooking, which is what we've been eating since my grandfather arrived."

"I'll tell you something else. You're exactly the person I would have chosen to eat lunch with." Shane dug into his corned-beef-and-rye.

"You could have called," CeCe said.

"I figured you'd be up to your eyeballs in couturiers," he admitted.

"Well, I have been, sort of." She found herself wanting to share every detail of the week with Shane. The luxury of choosing a dress at Yuki Yamazaki's salon. The meetings with the floral designer, the wedding planner, the music consultant... "Oh!" she said. "I've been meaning to ask you, is there any special music you'd like to hear at the wedding?"

"Music?" He cleared his throat. "Well, uh, something with a tune, I guess."

CeCe stared at him in disbelief. "As opposed to what—people beating on drums?" she said. "I meant a specific song."

"I can never remember the names of them, so I guess I don't care." Shanes snared a dill pickle slice from her plate. "Anything else you'd like my opinion about?"

"Did it ever occur to you I might want that?" she asked.

"What?" The pickle disappeared down his throat. "Oh, you mean what I just ate?"

"Never mind." CeCe chuckled. She hadn't really cared about the pickle; she'd simply wanted to see his reaction when she challenged him. "Okay, how about favors for the wedding dinner? You know, little mementos for the guests."

"I suppose funny hats are out of the question," Shane said. "I used to be partial to balloons, but that was in my younger days."

"The wedding planner suggested silver kaleidoscopes," CeCe said. "They'd be inscribed with our names and the wedding date."

"Do I get to keep one, too?" He regarded her hopefully.

A wistfulness in his expression touched CeCe, because it showed the boy he had once been. "Of course!"

"Besides, I get the best souvenir of all." Leaning forward, Shane took her hand in his. "I get to keep the bride."

At his touch, prickles ran down CeCe's arm. His words warmed her, too, even though she knew his idea of keeping her didn't involve being around very often.

"So how are you feeling?" he asked. "Pregnancy must be a big physical change."

"I'm so busy I scarcely have time to think about it," she admitted.

Her cell phone rang. Reluctantly, CeCe removed her hand from his to answer it.

It was Charlotte, practically having a heart attack since she'd discovered her daughter was missing. None too happily, CeCe agreed to return home. There was no point in provoking her mother, and she knew Shane needed to get back to work.

They would be seeing each other during the weekend, but only in the presence of other people, CeCe reflected as they made their way out of the restaurant. She was grateful for this brief, unexpected encounter.

On the sidewalk, they started to kiss goodbye, then drew back at the realization that heads were swiveling toward them. "No point in putting on a show," Shane said. "I'll take a rain check, though."

"You bet," CeCe said. And meant it.

SHANE HAD TO HAND IT to publicity: unwelcome as it might be, it was good for business.

Wuhan Novelty couldn't wait to sign a contract with the two stars of New York society. Other prospective clients from around the world kept the phones ringing.

"You ought to get married more often," Tawny told him the following Monday.

"Less than a week to go." Shane stifled a yawn. He'd had to cut into his already abbreviated sleep schedule in order to get all the work done and accommodate the social schedule set up by CeCe's family.

Charlotte didn't want to slight any of her friends, who included the mayor, a U.S. senator, business leaders, Broadway stars, socialites and publishers. All of them wanted to toast the bridal couple, and as a result there'd been a series of dinners and after-theater gatherings at homes and in the private rooms of restaurants.

Tonight's event was a gathering for embassy staff and local leaders of the Korosol community. Shane assumed the king wanted to introduce them to CeCe as a first step toward announcing her ascension to the throne.

He hoped the coronation wasn't going to take place too soon. He wanted time alone with his wife before other duties pulled them apart.

"There's a call for you on line three. She says it's personal," Tawny told him.

"Thanks." Shane swung into his office and closed the door.

He hoped it was CeCe. Maybe they could sneak off together during their lunch hour, although eating wasn't what he had in mind. Last Friday, it had been fun dining together, but there was no substitute for the privacy of the bedroom.

"O'Connell," he said into the phone.

"Shane! I meant to call you sooner with my congratulations but I was in San Francisco on a case." The caller was Janet, the recently separated lawyer who'd invited him to dinner a few weeks ago.

"Thanks." He wondered why she'd bothered to contact him.

"It occurred to me that a man about to lose his bachelor status ought to celebrate. And I do mean celebrate." Her sexy emphasis left no room to doubt what she meant.

Was this the way women behaved toward almost-married men? "Janet, I'm engaged. That means I'm no longer available."

"It means you're more alluring than ever," she corrected him. "I'd like a taste of what the princess is getting. Who wouldn't?"

"How flattering," he said dryly. "Look, I don't want to offend you but…"

"Oh, don't worry about me. I just got rid of the stuffiest husband on the eastern seaboard and I'm going a little crazy," Janet said. "Call me if you change your mind." She clicked off.

That was a weird conversation, Shane thought. Not entirely unexpected, however. He'd heard from Amy, the divorced stockbroker, a few days ago with a similar although more subtle invitation.

He hoped idle speculation about the ladies pursuing him didn't reach Krissy Katwell's column or any of the Korosol embassy staff. It would needlessly embarrass the royal family, because it would be utterly and completely off target.

He and CeCe might be entering a marriage of convenience, but Shane intended to be faithful. He had too much respect for his future wife and for himself to do otherwise.

He put in a call to CeCe's home, since her cell phone was turned off. She and her mother were away, meeting with the caterer, her housekeeper said. Since his purpose had been to invite her to lunch, Shane left no message.

He worked steadily for a few hours and ate a sandwich at his desk. By the time he came up for air, afternoon had flowed into evening.

Shane saw with a start that he didn't have time to go home and change clothes before heading to the embassy, located across the street from the United Nations building. Since he was already wearing a dark suit, he'd have to be satified with cleaning up in his private bathroom.

He emerged a short time later to find the office staff reduced to its skeleton night crew, whose members dealt with customers on the other side of the globe. Shane wished them a good evening and was rewarded with waves and a cheerful wolf whistle from one of the women.

The elevator, when it arrived, contained a mother and a baby whose stroller took up most of the space. If Shane hadn't been in a hurry, he'd have waited for another lift.

He stepped inside and hoped the infant wasn't going to start screaming. Also that the mother didn't plan on babbling cutesy words to her precious child. After hours of having a phone pressed to his ear, he yearned for silence.

Mercifully, she said nothing. The baby gurgled a bit, sounding happy. Shane found the noise rather soothing.

Between the tenth and ninth floors, the elevator stopped.

"Oh, great." He pressed the lobby button. Nothing happened.

"My husband said one of the elevators got stuck earlier but he couldn't remember which one," the woman said.

"Were the people trapped for long?" Shane checked his watch. He was already running late.

"I don't know." His companion had a pleasant, open face and a slightly chubby build. "I'm glad you're here. I get panicky in closed spaces."

"I just get impatient." He pressed a few more buttons, not caring whether they went up or down as long as they got off. No luck.

"I was bringing my husband his dinner." Apparently, talking helped calm the woman. "He's an accountant. You know how busy they are in March, with income taxes coming due."

"Sure."

The baby started to fuss. "Is he all right?" Shane said, guessing the gender from the blue blankets.

"Anthony's fine. Aren't you, little fellow?" As soon as the mother scooped the baby into her arms, he stopped fidgeting. "He's nine months old."

"Does he talk yet?" Shane asked.

She laughed. "He'd have to be a genius!"

"When do they talk?"

"It varies. Most babies manage a few words before they're a year old, and maybe short sentences by the time they're two," the woman said.

"Ga-ga," the baby said gravely, as if joining the conversation.

"He puts a lot of expression into that." Shane had never expected that a child could communicate until it could speak recognizable words.

"Oh, he's quite a character!" The mother seized on the topic. "He holds out his arms and makes a kind of Tarzan yell when he sees his daddy. He prefers apple juice to orange, and sweet potatoes to the regular kind. I tried feeding him beets once and he threw his spoon against the wall."

"I should think so," Shane said. "Beets. Ugh."

"Buh! Uh!" cried the little boy.

"Is it my imagination, or is he imitating me?" Shane asked as he resumed pressing buttons on the panel.

The woman smiled. "He's a great mimic. You should see him try to bark like our dog."

"Really?" He was on the point of asking whether the little guy could walk yet when the elevator gave a lurch and started downward.

"Hurrah!" said the mother.

"Uh-ah!" cried her son.

"I'll make sure this elevator gets labeled 'out of order.'" A check of his watch made Shane realize he'd lost valuable minutes. Still, he hadn't truly lost them, he reflected as they arrived in the lobby. He'd learned some fascinating information.

He'd also made himself later than ever to the embassy party.

Chapter Eight

CeCe always felt close to her father when she visited the embassy. The ornate facade of the narrow, eight-story building brought back childhood memories of the old country.

Drake would have been proud of her, she thought, and wished with all her heart that her father was alive to attend her wedding. At least, here at the embassy, she felt as if he watched over her.

Shane was supposed to meet them in front of the building. When he failed to arrive promptly, the king shepherded the Carradignes inside. "We can't keep our people waiting," he said.

Charlotte, CeCe and Amelia dutifully obeyed. Lucia had begged off, to her mother's disapproval, saying she had fallen behind in her work.

They passed through the ground floor, which during business hours was devoted to assisting citizens and providing tourist information. The interior of the embassy was beautifully maintained, CeCe noticed as they wound their way up the main staircase past the second-floor trade office.

On the third floor, they approached plush rooms reserved for entertaining. The soft melody of folk songs, played by a small string band, greeted them from outside, and CeCe heard the clink of glasses and the murmur of voices.

The music and chatter halted when they entered. A sea of Korosolans, including servers carrying trays of hors d'oeuvres, bowed or curtseyed to the king. They formed a colorful array, especially those wearing traditional folk costumes.

Although CeCe and her family had been a center of attention all their lives, the New York social set didn't bend their knees to royalty. With a jolt, she realized that someday people would be bowing this way to her. It was a strange notion.

Her grandfather gave a slight bow in return. The three Carradigne women, led by Charlotte's example, managed curtseys toward the crowd.

Acting ambassador Cadence St. John, a black-haired, blue-eyed duke who looked more like a man of action than a diplomat, approached to greet his monarch. Then, to CeCe's embarrassment, she was guided to the front and introduced to the assembly as the eldest granddaughter, about to be wed.

More bows. More curtsies. Welcoming smiles were tempered by frank curiosity as everyone focused on the princess bride.

It was only a taste of what lay ahead, CeCe reminded herself. She hoped she would get used to it.

If only Shane would get here! When he failed to arrive on time, she'd blamed it on traffic, but he should be here by now. Why didn't he at least phone?

"Ah, the lucky groom," said the ambassador, as if on cue.

Relieved, CeCe turned. Through the door sailed Shane, straightening his tie. He halted abruptly as he saw an entire roomful of people studying him.

On his face she read a discomfort to match her own,

and experienced a wave of sympathy. At least she'd been born to the spotlight. For Shane, this was new.

"Sorry," he said in a low voice as he reached her. He looked strikingly masculine in his dark suit, she thought with pleasure. "Got stuck in an elevator. I was afraid if I called I might interrupt some important ceremony."

"I'm glad you're here."

Cadence St. John presented a series of special guests and staff members to the king and his family. Although CeCe's feet hurt as she stood in line, she did her best to greet each person as if he or she were the most important individual in the room.

Some of them would talk about this day for the rest of their lives, she reflected. For once, it felt like an awesome responsibility to be a princess.

Between shaking hands and making polite conversation, Shane touched her elbow, lending support. She sensed the tension in his muscles and saw the hungry way he regarded her. Instinctively, her body responded.

If only he were coming home with her tonight…

CeCe forced her attention back to the receiving line. It was a relief, a few minutes later, when the last person passed through and dinner was announced. One benefit of being a member of the royal family was getting to go through the buffet first.

A round table had been set aside for the Carradigne party, the ambassador and the king's adviser, Sir Harrison Montcalm. Once seated, CeCe slipped off her shoes under the table. Not even the risk of incurring her mother's wrath dissuaded her.

A server set a glass of Korosolan wine in front of her. "You aren't supposed to drink that while you're pregnant, are you?" Shane asked.

"No." CeCe didn't even get a chance to call the server back before the woman, overhearing them, removed the glass and apologized profusely. "It's all right. No harm done."

"I really am terribly sorry, Your Highness." The woman scurried off.

"I wasn't expecting such a strong reaction from her," Shane said.

"Neither was I," CeCe admitted.

"We'll have to learn to keep our voices down. I thought the poor woman was going to faint." He looked so rueful that only the awareness of people watching kept CeCe from smoothing the fabric of his jacket and brushing her lips against his jawline.

She could just imagine how her mother would react if she did that! Other brides might nuzzle their grooms in public, but not a Carradigne princess.

They ate and talked with the people at their table. Gradually, the others finished eating and drifted away, leaving them alone.

"Let's see," Shane said, "you're two months along, right?"

"Uh, right." This past week, CeCe had been too busy reviewing wedding plans to think much about her pregnancy.

"Which stage is that?" Shane asked.

"The queasy stage," she said.

"I mean, the baby. Do you call it a baby at this point?" he asked. "Or is there some other term?"

"You can call it Junior if you like," CeCe said. "Or Buster."

"It's a boy, then?" he said. "You didn't tell me!"

"I don't know the sex." CeCe smiled at the thought of a little boy that would look like Shane. "What's with the questions?"

"I'm trying to picture what our son or daughter is like," he said. "Has it shown any signs of a personality yet?"

"Excuse me?" CeCe asked. "Shane, I can't even feel the baby moving."

He leaned closer. "When will that happen? Would I be able to feel it moving, too?"

"I'm afraid I don't know. This is my first child." She was torn between amusement and exasperation. The last thing she'd expected was for Shane to get obsessed with fatherhood. "I thought you didn't like kids."

"It's different now that it's mine." Only half seriously, he added, "What chance has this poor kid got, with two amateurs for parents?"

"Just remember, amateurs built the ark and professionals built the *Titanic,*" CeCe said. "That's a shipping joke, in case you hadn't heard it."

"I hadn't," Shane said.

The music started again. Charlotte, who had left for the rest room a few minutes before, hurried toward the table.

"Your grandfather would like for you and Shane to dance," she said. "Since we can't invite everyone to the wedding, he says it's a way of sharing the festivities."

CeCe wasn't sure she wanted the whole assembly to watch her with Shane. On the other hand, that was as much contact as she was likely to get with him until her wedding night. Besides, she had better get used to performing state duties.

"What my grandfather wants, my grandfather gets," she said.

SHANE HAD EXPECTED a traditional European-style waltz. Instead, he discovered a large circle of Korosolans waiting for them.

"What's this?" he asked CeCe.

"It's a folk dance," she said. "Kind of like a square dance. Just follow along and you'll pick it up."

Shane's mentor had instilled in him the importance of social skills, so he'd taken a course in ballroom dancing.

It hadn't involved any circles of people stomping their feet and weaving around one another, however.

He soon found that CeCe had been right: the steps were easy. In addition, the high spirits of their fellow dancers proved contagious.

CeCe flashed him a merry smile as they twirled around each other, arm in arm. In a twinkling, she disappeared down the line of dancers.

She looked wonderful tonight, uncharacteristically sweet in a pink skirt and pearl-embroidered sweater that emphasized the feminine way her figure was filling out. Impending motherhood was much underrated as an aphrodisiac, Shane decided.

He realized that an entire roomful of strangers was also keeping one eye on his bride. These people had a claim on CeCe. Soon, their claim would be as strong as his own and perhaps, in time, even stronger.

It almost made Shane jealous.

At last she came back to him, breathless and laughing. He was so glad to have her in his arms that he nearly hugged her in front of everybody.

He didn't look forward to living an ocean away, not knowing what CeCe was doing or whether she was completely safe. There wasn't a country in the world that didn't have its share of political intrigues, and being queen might make her a target.

A determination fired within Shane, stunning in its ferocity, to protect his woman and their baby. The watchful guards could never care as much about Cecelia as he did.

He had to abide by their agreement, which meant he couldn't be with her all the time. Even so, Shane swore silently that he would fly to her any time she needed him.

When the music stopped, his heart was racing. He wasn't sure why at first, and then it hit him.

He was falling for CeCe.

The discovery drove every other resolve from Shane's

mind. For most men, tumbling head over heels for their own fiancée was natural and right. For him, it could prove catastrophic.

He'd promised CeCe a marriage of convenience. He couldn't betray her trust by demanding more now. What made him think he had the ability to protect her once she reached Korosol, anyway?

He had to wrestle down this rebellion in his heart. She didn't want him to fall in love with her, and he didn't want it, either.

There was no backing out of the wedding, not that he would choose to. But once the honeymoon ended, he intended to get as far away from her as possible until he recovered his sanity.

IT WOULD BE BEST, King Easton decided a few days later as he relaxed in his daughter-in-law's whirlpool bath, to take his granddaughter back to Korosol soon after the wedding, with or without her bridegroom. The reception at the embassy had brought home to him how much Cecelia needed to learn before she wore the crown.

Not that the young woman had disappointed him, he mused, enjoying the ebb and flow of hot water and the filtered glow from a high octagonal skylight. Her behavior had been perfectly correct for a young bride-to-be. It simply hadn't been queenly.

She should have paid less attention to her bridegroom and more to her subjects. Also, although Easton had made certain she was introduced to the embassy staff, she hadn't taken the initiative to get to know each of them personally or to inquire about issues affecting their country.

He didn't expect the learning curve to be difficult. Once CeCe understood that she needed to approach the monarchy the way she'd approached becoming a shipping executive, she would tackle the job with gusto.

This business of organizing a wedding was also distracting her from her future role. It was distracting Easton, too. Accustomed to having Cassandra and various aides plan social events without troubling him, he hadn't realized what a production he was setting in motion.

A large percentage of New Yorkers obviously made a living from one aspect or another of the wedding industry. Wedding planners, designers, florists, music consultants, program printers—despite security precautions, they all managed to find their way into Charlotte's apartment.

Not knowing his identity, they took him for an ordinary, elderly relative. One chirpy young fellow with a tape measure looped around his neck had blithely addressed the king as "Gramps." Although Easton had been sorely tempted to grab the tape measure and choke the dolt until he learned a few manners, he had refrained.

Refreshed, he emerged from the bath, dried off and donned a robe. Before Charlotte left for DeLacey Shipping earlier, she'd assured him that no tradespeople were expected, so he didn't need to wear his usual meticulous apparel around the apartment.

As Easton padded through the hallway, the housekeeper appeared. She assured him that if he wanted a snack, he would have the kitchen to himself.

"There's no one around but the girls and your secretary," she said. "They're in the family room."

The king thanked her, declined her offer of help and went to the kitchen alone. It had been a long time since he'd been free to raid a refrigerator in peace.

He found it stuffed with delicacies. Deciding to try a local favorite, Easton selected a bagel, cream cheese and lox. At first, he couldn't remember how to use a toaster, but it came back to him.

While waiting for the bagel halves to pop up, he wandered to the entrance to the family room. Remaining out of sight, he peered into the cozy chamber.

His three granddaughters sat around a coffee table, Cecelia and Amelia on chairs and Lucia on the floor. Three blond heads, each a different shade, leaned together. Eleanor, her light brown hair providing a charming accent, sat a little apart.

The king could hear them discussing names and numbers. After a moment, he realized they were discussing who to seat at which table for the wedding dinner.

What a sweet picture they made, he thought, his eyes stinging. If only Cassandra were here to see them.

But she *was* here. In CeCe, he saw her zest for life and heard her melodious voice. And somehow he felt that Cassandra was looking down to watch over her goddaughter, Ellie.

Behind him, the toaster clicked. Cheerfully, the king retrieved his bagel and took his snack upstairs to his room.

"I THINK THIS WILL WORK," Amelia said, regarding the seating chart they'd drawn up. "We'll need mother's approval, of course."

"If you ask me, we ought to seat a few enemies next to each other just to keep things interesting," Lucia said. "What's a wedding for, if not to resolve old feuds and stir up new ones?"

Although CeCe hoped her sister was kidding, it was hard to tell. "I don't want any quarrels at my wedding," she said.

"No one would dare!" Ellie said. The secretary had been invaluable when it came to assigning seats to Korosol dignitaries. "They'd be outcasts if they behaved so disgracefully."

"What really ought to happen at a wedding," CeCe said mischievously, "is that one of my sisters should meet the man of her dreams. By the way, which of you wants to catch the bouquet?"

"Not me!" said Lucia. "I doubt I'll ever get married."

"Why don't you toss it into the air and let it fall where it may?" Amelia suggested.

"Fate should decide who's the next to get married," Ellie agreed.

CeCe nodded, pleased to be free of making the choice. "Good idea."

"This has been fun, getting together without Mom," Lucia said. "We ought to do it more often."

"It feels like old times." CeCe tried not to think about the fact that, once she was queen, the three sisters might never have this much time together again.

"I'd like to give you your gift now, if you don't mind," Lucia said.

"I'd love to see it." Her sister had mentioned making an item of jewelry, CeCe recalled. Given Lucia's talent, she was sure it would be something special.

From her purse, her sister retrieved a small package wrapped in white paper and tied with a frilly bow. Gingerly, CeCe slipped off the ribbon and parted the paper. Removing a green velvet jeweler's box, she flipped it open.

Inside nested a shield-shaped brooch that recreated the Korosol coat of arms, worked in tiny blue stones on silver with rich gem accents. In the upper left quadrant stood a lion, the ancient symbol for courage, and in the upper right, a dove for peace. One lower quadrant depicted mountains, the other a ship at sea.

"It's exquisite," said Ellie, who had moved closer. "I can't believe you made it yourself!"

"My sister is very talented." CeCe examined the piece with growing delight. "I'm going to wear it on the collar of my wedding gown."

She could tell from Lucia's expression that her sister was pleased. "I'd be honored."

"It's light enough," Amelia said, fingering the brooch. "And a bride *is* supposed to wear something blue."

"Is she?" Ellie inquired.

"Something old, something new, something borrowed and something blue," all three sisters recited, and burst into laughter.

"You know what?" CeCe said. "I'm glad the news of my pregnancy broke while grandfather is here. Otherwise, we wouldn't be having this wedding."

"How do you suppose the news got out?" Amelia asked.

"I'll bet someone at your doctor's office took payola," Lucia said.

"I never told my doctor the father's name," CeCe said. "I didn't tell anyone except Hester, and she wouldn't have repeated it." That reminded her of the circumstances of that afternoon. "Amelia, you came into the kitchen a few minutes after our conversation. Earlier, I'd heard a noise on the stairs, and the guards said later they found a connecting door pried open. Did you see anyone?"

"It certainly wasn't me, because I had no idea you were pregnant," her sister said. "I'm afraid I didn't see anyone, either."

"I wouldn't be surprised if cousin Markus is behind it," Lucia said. "Grandfather's passing over him to make you queen, and everyone knows how much he covets the throne. He'd probably leap at the chance to discredit you, although if this is his doing, it backfired."

Markus's adviser had been on the premises that day, CeCe recalled. She didn't like to think that her cousin would have stooped so low as to have his man spy on her. "He probably doesn't even know I've been chosen as the successor."

"There isn't much Markus doesn't know where his own interests are concerned," Lucia said darkly. "I'll bet we haven't heard the last of him."

Amelia shuddered. "Don't talk that way. Besides, he's

on the guest list for the wedding, so of course we'll hear from him.''

"His aide already replied," Ellie said. "Markus can't come. Something about pressing business.''

"So that's why he wasn't on our seating chart," Lucia said. "I'm glad he won't be here. He used to be fun, but recently he gives me the creeps.''

CeCe felt a little guilty about Markus. It didn't seem right that he should be deprived of a position he'd always assumed would someday be his. But the king had seemed determined to bypass him.

As a result, she was going to be starting a whole new life. "Ellie, what's it like to live in Korosol?" she asked. "I know it'll be a big change for me.''

"It's nothing like New York," the young woman agreed, her expression softening. "I grew up on my parents' sheep farm in the western part of the country, so it was fairly isolated. I enjoyed it, though. I knew everyone on the estate and I had my own horse.''

"What fun!" CeCe had taken riding lessons for years.

"I've traveled more since I became His Majesty's secretary," Ellie said. "Korosol la Vella, the capital, is a mixture of the old and the new. It's funny to see video stores and cyber cafés tucked among the curio shops and medieval inns.''

"Where do people go on vacation?" Lucia asked.

"My family spends part of the year taking the thermal waters in Esperana, up in the mountains," Ellie said, warming to her subject. "Things get more lively in Serenedid, in spite of the *serene* in its name. It's both a beach town and a port, so it's quite international.''

"CeCe can run up to Paris if she wants to go shopping, right?" Amelia said.

"Or she can go to Barcelona," the secretary said. "That's a beautiful city. There's no place like New York, though. I didn't know how magnificent it was until I got here.''

"Maybe you'll decide to stay," Lucia teased.

"Oh, no!" Ellie looked taken aback. "I could never leave home permanently. Especially now that my brother's moved back. He was wild in his younger days, but he's adopted two children from abroad and they're so cute!''

"Your brother adopted children abroad?" Amelia's voice had a strange, choked sound. "I didn't think about...your last name is Standish, isn't it?''

"Maybe he went through the International Children's Foundation," Lucia said. "Wouldn't it be funny if you'd met him?''

"If you're worried about little Jakob and Josie, don't be," Ellie said. "Nicky adores them. He's a great father.''

"Nicky would be short for...?" The words seemed to stick in Amelia's throat.

"Nicholas," Ellie said. "I'm glad he's settled down. He ran off years ago and my parents were furious. I was afraid he might not come back.''

"That must be hard," Lucia said. "Even though we have our flare-ups with Mom, we're all pretty close.''

Amelia gave a light cough. "Talking about the ICF— I've got work to do. Please excuse me." She practically ran out of the room.

"Did she look upset to you?" CeCe asked. "I hope she wasn't offended when I asked her about that noise on the stairs. I didn't mean to imply she might have talked to Krissy Katwell.''

"Maybe she doesn't approve of single fathers," Ellie said. "In Nicky's case, though, he's perfect for those kids.''

The phone rang with yet another question from Charlotte's secretary about a detail of the wedding. As soon as CeCe hung up, she had to race to a fitting at Yuki's salon.

Only two days remained until she and Shane walked down the aisle. Her mood swung between impatience for the day to arrive and abject fear.

She knew she would survive. She just wasn't sure how.

Chapter Nine

The wedding rehearsal took place on Friday afternoon at the rented mansion. Workmen were still hammering and painting, but already the theme, A Fairy-Tale Castle, was unmistakable, Shane saw when he entered.

His only groomsman was his best man, Ed Ferguson. It saddened Shane that there was no family on his side. Under the circumstances, however, perhaps that was a good thing, since it would save him from having to make explanations when he and CeCe began living apart.

"This is impressive," Ferguson observed when they entered. "I never saw such an elaborate production for a wedding."

"You'd think we were mounting a Broadway show." Shane suspected the event was costing almost as much. It was worth it, though, if it made CeCe happy.

Last night, they'd attended a cocktail party hosted by the mayor. The bride had looked cheerful but a bit strained.

He hoped she would relax on their honeymoon. He'd planned a secluded trip during which they'd be left alone to dine and make merry. Since he'd resolved to put as much space between them as possible afterward, they ought to make the most of the time they had.

"Ladies, gentlemen and Your Majesty." It was the

minister, a short, thin man of Korosolan background. "I know you have busy schedules, so I suggest we get started."

He seemed nervous, especially when directing the king to escort CeCe down the aisle. He kept saying, "If Your Majesty pleases" and "A little slower, Your Highness, if you don't mind."

The king took the instructions good-naturedly. He even apologized once for a mistake, and commented wistfully that since he'd never had daughters, this was his first experience at giving away a bride.

"Who'd have thought you'd be marrying royalty?" Ferguson murmured into Shane's ear. "It couldn't have happened to a nicer guy."

"We've come a long way," he said.

Ed beamed at being included in the "we." "Damn—I mean, darn right." He'd worked hard to clean up his language since his younger days, but occasionally he slipped.

When CeCe reached Shane, excitement stirred inside him. Tomorrow, this ceremony would be for real. Tomorrow, she'd become his wife.

All week, he'd dreamed about CeCe. Why did he have to fall for her now? It was maddening, annoying and exhilarating the way she invaded his thoughts.

The two of them turned to face the minister. He began racing through the ceremony, skipping large portions, then halting to point out when it was time for CeCe to say "I do."

She looked so elegant and so unsure of herself that Shane's heart squeezed. Every day, he seemed to care more about CeCe.

Nevertheless, in due time, he was certain he'd get over her. Once an ocean lay between them and she belonged to her people, only their child and a marriage contract would tie them together.

Most married couples he knew found their affections

waning over the years, even though they lived together. Throw in a few thousand miles, and he'd be safe enough.

"Mr. O'Connell?" the minister said.

"What? Oh." He saw Ferguson making a circle with his thumb and forefinger. "We've reached the part about the ring?"

"Correct," the man said. "You'll place it on the bride's finger and repeat after me…"

At last, they finished. The rehearsal dinner was slated for a nearby private club.

"The DeLaceys have been members for over a hundred years," CeCe explained as they walked the four blocks to the club. "I've only been there a few times, but I remember they have great dining facilities."

A doorman scrutinized the party as they approached. Recognizing Charlotte, he hurried to hold the door for them.

Inside, the scent of plush furniture and wood smoke hit Shane. The place might as well have Rich and Exclusive stamped on the carpet and wallpaper.

They walked past hushed rooms toward the reserved dining area. Well-dressed people sitting in high-backed chairs turned to watch as they passed, and Shane could hear the murmurs of recognition.

Some mentioned Charlotte, and a few guessed that Easton might be the king. Surprisingly, most of them seemed more fascinated by the bride and groom.

It was hard to believe that he, Shane O'Connell, belonged in a place like this and that the people were talking about him with fascination instead of disdain. He could probably take out a membership himself, if he liked.

Shane wondered how the other members would react if he showed up with a bunch of his raffish friends from the old days. No, he decided, the club might accept him as a member, but this wasn't the kind of place where he wanted to hang out.

"What's going through your mind?" CeCe asked. "First you frowned, then you grinned, then you frowned again."

"Part of me is still a street kid from East L.A.," Shane admitted. "This place, well, they'd have thrown me out by my collar a few years ago."

"Do you feel like you're playing a role?" she asked.

"I do, sometimes."

"You?" That surprised him. "But you've always been a princess."

"My sisters and I weren't raised in a palace," she said. "Mother didn't spoil us, either."

"You got everything you wanted, didn't you?"

"Hah!" CeCe said. "At Christmas and birthdays, we each received one large gift and a single small one from our parents. Then we were expected to do charity work, and we still do. At Thanksgiving, we help serve dinner at a rescue mission before we go home to eat, and each year we organize a gift party for poor children in December."

"I'm on the board of the Foster Children's College Fund," Shane said. "Maybe we could persuade you to be guest of honor at one of our fund-raising events. That would draw a lot of interest."

Her grip tightened on his arm. "Shane, I'm going to be your wife. Of course I'll support your charities."

"Even when you're…?" He decided to avoid saying the word *queen* where outsiders might hear.

"I'll still be myself," she said.

Maybe they could take an extra-long honeymoon, Shane thought warmly. And he didn't have to flee her company immediately after the honeymoon.

That didn't mean he was going to dote on his wife. They'd just have a friendlier marriage of convenience than people had in the old days.

A FEW OBLIGATORY TOASTS punctuated the dinner. CeCe barely stifled a yawn.

Thank goodness she'd passed on the idea of a bachelorette party tonight. Although the wedding wasn't scheduled until 3:00 p.m. tomorrow, she'd be up early going over last-minute details and having her hair and nails done.

"Tomorrow night, after the reception," Shane said to Charlotte, who sat across the table from him, "what time do you think CeCe and I will get away?"

"Get away?" Charlotte repeated.

"For our honeymoon," he said. "I'll have one of my planes stand by."

CeCe blinked at him. She'd entirely forgotten about the honeymoon. Well, not altogether, since she'd fallen asleep most nights imagining herself in Shane's arms, but she hadn't given any thought to specifics.

"You'll honeymoon at Charlotte's apartment," said King Easton from the head of the table.

"Excuse me?" Shane regarded him in disbelief.

CeCe braced herself for a battle. Her grandfather was accustomed to having his orders followed without question. Shane, in his self-made rise from poverty, was about as typically American as a guy could get, which meant that he didn't like taking orders.

She had to admit that the prospect of honeymooning in her own rooms sounded about as sentimental as eating a candlelight dinner at a hot dog stand. Even so, this was one argument she intended to stay clear of.

"There's a question of security," Charlotte said placatingly. "Naturally, we want the royal guard to keep an eye on CeCe at all times."

"I hope you're not planning to send them into the bedroom," Shane shot back.

"Young man, I appreciate your concern for my granddaughter," the king said. "However, there's more at stake here than our personal preferences. For the good of my country, I must insist on protecting CeCe's safety.''

Shane stared at Easton for a long moment, a muscle twitching in his jaw. The rest of the long table fell silent as everyone awaited his response.

Despite her own feelings, CeCe wondered why Shane was making such an issue of the honeymoon. He'd only decided to marry her because of the pregnancy and the threat of a scandal, after all.

Leaning close, she said in a low voice that only he could hear, ''Remember what you said? Neither of us is romantic. This seems like a good time to be practical.''

He released a sharp breath. ''Very well,'' he told the king. ''We'll honeymoon in CeCe's suite. Undisturbed, I presume.''

''We'll pretend you aren't there,'' Charlotte said, clearly relieved.

''Naturally,'' agreed the king.

CeCe felt the tension seep from the room. The problem was that although she was the one who'd persuaded Shane to back down, she wasn't entirely happy about it.

Soon they'd be thousands of miles apart. She wanted a little time with her husband before they became strangers, perhaps forever.

IN HER SUITE THAT NIGHT, CeCe couldn't sit still. The wedding gown hanging in its transparent covering, the scent of flowers from an arrangement Shane had sent—everything reminded her that tomorrow her life was going to change.

She was more thrilled about becoming Mrs. Shane O'Connell than about her future as Queen Cecelia. It was foolish, CeCe told herself. Despite his desire for a honeymoon, the man had made it clear they only suited each other because...because...

What exactly had he said, two weeks ago here in her

suite? Oh, yes—he'd mentioned how much they seemed to have in common and that they could talk openly. Gee, compliments like that really made a girl's head swim!

Yet during these past few days, she'd caught Shane looking at her as if he couldn't wait to get her alone. Was it possible that's why he'd pressed for a real honeymoon? If so, CeCe didn't know whether to be pleased or irked.

When the phone rang, she nearly didn't answer, although it was her private line. She was in no mood for chitchat with anyone, even Shane.

But, as future queen of Korosol, she couldn't afford to indulge her moods like a teenager. CeCe swallowed hard and picked up the handset. "Hello?"

"You didn't think I'd forgotten my own dear cousin, did you?" Although Markus failed to identify himself, she recognized his slightly nasal voice. "I'm calling to wish you well."

"I'm sorry you won't be here." CeCe curled up on the couch with the phone.

Maybe everyone was wrong about Markus, she thought. This friendly call was more like ones she'd shared with the cousin she'd known while they were growing up.

Six years older than CeCe, he'd been like an older brother. She'd felt the connection to him even more strongly after he barely survived the plane crash that killed her father and maternal grandfather.

During the last decade, though, Markus had begun to seem like a stranger. He was spending more time in Europe, and now, when he visited New York, her cousin always had a different woman on his arm.

He'd always thrown around his wealth, and the pace had accelerated since he inherited the bulk of his parents' estate last year. He never appeared to seek a serious center to his life, perhaps because he'd assumed that someday he would be king.

"I regret that I can't join you." As Markus spoke, she

pictured him self-consciously finger-combing his dark, wavy hair to cover the receding hairline. "Such an important occasion! You know, people are talking about you all over town."

"Which town?" she asked.

"New York, of course," he said. So he'd been collecting gossip from Rademacher.

"Yes, the newspapers love royalty, don't they?" Krissy Katwell had been running a "Wedding Watch" item daily with tidbits about CeCe's gown, the flowers, the cake, et cetera.

"I think it's noble of you, no pun intended, to…" Markus's voice trailed off suggestively. "Well, never mind that."

"Noble of me to do what?" CeCe asked.

"To bear Shane O'Connell's child," Markus said. "Under the circumstances."

"The circumstances are that we're getting married." She found her cousin's innuendos annoying.

"Yes, of course, now that that gossip columnist brought everything out in the open," her cousin said. "Well, not *everything*. I must say, your fiancé is doing a good job of keeping up appearances."

Apparently, Rademacher had uncovered some rumor that CeCe hadn't heard. "Tell me what you're talking about," she said. "Whatever it is, it's probably wrong."

"I certainly hope so." To her ears, Markus sounded smug, although perhaps it was CeCe's irritation that made her think so. "Very well, I'll tell you straight out. You asked me to, so don't get angry."

"I'm already getting angry," she said. "Quit dodging."

He heaved a sigh. "It's all over town that Shane's having an affair with a married woman. I believe she recently separated from her husband because of it."

CeCe went cold. It was true that she and Shane had

only made love once, two months ago, and there'd been no promises of fidelity afterward. They hadn't discussed the issue of exclusivity when they got engaged, either.

She supposed that, in a marriage of convenience, a woman might have to put up with her husband's straying. But now, on the eve of her wedding? And it was all over New York?

"Who is she?" she asked.

"I don't know," Markus said. "She must have a big mouth, though, because I'm sure your ambitious bridegroom wouldn't be stupid enough to talk about the affair himself."

CeCe didn't miss the implication that Shane's ambitions were his motive for marrying her. She didn't believe that. The rumored affair was another matter.

Something deep inside her twisted painfully. She didn't want to share Shane. She certainly didn't want him tumbling into bed with anyone else.

She'd believed she could go through with a marriage that wasn't really a marriage. What she hadn't counted on was this agonizing sense of betrayal. It hurt like fire to think that Shane would do such a thing.

"I'm afraid there's more," Markus continued, his voice like a spike in her heart. "According to the grapevine, Shane can't stand you. He calls you an ice queen."

"That's not true!" CeCe blurted, then clamped her mouth shut. Markus was the last person to whom she would confide how wildly the two of them had gone at each other during their night together.

"I am sorry to be the bearer of bad news," said her cousin. "Your child needs a father, or it would be a terrible scandal, so I suppose there's no choice. I do hope I haven't spoiled tomorrow's big event."

He hoped he hadn't spoiled the wedding? That was precisely the reason he'd called, CeCe thought.

"Goodbye, Markus," she said coldly.

"Goodbye, my dear." He didn't try to hide the jubilation in his voice.

He wants the throne. And he'd willingly tear me apart to get it. Yet if even half of what Markus had said was true, CeCe couldn't possibly marry Shane.

AFTER THE REHEARSAL DINNER, Shane went home and spent a couple of hours on the Internet. He planned to take a break from business during the honeymoon, so he needed to get as much done tonight as possible.

The doorbell rang repeatedly during the evening. Each time, Ferguson appeared moments afterward with a congratulatory gift. The latest one was balloon-shaped and decorated as a bikini-clad woman. It and a bottle of wine had been sent by Janet, the attorney.

"I read in the paper that you aren't having a bachelor party, so here's my contribution," her note read. "Give me a call if you want a real send-off."

Shane showed it to Ed. "Can you believe this?"

"I can't believe any of it," his assistant said, indicating the other gifts. They ran the gamut from the practical—a digital camera—to the fanciful—a remote-controlled toy helicopter. "Since when do people send presents to the groom?"

"Since they figure I'm going to be richer and more powerful than ever, and they want to get on my good side." Shane stretched his long legs under the desk. "I like being respected. I don't enjoy having people curry favor, however."

"If you don't want the helicopter..."

"It's yours," he said. "But you have to write the thank-you note."

"I'll say it's on your behalf, of course." Grinning, Ferguson scooped up the toy. "Guess I'll head downstairs, if you don't need me."

"You're off-duty any time you want to be," Shane said. "I've told you that."

"Well, I didn't want to be until now," said his friend. "See you tomorrow."

Shane regarded Janet's note again. Although he hoped this kind of thing was going to stop once he got married, he doubted that it would, especially after people realized he and his wife weren't living together.

Oh, Lord, he must be crazy to enter into a marriage like this. Of course, he'd been out of his mind to go to bed with CeCe in the first place.

The woman came with strings attached. He'd always known that, although he hadn't expected the strings to metamorphose into iron chains.

Shane rested his head in his hands. A king for a grandfather-in-law, a queen for a wife, a honeymoon practically under her mother's nose, a daily item about their wedding in the newspaper—whatever happened to two people running off to the justice of the peace, and living happily ever after?

Oh, the heck with worrying. He'd sail through this, and so would CeCe. They'd have fun for a few days, and then things would get back to normal. For him, anyway.

Shane was no longer apprehensive about the baby. He planned to maintain enough distance between them so he didn't reopen painful old wounds, while keeping tabs on the kid's development.

This ought to be interesting, a new life experience. Every guy should have a child, as long as it didn't distract him from his work. And he was beginning to suspect he might enjoy the time they did spend together.

The phone rang. Shane's first thought was that it might be Janet. If so, he needed to set her straight once and for all.

"O'Connell," he said into the phone.

"Carradigne here."

"What's going on?" Something must be seriously amiss. She hadn't even used her given name.

"I don't like to repeat rumors," she said. "However, I've come across one that disturbs me. I want your official denial."

From her phrasing, he assumed that this was a business matter. "Does it concern Wuhan Novelty?"

"No, it concerns your mistress," CeCe said. "Excuse me, I mean alleged mistress."

Mentally, Shane shifted gears. Something personal had distressed his bride-to-be, yet she was handling it with the crispness of an executive. "I don't have a mistress. Is that what you wanted to hear?"

"Maybe that's the wrong term," she said. "It could be more casual than that."

"I'm not sleeping with anyone," Shane told her. "Mind filling me in?"

He listened while she explained that her cousin, Markus, who apparently was something of a busybody, had telephoned from Korosol to tell her that Shane was supposed to be carrying on with a married woman. "Or recently separated," CeCe concluded.

As she spoke, her tone lost its businesslike edge. He knew she'd taken that approach as a way of shielding her feelings, and it touched him.

"I think I know where that story originated." Shane described Janet's overtures. "She's not the only one, either. I've had several ladies after me. I wouldn't put it past one of them to spread tales."

"You must be flattered," she said dryly.

"I'm not flattered. It makes me feel like a trophy," he said. "Have we cleared this up? Come on, wife-to-be, I can tell this was bothering you."

"It made me feel lousy." From the ragged note in CeCe's voice, he pictured her with rumpled hair and shadowed eyes. She needed someone to take that beautiful face of hers in his hands and kiss her senseless, Shane thought.

"For the record, I don't plan to cheat on you," he said. "Not now, not ever."

"Really?"

"Cross my fingers and hope to die."

She laughed. "Let's not go to extremes." More soberly, she said, "Are you angry that I questioned you?"

Shane wished he could pull her onto his lap and demonstrate just how angry he wasn't. "I'm glad you called. It's a bad idea to let suspicions fester. Frankly, I'm surprised your cousin would repeat such a thing."

"He expected to be king himself," she said. "His father, who was first in line for the throne, died last year. For some reason, my grandfather doesn't like Markus."

"I can understand why. He has no business pestering you with idle gossip." Shane wasn't pleased to discover that he'd been right about the existence of political undercurrents. Mentally, he made a note never to turn his back on this guy Markus. "So your cousin's trying to get you to break off the marriage so you won't be chosen queen?"

"Grandfather hasn't announced his decision," CeCe said. "I'll bet Marcus puzzled it out, though. His adviser, Winston Rademacher, is wandering around New York, snooping on people. He might be the one who found out about my pregnancy and leaked it to the newspaper."

"Do you think they're dangerous?" Shane's pulse speeded. "If there's a threat to you..."

"I've got the guards to protect me," CeCe said. "Besides, if anything happened to me, my grandfather would choose one of my sisters."

"That's not a very reassuring thought," Shane grumbled.

"I'll be fine."

Under other circumstances, he'd have hurried to her

side. However, the press had begun staking out her apartment and her family wouldn't appreciate the scandal of the bridegroom sneaking into his intended's bedroom on the eve of their nuptials.

Her bedroom. Thinking about it sent heat rushing through Shane. "What are you wearing?" he asked.

"Excuse me?" CeCe asked. "I haven't put on a bullet-proof vest, if that's what you mean."

"It isn't." He'd shifted gears abruptly, he supposed. "Humor me on this. Are you dressed?"

"I'm wearing my nightgown," she said. "It's kind of old. I bought a new one for my trousseau."

"You're not wearing something flannel with teddy bears on it, I hope." His fantasy was sheer and lacy. Or completely see-through.

"It's silk," she said. "And short."

"Low-cut?"

"Please tell me you're not expecting cleavage," CeCe said. "If you are, you must have a short memory."

When they'd made love, she'd showed only one moment of hesitation and that was when Shane removed her bra. His future bride must be self-conscious about her small breasts. As far as he was concerned, their sensitivity was what counted and boy, were they sensitive.

"I'm not expecting anything," Shane said. "Or rather, I'm expecting a lot because I've already had a taste, and you're one special lady."

"Okay, I'm following you now," CeCe said. "We've moved on from rumors, right?"

"All the way to sheer wedded bliss," he said. "I'm looking forward to it."

"Are you really all right with this?" she asked. "We haven't had a chance to talk. I know what you said when you asked me to marry you, but Grandfather didn't give you much choice."

"I had all the choice in the world," Shane said. "You suit me fine."

She didn't answer. Perhaps she was waiting for more reassurance.

He wanted to offer it, but flowery phrases weren't his style. "There are no other women," he said at last. "There never will be."

"I'll see you tomorrow, then," she said.

"We're still on for the wedding?" he teased.

"You bet." He heard the smile in her voice. "I have to marry you now, if only to spite Markus."

"We'll show him," Shane said.

After she hung up, he took off his tie tack and pierced the sexy-lady balloon. It shot around the room with a satisfying hiss.

So much for rumors. Shane was almost grateful for this one, though. He wouldn't have missed tonight's discussion for anything.

Chapter Ten

"We've searched the premises thoroughly. Security is checking everyone's ID and invitation," Sir Devon Montcalm told King Easton as they stood at a second-floor window in the wedding mansion, looking down on the crowd gathered in the street.

"No sign of either Rademacher or my grandson?" Easton asked. "I wouldn't put it past either of them to wangle diplomatic credentials and try to impress the guards."

"I've warned everyone to be on the lookout," said Cadence St. John, who stood on the king's other side.

Easton wished Sir Harrison were here as well, but the royal adviser was at the embassy, checking to see if there were any rumors from Korosol or within the local Korosolan community about Markus's activities. With luck, Harrison might finish in time to attend the reception.

Late last night, CeCe had told her grandfather about Markus's calling with a vicious rumor. She'd repeated it to him so that if the same gossip reached his ears—probably via the same source—he would understand that there was no truth to it.

Easton had assured her that he took her word and Shane O'Connell's over Markus's. He didn't care to explain further.

The allegations of his grandson's involvement in his parents' deaths were still too painful and infamous to be revealed even within the family. The accusations served a purpose, however: they put the king on the alert.

He didn't believe Markus would use violence on CeCe or her wedding party. However, he was taking no chances.

Below in the street, he saw the swarm of onlookers shuffle back obediently at the command of a couple of police officers, clearing room on the sidewalk for passersby. News crews moved aside only by inches, and quickly resumed their places.

From the windows of buildings opposite him poked a number of minicams. Obviously, the press wanted to capture this event from every angle.

The morning newspapers had been filled with juicy details of the wedding, some of them provided by Charlotte's public relations staff and some fabricated. Contrary to certain reports, the wedding party did not plan to dine on peacocks like the ancient Romans, nor had the guests been instructed to wear the royal colors of blue and silver.

From overhead intruded the whir of a helicopter. "What's that?" Easton demanded. "I mean, I know what it is, but what's it doing here?"

Devon spoke into a handheld communications device and listened attentively to the response. "It belongs to a local TV station," he said.

A collective gasp from the crowd below drew the king's attention to the street. Down the block, a fairy-tale coach was approaching, pulled by four white horses.

Charlotte had outdone herself, he thought. What a splendid sight the carriage made, its brass fittings agleam in the sunlight, the horses steaming in the cool March air. As he gazed down in satisfaction, Easton realized that the entire street and many of the windows were lined with rapt faces.

The carriage halted in front of the mansion. Two footmen outfitted in ruffed medieval-style costumes hurried to open the door.

Charlotte emerged first, a hat perched rakishly atop her short white hair. Her peach-colored suit swirled around her, drawing—to Easton's amusement—applause from the crowd.

She was followed by Princess Amelia and Princess Lucia, willowy as fashion models and elegant in their coordinated gowns. There was a cool splendor about the young women, brightened by their bouquets of blue and white flowers tied with silver ribbons.

The onlookers oohed and aahed. Easton held his breath for what would come next.

A footman reached into the coach and a white gloved hand appeared. A moment later, a delicate foot encased in a silken slipper touched the coach's step.

From this angle, he saw his granddaughter's tiara next, the diamonds sparkling against her upswept blond hair. A froth of white fabric surrounded her as she emerged to a collective cry of delight from the observers.

CeCe hesitated, clutching her bouquet. Was she feeling the awkwardness she'd described to him? Did she fear a tumble to the sidewalk?

She tipped back her head to look upward, lifting one hand to hang on to her tiara. Her bright emerald eyes met Easton's, and she smiled.

Fifty years vanished like morning fog, and Easton saw Cassandra at their wedding. Joy and anticipation rushed through him, as if he were a bridegroom all over again.

She was here, he thought suddenly. He could feel Cassandra standing beside him, where Devon Montcalm had been a few moments before. Her hand brushed his, sending shivers down his spine.

Tears of happiness blinded the king. When his vision cleared, his granddaughter and her entourage were vanishing into the mansion.

He noticed details about the crowd that had escaped him before: the flash of cameras, the fact that quite a few onlookers had dressed in blue and silver, the way a little girl balancing on her father's shoulders was waving a bridal doll. Good heavens, the doll had chin-length blond hair like CeCe's.

"Your Majesty?" Devon said. "Perhaps we should go downstairs."

"Yes, yes." The king declined to lean on the captain of the Royal Guard, although he could tell the man expected to assist him. After his rush of emotion, he was feeling a bit weak, however, so he consented to ride in the elevator instead of negotiating the curved staircase.

He must save his strength for the walk down the aisle. After all, Cassandra would be watching.

As CeCe waited for her cue to walk down the aisle, she almost wished she'd worn a veil. She hadn't been expecting such a large audience outside the mansion, although she supposed she should have been.

In the tiara, she'd felt rather exposed. Then she'd spotted her grandfather and experienced a surge of pride. Pride in her heritage, in her father's country, in her future.

Now the king stood beside her, tall and strong. CeCe hoped she possessed equal strength, although right now she didn't feel like it. Her hands, from which she'd peeled the gloves a short time earlier, were damp and her knees felt hollow.

Nearby, Lucia swatted at a gnat circling her bouquet. Amelia pushed a curl of hair off her temple. They were both fidgety, too.

CeCe's fingers flew to the brooch she wore on her collar. The Korosol coat of arms, created with her sister's love, steadied her.

She wouldn't let the king down. She wouldn't let anyone down. Fortunately, the baby was cooperating today.

Despite her butterflies, CeCe's stomach remained mercifully calm.

As if from a distance, she watched Shane's friend, Ferguson, escort Charlotte down the aisle to a front-row seat. Peeking from the vestibule into the transformed ballroom, CeCe felt as if she were gazing at another world.

The designers and floral artists had created a garden courtyard surrounded by a stone-walled castle. Wondrous plants, painted to look superreal, climbed to great heights, while real and painted blooms formed a profusion of colors and shapes.

Although she couldn't see all the way to the altar, she knew it was framed by a trellis covered with silver roses. Was Shane already there? CeCe wondered, and strained to catch a glimpse of him. No luck.

A movement to one side of the room caught her eye. A lovely singer costumed in a medieval dress appeared on a balcony halfway up the wall. The organist played the opening bars of a traditional Korosol melody and the singer's sweet voice silenced the rustling of the guests.

They probably thought the French words had something to do with love. CeCe knew that the singer was asking God to grant her courage and steadiness. She herself had chosen the song because she knew she was going to need both those qualities today.

When the song ended, the organist played a prelude that heralded the bridesmaids' entrance. "Here goes," said Amelia, and set off down the aisle at a measured pace. Someday, she would make a beautiful bride herself, CeCe thought, and wondered when that might happen.

"My turn!" Lucia started after her sister, going too fast but slowing before most people had time to notice. Despite Lucia's low-key running battle with their mother over her lifestyle, CeCe knew her sister would never intentionally disrupt the wedding. She might kick up her heels a bit at the reception, though.

The music segued into Mendelssohn's wedding march. In the ballroom, CeCe could hear people turning in their seats.

"Ready?" asked the king.

"As ready as I'll ever be." She took his arm. "One, two, three, go!" Her grandfather chuckled, then grew solemn as he escorted her into the main room.

Faces came into focus as they walked together. There was her secretary, Linzy Lamar. Hester and Quincy Vanderling. Friends from high school and college, executives from DeLacey Shipping, relatives on her mother's side, and Charlotte herself, tears coursing down her cheeks.

At last CeCe dared to look at the altar.

Shane stood beneath the trellis, straight and true in his black tuxedo. His dark eyes transfixed her and his warm mouth curved as she neared him. He looked every inch the Prince Charming she had dreamed of.

If only this were a real marriage, she thought, and her heart leaped into her throat.

SHANE HAD NEVER UNDERSTOOD why women made such a fuss about weddings. From a guy's point of view, it made more sense to sign the legal documents and cut right to the honeymoon.

Still, this place looked terrific. The music was beautiful, and he enjoyed the singing in French even though he didn't understand it. And the costume parade, with glamorous dresses and elegant hairstyles, was fun to look at.

Judging by Ed's awestruck expression, he was getting an even bigger kick out of the whole business than Shane was. The assistant had turned into a wedding devotee, collecting clippings, invitations and other paraphernalia in a scrapbook. Today, the man was nearly delirious with excitement.

Shane snapped to attention as his two sisters-in-law-to-be strolled down the aisle. They both looked stunning, which made them fitting attendants for the most beautiful woman of all.

As the wedding march began, something inside him quivered. Had the melody always been this soaring, this magnificent?

When CeCe appeared, it seemed to Shane that rays of light converged on her, casting the rest of the room into shadow. She was like a beacon, illuminating his future.

He'd never before noticed the delicacy of her features with such clarity, or the trembling vulnerability in her eyes. She needed him. They needed each other.

He reached for her hand. Vaguely, he heard the minister ask, "Who gives this woman to be married?" and heard her grandfather answer, "I do."

Shane wished the minister would hurry so they could pledge themselves to each other. Instead, the man launched into a talk about the mystery of matrimony and how two spirits merged to become a greater whole.

Shane didn't usually subscribe to that kind of sentimentality. He wondered now if the pastor hadn't hit on something, though, because what Shane was experiencing was definitely out of the ordinary.

He wanted to whirl CeCe around and kiss her. He wanted to hear her laugh, and feel her mold herself against him.

Joy. Mania. Ecstasy. All from standing beside a woman in a white dress, a woman who could provoke him with her stubbornness and pierce him with her sharp tongue.

The woman he loved, in spite of himself.

"Shane O'Connell, do you take Cecelia DeLacey Carradigne…"

"Yes," he said, before the minister could finish. "I mean, I do."

A ripple of amusement spread through the room. Shane didn't care.

"To honor and cherish, in good times and bad, in sickness and in health, as long as you both shall live?'' the pastor concluded, and stopped.

Silence filled the room. ''Say it again,'' Ferguson whispered.

Shane blinked, and realized everyone was waiting for him. ''Like I said, I do,'' he answered. This time, the laughter was more open.

CeCe gave her dignified consent at the right moment. How could she exhibit such self-control? Shane wondered.

He supposed it had something to do with being a princess.

THE RECEPTION WAS IN FULL swing by the time CeCe came out of her daze. Since the moment when she first gazed into Shane's face at the altar, she'd been virtually hypnotized.

In front of so many people, she should have been self-conscious as they stood side by side, but she wasn't. All she could think about was him. All she could feel was his strength and eagerness.

When he kissed her, she'd had a sudden impulse to grab his hand and dash out of there. Thank goodness a couple of faces in the front row had penetrated her absorption: her mother's and her grandfather's. No way would she misbehave in front of them.

Instead, she'd squared her shoulders and turned to face everyone with a smile. Then she and Shane had strolled down the aisle in a courtly manner.

Each guest was greeted personally in the reception line, which formed immediately afterward in the vestibule. Although CeCe's legs were shaky, the steel in her character ran true. She looked directly at each person and made an appropriate comment, taking her time as if she weren't in an agonizing hurry to be alone with Shane.

This was, she reminded herself, merely a prelude to a

lifetime of standing in receiving lines. And, perhaps, a lifetime of longing for Shane and having to wait.

She could handle it. CeCe never gave in to weakness when there was something important at stake.

The reception was held in another ballroom upstairs, which was decorated like the interior of a castle. Great tapestries had been hung along one wall, and a small orchestra occupied a corner.

By the time the bridal party arrived, waiters were circulating among the tables, offering selections of salads and hors d'oeuvres. CeCe was about to sit down when the orchestra leader signaled her.

"He wants you and Shane to have the first dance," Charlotte said. "Until you do, no one else can use the dance floor."

"Shall we?" Shane asked, offering his arm.

"Indeed yes, good sir," CeCe joked.

They moved onto the smooth wooden floor. She'd chosen the melody in advance, a Strauss waltz. "I hope this isn't too formal for your taste," she told Shane. "I did clear it with you, remember?"

"I didn't know what you were talking about." He encircled her waist with his arm. "Don't these guys do rap?" He indicated the bandleader, a fiftyish fellow in a tuxedo.

CeCe hoped he was kidding. "I suspect the only rapping he does is with his baton."

The infectious opening bars cut off conversation. Smoothly, Shane swung her across the floor in a vigorous but polished ballroom waltz. He *had* been kidding.

CeCe felt powerfully drawn to her new husband as he led her through the movements. His focus enveloped her, merging them into a single will. For once, CeCe didn't try to take charge, because she didn't want to.

The space between their bodies, required by the formality of the dance movements, only increased her longing to touch him all over. She knew this moment didn't mean as much to him as it did to her, but she wanted this dance to last forever, just the two of them, newly sworn to each other.

She wanted to pretend that Shane loved her. She wanted to imagine that they were a real husband and wife.

The waltz ended too soon. Applause accompanied them to their table.

"You look beautiful," Charlotte enthused. "Both of you."

"Magnificent." King Easton's eyes were suspiciously moist.

"Can we eat now?" Amelia asked. "I'm starving."

"Who wants to eat?" Lucia reached up and pulled the pins from her hair, then fluffed it with her hands. "I'm in a dancing mood. Has anybody seen my date?"

"You brought a date?" CeCe hadn't realized her sister was seeing anyone. Of course, since Lucia lived in her own loft, her comings and goings were unknown to the family.

"There he is." Lucia waved to a young man across the room. Among so many people, CeCe couldn't get a clear look at him, but she saw enough to note that his idea of formal dress definitely wasn't a tuxedo, and that he had even longer hair than her sister's.

"Isn't that…?" Amelia began. "I'm sorry, I can't think of his name. He's a rock singer, isn't he?"

"See you guys later." Lucia bounced to her feet and zoomed across the room with unladylike haste.

"I don't know where she found him, but I'll bet she did it to spite me," grumbled Charlotte. "What a disreputable young man!"

"You shouldn't judge him by his appearance," Amelia said. "He might have a good heart."

"I'd rather he had a good haircut," said her mother.

"You should be glad if she brought him to spite you,"

CeCe told her mother. "That would mean she isn't serious about him."

"Lucia's never serious about anyone," Charlotte said, more cheerfully.

"That may be because she's never met the right sort of fellow," King Easton said. "She needs someone brave and handsome. Reliable, too, of course."

"I already married him," CeCe teased.

Her grandfather patted her hand. "So you did. I was thinking of someone like Sir Devon, to tell you the truth. Your sister could do worse."

"Don't let her know what you're thinking!" Charlotte warned. "I know she adores you, Your Majesty, but she's got a rebellious streak a mile long."

"I'll remember that. Now, if you'll excuse me, my royal adviser just arrived from the embassy," the king said. "We have a few matters to discuss."

After he left, Amelia said, "Did I misunderstand, or is grandfather matchmaking?"

"I'm sure he wants what's best for all of you." Charlotte paused as a waiter served their dinners of poached salmon, asparagus and crab-stuffed potatoes.

"I can't imagine Lucia marrying a man with a military background," CeCe said. "Someone artistic is more her style."

"Oh, I don't know," Amelia said. "She might like a man who's stable and has his act together, as long as he doesn't try to control her."

"Sorry to interrupt, but have you noticed the lady with the red hair?" Shane asked. "She's wandering toward us. Somehow she doesn't fit in with everybody else."

He indicated a short, curvy woman in a shocking-pink dress. CeCe recalled having seen that gown somewhere before, but she couldn't place the sharp-eyed woman with masses of unnatural-looking auburn hair.

"That's the ugliest wig I've ever seen," Charlotte sniffed.

"It's Krissy Katwell!" Amelia said.

"The nerve!" Her mother smacked the table for emphasis.

CeCe rose. "I'll tell the captain of the guard. He'll see to her at once."

"Let me do it." Shane sprang to his feet, then checked himself. "I forget that you're going to be qu—in charge. I feel like it's my job to protect you."

A part of her wanted him to do exactly that. "Don't lose that impulse," CeCe said. "You're my husband. There may be times when…"

"When what?"

When I need you by my side. That was what she'd meant to say. She'd almost forgotten that she had no right to make demands on him. "I'd better tell Sir Devon about Krissy."

After being informed, the captain strode toward the columnist. She scuttled away like an alarmed crab.

"Madame, please!" Devon said. When Krissy tried to dodge past him, he caught her arm, halting her so abruptly that her red wig slid sideways to reveal disheveled knots of black hair.

The gossip columnist blistered the air with insults, none of which appeared to faze Sir Devon. He calmly accompanied her out of the room and, no doubt, out of the building as well.

King Easton rejoined them. "That woman is determined, isn't she?"

"She's a pain in the crown jewels," replied Charlotte. "Do ask General Harrison to join us, won't you? He looks so wise, I'm sure we could all use a bit of his advice."

"It's better if he keeps an eye on things while his son is busy removing Miss Katwell," the king said.

"I hadn't realized Sir Harrison was Sir Devon's father," Amelia said. "How convenient for them to work near each other."

"They're not close, I'm afraid," Easton said. "It's easy for families to drift apart, isn't it?"

"Not ours," CeCe said. "At least, I hope not."

"My dear," said her grandfather, "if you're feeling up to it in your delicate condition, I would appreciate the honor of a dance."

"I'd love to."

When the two of them took to the dance floor, the band segued into a slow waltz. The other dancers fell back to watch.

What a splendid partner the king was, CeCe thought. She could feel the thinness of his shoulder beneath her hand, yet he never faltered, and he'd lost none of his youthful grace and dignity.

When they finished, he bowed and she executed a curtsey. Her knees gave off a loud crack that to her ears sounded like a sonic boom.

"Pay no attention, my dear," her grandfather murmured as he escorted her away. "Pretend it didn't happen and everyone else will, too."

"Absolutely right." CeCe was too happy to let a little embarrassment get in her way.

En route back to their table, she noticed Lucia in conversation with Sir Harrison and wondered what they were talking about. Judging by her sister's animated expression, the adviser had engaged her interest, or perhaps her annoyance. It was hard to tell with Lucia.

The king's secretary was sitting at a nearby table, looking pretty in a subdued pale-pink dress. When a man tried to catch her eye, she stared down at her hands, and he walked away without asking her to dance.

"I don't know what's wrong with men today," Easton said, apparently having observed the same interaction. "They're so easily discouraged."

"Ellie seems like a nice person," CeCe said. "But very shy, I gather."

"The right man could bring her out of her shell," her grandfather said.

When they rejoined Shane, he stood and reached for CeCe's hand. The contact shivered through her deliciously, and she forgot all about Ellie Standish.

"Don't sit down yet," Shane said. "The caterer seems anxious for us to cut the cake."

"I wish Amelia could cut it for me," CeCe said. "I'm so clumsy at these things."

"Think of the cake as one of our rival companies," Shane advised. "You'll slice right through it."

And so she did.

Cake was served and champagne flowed freely, and gradually the party grew louder and merrier. Amelia danced with a young man of her acquaintance, and Charlotte whirled about in the arms of one of DeLacey's executives.

"They're all having such a good time," CeCe said wistfully.

"Aren't you?" Shane asked.

"I just wish things were simpler," she admitted. "That there wasn't so much depending on me. That you and I had more time together."

"The least we can do is enjoy the time we have," Shane said. "Do you suppose anyone would notice if we sneaked out the back?"

"We'd probably run right into Krissy Katwell staking out the alley," CeCe said. "Besides, I imagine there are people still standing on the sidewalk, waiting for us to come out."

"We can't disappoint our public," Shane said gamely.

It took far too long, as far as CeCe was concerned, but finally the pair managed to take their leave of everyone.

The royal guards formed two protective columns as they exited through the front door.

Soap bubbles filled the air in a salute from guests and the public. CeCe waved, and was touched when cheers of approval rang out.

Shane handed her into the waiting coach, then settled beside her. Sir Devon closed the door and hopped onto the running board, keeping an eye out for trouble as the horses carried them away.

Next stop: honeymoon.

Chapter Eleven

Shane hadn't expected to find Ferguson in CeCe's private suite when they arrived. The last time he'd seen his friend, Ed had been dancing at the reception and from all appearances having a great time, but apparently he'd rushed here ahead of them.

"I wanted to unpack your suitcases," the best man explained. He was bustling around the bedroom, hanging up shirts and trousers.

"I appreciate the concern, but I'm not helpless, you know." Shane grinned at his friend. "You're on vacation this week, remember?"

"I'll start tomorrow." Ferguson hesitated in the middle of the room, a pile of neatly folded undergarments in his hands. "Where do I put these?"

Although usually impervious to embarrassment, Shane could feel the heat rising in his cheeks. He snatched the stack from his assistant. "I'll figure out something."

"I cleared a drawer for you." CeCe, who'd been observing the scene with amusement, strolled to the bureau. "Right here."

Shane stuffed his garments inside. Ed's fingers curled, as if he was barely restraining the impulse to rush over and refold them.

The man was too absorbed in his job, Shane thought. "You need a hobby."

"I have a hobby," Ferguson said stiffly. "I keep scrapbooks."

"About what?" CeCe asked.

"You and Shane," the assistant said. "Also about O'Connell Industries and DeLacey Shipping. I've begun a separate scrapbook for Korosol."

"My secretary, Linzy, keeps scrapbooks for her daughter," CeCe said. "She was widowed two years ago and she doesn't want her little girl to forget her father, so she started by putting in pictures of her late husband. Now she collects items about every outing they take and about people she knows."

"Including you?" Ferguson's interest was clearly piqued. "Maybe she has some duplicate pictures she would share."

"You can contact her at my office," CeCe said. "Be sure to tell her I suggested it."

"I'll do that. It would be interesting to meet somebody else who keeps scrapbooks," Ed said. "I guess I'll run along, then." He brushed a speck of lint off his tuxedo, then shook hands with them both and departed.

"He's devoted to you," CeCe said, removing the brooch from her collar and setting it on her dressing table.

"I hope you weren't sending him on a wild-goose chase." Shane unclipped his bow tie and removed the cummerbund from around his waist. He couldn't wait to get undressed. All the way undressed.

"Of course not!" The bride strode to the apartment entrance and locked it behind Ferguson. "Not that I'm matchmaking, but he and my secretary have a lot in common."

"Come here." Shane reached for her hand.

CeCe ducked into the kitchen. "Aren't you hungry?"

"After that huge meal?" he said. "The only thing I'm hungry for is you."

He'd scarcely been able to take his eyes off her all evening. CeCe exuded a special radiance today. The sheer fabric across her shoulders and chest tantalized him, and so did the color in her cheeks and the fullness of her mouth.

She was his wife. Part-time wife, perhaps, but his for tonight and the rest of the week. Shane couldn't wait to get intimate.

"I'm a little nervous," CeCe said.

"About what?"

"Making love this way seems so—cold-blooded. Like we planned it," she said.

"That's what people do on their wedding nights," Shane pointed out.

"Of course you're right!" She sighed. "It's just that last time it was so spontaneous between us."

"Yeah, wasn't it great?" Shane said. "Listen, once we get started, I promise you won't remember whether we planned it or not."

CeCe paced past him into the living room. "I don't know what I am. I don't feel like a typical bride."

"What do you feel like?"

"An executive," she said promptly. "Like I ought to get to work. Do something useful. Can you picture me, the barracuda, as a sex kitten?"

With her luminous green eyes and the sensual white fabric billowing around her slim body, Shane could picture that very well. The avid expression on her face might indicate the killer instinct at a business meeting, but it also quickened his blood.

"I guess that depends on whether or not you can picture me as the hunk of your dreams," he replied. "What do you say, princess?"

WHAT COULD SHE SAY? CeCe wondered. Yes, Shane was her dream man, but in her dreams he didn't spend a week with her and then wave farewell. Until recently, she'd assumed that if she ever met Prince Charming, they'd live happily ever after.

CeCe was afraid. Afraid of her feelings for her husband, afraid of his effect on her, afraid of losing control over her heart.

"Maybe we shouldn't make love," she said. "Not tonight, anyway. I mean, we've had a long day."

Shane clenched his teeth. They didn't gnash, exactly, but close. "It's our wedding night."

"We already had our wedding night, two months ago," CeCe reminded him. "That's how we got into this situation."

"What's so terrible about this situation?" He advanced on her. At six foot one, he stood five inches taller and had the advantage of impressive muscles, which bulged beneath his jacket.

"Threatening me won't do you any good." She stood her ground until he was almost on top of her, then took a step backward.

"I haven't threatened you." Shane looked mildly insulted.

"Your presence is intimidating," CeCe said.

"My presence is required. We're supposed to consummate our marriage," he said. "And don't tell me we did it two months ago. I've practically forgotten how it felt."

"You've forgotten?" she sputtered.

"I said 'practically.'" He'd managed, she discovered, to back her against a wall, and now he stretched his arms on either side of her and leaned against his palms.

Ducking underneath to escape would be undignified, CeCe reckoned. "If you were a gentleman, you'd respect my wishes."

"But I'm not. I'm a ruffian," Shane teased. "However,

in the interests of world peace, let me volunteer to assist the bride in removing her tiara.''

Since the pins were digging into her scalp, CeCe had to admit this wasn't a bad idea. ''Okay, I'll let you do that.''

''Thank you so much, Your Highness.'' Humor laced his deep voice.

He shifted away from the wall and reached to touch her hair. CeCe's eyes closed instinctively as Shane's fingers fumbled with the hairpins holding her tiara. He tugged, then tugged a little harder.

''If they'd fixed these any more tightly, I'd need a staple remover,'' he said.

''The hairdresser promised my mother it wouldn't fall off, no matter what,'' CeCe said.

''Including a nuclear blast,'' he muttered. ''There we go.'' She felt the pins slide free, and the tiara lift from her hair.

Shane wasn't finished, though. He removed the additional pins holding her coiffure in place and ran his fingers through her hair to free it. His fingers massaged her scalp, soothing away the faint itching.

''That's good,'' CeCe said. ''Fabulous, in fact.''

His hands stroked down her temples and framed her face. She opened her lids in time to catch a shimmer of desire in his eyes, and then his mouth covered hers.

It wasn't a gentle kiss. He commanded her to yield, and she did, letting his teeth graze her lips and his tongue enter her mouth. Just for a second, CeCe told herself. Just to refresh her memory of how it felt to taste him.

A second wasn't long enough. Eager for more, she wound her arms around Shane and kissed him back.

He caressed the edges of her breasts and cupped them through the luxurious fabric. She felt him grow hard against her.

Longing fired through her body, stiffening her nipples

and making her knees go weak. This was how she'd reacted the first time they came together. No wonder they'd both flung off their clothes and thrown caution to the wind.

Slowly, Shane drew away. "I guess that's enough for now."

"What?" CeCe glared at him.

His eyebrows quirked mischievously. "You said you didn't want to make love tonight."

She recovered a trace of her defiance. "I—I meant it."

Shane checked his watch. "It's nearly ten o'clock. Tonight ends officially at twelve, so we'll have to wait two hours and do it then. Got any good movies in that home theater of yours? Something with cars blowing up and guys shooting each other?"

The man couldn't be more infuriating if he tried. Actually, CeCe suspected, he *was* trying. "No, but there's lots of romantic comedies and tear-jerkers."

"Not in the mood." Shane picked up the remote control and flopped on a couch. "Let's see what's on TV."

"You're out of your mind!" Dropping beside him, she grabbed the controller and threw it across the room. "Don't you dare turn that thing on."

He grinned, looking wonderfully rumpled. Somewhere along the line he'd removed his tuxedo jacket and his shirt had come untucked.

"Change your mind?" Shane asked.

His cheeky comment aroused her fighting spirit. "You make a lousy bride's attendant," she said. "You didn't finish your job."

"I got the tiara off!" he protested. "Oh, you mean the dress?"

"I couldn't possibly unwork all these snaps and buttons up the back," CeCe said.

"Turn around. I'll take care of it." When she obeyed,

he reached for her dress. "Wait a minute. There's nothing but a zipper."

"Lucky for you," she said.

Shane lowered the zipper inch by inch. "Sure is tough getting this dress off you."

"It's going to be a lot tougher when I put my suit of armor over it," CeCe said.

"Is that what a well-dressed queen is wearing these days?"

"Yes, along with a lance, a dagger and a couple of hand grenades," she said.

"Sounds like a scene from one of my favorite movies." Having finished with the zipper, Shane eased the dress down CeCe's shoulders. His lips grazed the bare skin between her shoulder blades.

As his kisses trailed up her spine to her neck, she forgot the riposte she was about to make. When Shane lifted her hair and nuzzled the edge of her jaw, CeCe leaned back against him.

A small cry escaped as he encircled her with his arms and teased her nipples with his thumbs. She reached down and caressed his hips, moving suggestively against him.

He peeled off her dress and left it in a heap on the floor. CeCe found herself stripped to her pink lace lingerie. The experience was exhilarating.

Shane studied her with relish. "My wife," he said hoarsely. "This is exactly the way I like you."

"You're a little overdressed for the occasion, aren't you?" CeCe shot back.

"I can't seem to get these cuff links off," he said, although he hadn't tried. "I guess I need help, too."

She lifted each of his wrists in turn and unworked the gold links. As she bent over him, CeCe became acutely aware of the power in his arms. Especially when he caught her wrists and held them so she couldn't escape.

"Well, wench," Shane said. "Methinks I have the queen at a disadvantage."

"Methinks you are a cad," she said, laughing. "Do you want me to take your shirt off, or do you prefer to do it yourself?"

He released her. "Got a razor blade?" he said. "Let's cut the darn thing off. I'm in a hurry. You have no idea how enticing you are."

Desire welled inside her, too. "We should take our time. I mean, tonight is special."

"Take as much time as you want," Shane said. "Just don't get in my way."

"You rogue!"

"I never pretended to be anything else. Allow me to demonstrate."

Before she knew it, he stripped off his shirt and pants in record time and pulled her onto the couch. It was wildly undignified and incredibly arousing, the way he climbed on top of her and the two of them tussled playfully.

CeCe wore nothing but her wispy undergarments and garter-held stockings. As for Shane, he was magnificent in his briefs, which were rapidly becoming inadequate to cover him.

She didn't intend to let him know he'd conquered her this easily. "Maybe we should go watch that movie now," she deadpanned.

"Woman!" he roared. "Submit!"

"Never!"

Shane stripped off her panties in one feral gesture. How he managed to shrug out of his own undergarments, CeCe never did figure out. The next thing she knew, he was driving into her like a man possessed.

"Okay, I think I'll submit," she whispered.

As his tautness filled her, CeCe stopped trying to hold back any part of herself. It was a useless effort, anyway. She wanted him too much.

Her body writhed eagerly beneath his. When he bent to kiss her again, her tongue met his with pure exuberance.

They rocked in a private rhythm, a dance beyond all others. Their spirits merged for a precious instant, and the excitement that shot through CeCe's body was nothing compared to the joy in her spirit.

Shane thrust into her, his own climax louder and longer than her own. But no less profound, she thought with spreading satisfaction. That simply wasn't possible.

SHANE WASN'T THE SORT OF MAN to separate sex from emotional contact. Even so, he'd never felt more than warm affection for his previous partners. That all changed when he met CeCe.

Now their connection obliterated any distance between them. He almost couldn't distinguish his reaction from his wife's, because every movement and sound she made vibrated inside him.

They were attuned, merging at a level he'd never known existed. He didn't understand what had happened, but he figured it would become clear in time. Right now, he wanted nothing more than to hold her.

They moved from the couch into the bedroom, chuckling at the pile of clothes they left on the carpet. "I'll straighten them tomorrow," CeCe said. "I wouldn't want Hester to see this mess."

"Send the pile to the dry cleaners and forget about it," Shane muttered, and fell happily into her comfortable queen-size bed. "Now, let's wreck these sheets, shall we?"

CECE AWOKE WITH SUNLIGHT on her face. It startled her. She hadn't slept past six since adolescence.

Rolling over, she gazed at Shane. He slept on his back with the sheets bunched around his waist, and she relished the sight of his broad chest. A faint stubble darkened his cheeks, giving him a scruffily appealing air.

Her heart swelled. *I love him.* He was the right man for her, in spite of how fiercely she'd resisted him.

A shaft of sunlight sparkled off something on her dressing table. Propping herself on one elbow, CeCe saw that it was Lucia's brooch.

The Korosol coat of arms. A whole country distilled to its essential symbols.

Painfully, CeCe came back to reality.

Shane might be the right man, but he would never give up his work to serve at the queen's beck and call. And she didn't expect him to.

She, on the other hand, had spent the past twenty years becoming the person she was meant to be. Hard-driving, even tough. Coming through for her mother and her family whenever they needed her. Living up to what her father would have expected.

She couldn't change who she was, any more than Shane could or would change himself. Maybe, if her grandfather and Korosol didn't need her, some compromise might have been possible. But it wasn't.

A heavy weight settling onto her chest, CeCe fell back against the pillow. Yes, she loved Shane, and she would do her best to please him during whatever brief times they spent together. But she must not fool herself into believing they could make each other ultimately happy.

"WE FORGOT SOMETHING," Shane said while they were taking a shower.

"What's that?" Beside him in the large stall, CeCe washed herself unselfconsciously. She didn't seem to have any idea how beautiful she was, with her velvety skin and long legs.

"You never got to wear your new nightgown," he said.

"We have half a dozen more nights left." She dabbed

almond-scented body wash on her cloth and smoothed it over her stomach.

Shane was getting hard again. How unfair that a man's passions were immediately evident to anyone looking at him naked. On the other hand, anyone looking at Shane clothed probably already knew he desired her.

Then he caught the implication of CeCe's last remark. "Half a dozen more nights left until what?" Shane said. "I mean, I know we don't get a long honeymoon, but we *are* married. Even though we'll have to get back to work, that doesn't mean we can't share our nights."

CeCe blinked at him, water running down her neck and trickling between her breasts. "My grandfather wants me to go back with him to Korosol," she said. "Next week."

"That soon?" Shane hadn't expected this much haste. "What's the hurry? He isn't planning to crown you five minutes after your plane lands, is he?"

CeCe looked rueful. "I thought he'd explained it to you," she said. "He told me last week that there's a lot I need to learn before the coronation. Protocol and treaties, the political lay of the land, his plans for the future."

"He'll be around to guide you, won't he?" Shane said.

"I certainly hope so!" CeCe massaged herbal shampoo into her hair. Shane leaned against the tile wall and watched her. The white lather atop her head might resemble a halo, but he had no illusions that she'd been transformed into an angel. Thank goodness!

"Then we can afford a little more time," he said.

CeCe met his stare. "Shane, let's be honest with each other. We're great together. It's too bad we can't play for a few weeks like normal newlyweds, but you knew the terms when you married me."

"The terms?" he said. "Hey, I'm not going back on my word. I just don't want my wife whisked away while we're still practically strangers."

"I wouldn't call us strangers." She smiled.

Shane couldn't explain his position very well because he didn't fully grasp it. He only knew that last night he'd experienced something precious, and he wasn't ready to let go of it yet.

He had to do his best to keep her for a while longer. "If you leave now, I think we're going to lose something essential in our relationship," he said. "It's like we're laying the foundation of a house. Or a palace, if you prefer. Once it's solidly in place, we can take our time about building the rest, but if we quit too soon, it will never hold up."

"We aren't building anything." CeCe resumed scrubbing her hair. "I mean, how can we? Anyway, my grandfather's counting on me and I know he's eager to get home."

"Let me take care of your grandfather," Shane said, although he had no idea how he was going to accomplish that.

"You can't come between him and me. I'd have to be the one to talk to him, and I won't," she said.

"We'll see about that." Shane didn't want an argument. He wasn't giving up, though.

In fact, he already had the germ of an idea.

Chapter Twelve

Sometimes CeCe wondered if her honeymoon had been choreographed by the Marx Brothers.

Not that the nights weren't wonderful. And, true to their promises, family members refrained from intruding on the happy couple.

However, there were a few glitches. For one thing, the whirlpool bath and sauna lay at the other end of the apartment, which meant that whenever she and Shane had a yen for a dip, they risked running into Charlotte or Amelia or even Easton himself.

One time the honeymoon couple arrived just as the king was lowering himself into the hot water. Courtesy required them to join him and make pleasant conversation, even though they wanted nothing more than to grab each other and make fizzy love.

The nearness of the home theater to CeCe's private quarters also proved distracting. One evening her entire family, including the Vanderlings, piled in to watch a travelogue about Korosol. Despite the partial soundproofing, the booming voice of an announcer drifted into the kitchen where she and Shane were trying to have a romantic candlelight dinner.

"This small European kingdom has held its own for

*more than eight hundred years, surviving turbulence that
swamped larger nations...."*

"You know what this reminds me of?" Shane said,
setting down his fork.

"I can't imagine," CeCe admitted, and wondered if
they should move the small table into her bedroom, which
was farther from the noise.

"When I was about nineteen and broke, I took a date
to one of those free dinners where you have to listen to a
spiel about buying into a time-share development," Shane
said. "Every time we started a conversation, the shill at
our table would work the subject around to vacation hide-
aways and why this investment was perfect for us."

*"The Royal Palace is located in a secluded valley ten
miles north of the capital city of Korosol la Vella."*

"I hope your date had a sense of humor."

"My date had no idea what kind of dinner it was," he
said. "When she found out that the hosts believed we
were married and that we were going to have to sit
through a half-hour presentation afterward, she stormed
out."

"What did you do?" CeCe asked.

"I told the shill we had marital problems and spent the
rest of the dinner inventing stories about ruined vacation
trips." Shane chuckled. "The sponsors couldn't wait to
get rid of me. I must have been scaring off the other
attendees, because they encouraged me not to stay for the
presentation."

*"Wool is one of the major exports of Korosol. How-
ever, tourism remains the chief industry."*

"Who can eat with all that racket?" CeCe hoped Bernice wouldn't be offended that they hadn't finished her
beef bourguignon with steamed vegetables and fresh-
baked French bread.

"I'm starved," said her husband. "However, I'm crazy

about leftovers. Let's go find something more interesting to do until our neighbors go away.''

"I wonder what we could possibly find to do in such tight quarters," CeCe said.

He showed her.

Yet there was no escape, not really. The only time they ventured onto the balcony, she heard a woman on the street below shout through a megaphone, "I see them! Look, there's the princess and her husband!"

She learned to keep the blinds drawn after a photographer sneaked into an adjacent building and started snapping away. One of the royal guards waylaid him and managed to "accidentally" expose the film, but it was a close call.

The morning papers, which Hester left outside CeCe's door, intensified her sense of being under siege. Unwilling to give up the fascinating subject of a royal wedding, Krissy Katwell ran daily recaps of the big event.

She made much of the fact that King Easton had attended his granddaughter's wedding, although it was assumed he had left or would soon be leaving for home. She provided details about the carriage in which the royal couple had ridden and quoted at length the reactions of people who'd watched from the sidewalk. She cited such profundities as "I liked Princess Amelia's dress better than Princess Lucia's" and "Lady Charlotte doesn't look old enough to be a grandmother."

CeCe's hopes that Krissy would turn her interest elsewhere faded when, on Thursday, Royal News gave way to a new heading: Royal Baby Watch.

The first item detailed how baby stores all over town were eager for the royal couple's business. One shop offered a "Princely Pram," which was available, at a hefty price, to the general public. The stroller came with velvet cushions and a built-in CD player.

She almost wished Shane would renew his demand that

they spend more time alone. However, he didn't mention it again.

He didn't even protest when the king informed her—by phone—that their departure was scheduled for Sunday. CeCe wished Shane at least cared enough to make a fuss. However, judging by her husband's good spirits, he was perfectly content to let her go.

It was for the best, CeCe told herself. Unknowingly, she'd been training all her life to take on the duties of queen. Surely her uncertainties would vanish once she assumed that role.

Otherwise, Shane was the perfect bridegroom, attentive and always ready for action. Like her, he kept his vow not to work during this special time, although on Thursday she awoke from a nap to hear him talking on his cell phone in the other room.

"Have them get Morris's memory ready," he was saying as CeCe wandered out of the bedroom. "Excuse me. Gotta go."

"Who was that?" CeCe asked after he hung up.

"Ferguson."

"Did he call my secretary about the scrapbooks?"

"He did better than that—he took her on a date," Shane said. "He likes her little girl."

"He met Betsy?" CeCe said. "Things are progressing."

"You wouldn't mind if Linzy took some time off, would you?" Shane asked.

What an odd request, she thought. "While I'm away, someone has to keep tabs on my office." That sounded ungenerous, she decided. Besides, Linzy almost never used her accumulated vacation time. "Forget I said that. If she really wants to go somewhere, that's fine with me."

"I'll tell Ferguson," Shane said.

Only later did she remember that she hadn't asked him what he meant by "Morris's memory." CeCe supposed she must have misheard, and besides, she didn't like to admit she'd been eavesdropping, so she let it pass.

On Friday, Hester tapped on the door. "I'm sorry to disturb you," she said when CeCe answered. "Before I pack for your trip, I wanted to take a look at your wardrobe to see what needs cleaning."

"We sent everything out earlier." Even on her honeymoon, CeCe was never less than efficient. "There's only what I'm wearing today, thank you, Hester."

"Why don't you go ahead and do some packing now?" Shane suggested. "I mean, for once we're both dressed. CeCe and I can take a stroll through the apartment and remind people that we're still alive."

Hester agreed that she'd like to get a head start, so the two went downstairs and made small talk with Amelia, the king, Ellie and Sir Harrison. The conversation was mostly about Korosol and Sunday's trip.

"Naturally, you're welcome to come with us, young man," her grandfather told Shane. "Although I'm afraid your bride will be terribly busy."

"She needs to get enough rest," he warned. "Don't forget her condition."

"Not at all," the king said. "I've arranged for her to be seen by the finest obstetrician in Korosol."

Shane frowned. "You expect her to give birth there?"

"Naturally," Easton said. "The baby will be heir to the throne, so he or she should be born in Korosol. You can come to attend the delivery. In fact, I'm sure everyone will expect it."

"I definitely want to be there, but babies don't always arrive on schedule," Shane said. "I'd like CeCe to return to New York in her seventh month. We have the finest medical facilities in the world—"

"Out of the question," said the king. "I'm sorry, young man, but starting Sunday, Princess Cecelia belongs to Korosol. Not to New York and not to you."

When her grandfather used that tone of voice, there was no arguing. Shane's jaw clamped shut.

On Saturday morning, the rest of the family departed for a daylong visit to some of Charlotte's relatives in the country. They set off early in the Carradignes' helicopter from the helipad on the roof, followed by a second chopper carrying Devon Montcalm and a contingent of guards.

CeCe would have liked to say goodbye to her cousins, but this was her last precious day alone with Shane. And, except for the staff, they had the entire apartment to themselves.

"What would you like to do today?" she asked him after they'd showered and dressed. "I mean, besides the obvious."

"Drop water balloons off the balcony on all those people trying to invade our privacy," he said.

"What's your second choice?"

"To tell the truth, I'm a little worried about security," he said. "I think I'll go downstairs and talk to the guards."

"Why?" Although she knew her grandfather conferred frequently with Sir Devon, CeCe tried not to think about possible dangers. As a future head of state, she'd drive herself crazy if she went around expecting the worst.

"The captain and a lot of the guards went with your grandfather today," he said. "If your cousin intends to pull any tricks, today is his best chance. I want to know what precautions they've taken."

Despite her resolve not to worry, CeCe felt a tremor of fear. She didn't want to think that Markus was capable of harming her, but his cruel attempt to break off her wedding made her suspicious.

And Shane had a good point. Although she felt safe here at home, Rademacher had penetrated security once. It certainly wasn't airtight.

"That's not a bad idea," she said. "I'll come with you."

"I doubt the guards will talk openly in front of you," Shane said. "Your grandfather probably left them instructions not to alarm you."

CeCe didn't like being sheltered or treated like a child, and she intended to set things straight with the guards and everybody else as soon as she assumed the throne. For the moment, however, Shane was right.

"I'll stay here," she said.

"Lock the doors."

"Okay." CeCe was growing increasingly nervous.

"I'm sure there's no problem," Shane added. "But we'll both be happier if I make sure they're on the ball."

"Agreed."

Without Shane, the suite seemed hollow, like a summer cottage the Carradignes had rented when she was a child. One September day when the family was departing, CeCe had run back inside to look for a missing doll. She still remembered the echoing emptiness.

Nonsense! Annoyed at herself, she smacked her hand against the wall. Why was the future queen of Korosol cowering in her rooms? She didn't intend to let Markus or anyone else turn the barracuda of DeLacey Shipping into a mouse.

CeCe yanked open the door and walked through the home theater into the upper gallery. Since she had no idea where she intended to go next, she stopped to consider.

What a big place her home was, she thought, noticing the back staircase to her left and the long stretch of hallway before her. It seemed unnaturally quiet. She'd assumed most of the staff would remain behind, busily vacuuming and mopping while the family was out of the way, but nothing stirred.

Beyond the staircase, from the direction of her grandfather's suite, she heard a board creak. CeCe's throat constricted.

She waited, frozen. No more sounds reached her.

Okay, false alarm, she told herself, and decided to descend to the kitchen. She found it hard to take the stairs, however, because she kept visualizing Rademacher sneaking up on them a few weeks ago.

How ridiculous. She'd lived here all her life and never been frightened before.

Besides, CeCe had taken martial arts and self-defense classes at Charlotte's insistence. Her mother had always been sensitive to the danger of kidnapping.

Below in the kitchen, she found everything neat as a pin. However, she missed seeing red-cheeked Bernice puttering at the stove or Hester sharing coffee with Quincy.

Today was Saturday, CeCe noted. Bernice usually took off on Mondays, but once in a while she chose to visit her grown daughter over the weekend. Hester and Quincy were probably deliberately staying out of the way of the honeymooning couple.

Well, she'd proved to herself that she was no coward. She'd demonstrated, just in case Markus was spying, that he couldn't frighten her into hiding in her suite. She could go back upstairs with a clear conscience.

By the time CeCe reached the second floor, she was practically trotting.

A *bang!* from the far end of the hall set her heart skittering. She spun to see Shane racing toward her from the side stairs that ran by the whirlpool bath.

"What are you doing in the gallery?" he said. "Never mind. Come on. We've got to get out."

"What?" Real danger couldn't be intruding into Charlotte Carradigne's home!

"The guards aren't there," he said. "The whole place is wide open. Somebody's been bribed or tricked, I don't know what, but we can't stay."

CeCe fought down panic. "Where should we go?"

"Let's grab our suitcases," Shane said. "We may need to stay hidden for a day or so."

In no mood to argue, CeCe hurried with him into her suite. They snapped their bags shut, hauled them out through a private entrance she rarely used, then climbed up the fire escape onto the roof.

"I've called for one of my helicopters," Shane said.

"Thank goodness." CeCe hoped the pilot would hurry.

She disliked the very notion of fear, yet there was no other word for the emotion squeezing her chest. She wanted desperately to get away.

Where had the guards gone? They were all deeply loyal, she knew, and hoped they hadn't been harmed.

Maybe it was a mistake. Maybe they'd assumed that the honeymoon couple had left with the rest of the family. That didn't explain why the doors were unlocked, though. Besides, Sir Devon Montcalm didn't seem like the kind of man to make such a mistake.

The crowd below, if it was still hanging around, must wonder at all the comings and goings today, CeCe thought. She hoped Krissy Katwell wasn't going to start a Helicopter Watch full of stupid speculation about what was going on.

The whir of an approaching craft quickened her pulse. For one alarming moment, as sunlight glinted off the door and hid the markings, CeCe wondered if it might belong to Markus. Then she saw the intertwined letters OCI, the O'Connell Industries logo.

"Thank goodness," she said.

At Shane's signal, the copter descended. As soon as it was safe, he and CeCe climbed inside.

"Let's get out of here," he told the pilot, who lifted off without further urging.

A deep sense of relief came over CeCe. They were safe. She peered down at the city spread below. Although she sometimes rode to work with Charlotte in the De-Lacey copter, CeCe rarely indulged in sightseeing. Now she reveled in her bird's-eye view of the skyscraping towers and the vast sanctuary of Central Park.

"Gorgeous, isn't it!" Shane called over the noise of the engine.

The bird tilted and swooped, leaving CeCe's stomach behind. "Where—where are we going?" she asked, shouting to make herself heard.

"The airport," Shane said. "I want you safely away from here until we get to the root of this."

Grandfather would be proud of him, she thought. So would Charlotte. And they'd both be indignant to learn that CeCe had been placed in peril.

"I should go directly to Korosol," she told him.

"I don't think that's wise," Shane said in her ear. "Suppose your cousin is attempting a coup?"

A coup d'état in quiet little Korosol? The idea was ludicrous. Yet if the king's own guard had been compromised, the possibility had to be considered.

They landed a short time later at an airfield, in a remote area reserved for private craft. Most of the planes on the ground bore the OCI insignia.

Shane grabbed his suitcase. "Let's make the transfer fast. I want to get you out of harm's way."

CeCe wasn't accustomed to working blind and relying on someone else. This wasn't just someone else, however; it was her husband. "You bet." Toting her bag, she followed.

The wind whipped her hair back as they crossed the tarmac. A mobile set of steps ushered them into a plane.

"My corporate jet," Shane explained unnecessarily as they deposited their luggage on the carpet.

The main room of the cabin was equipped with armchairs and sofas, a computer, desk, wet bar and large-screen TV. "It's almost as nice as DeLacey Shipping's corporate jet," CeCe teased.

"It's nicer," Shane said. "It's bigger, for one thing. Also, I designed it myself."

The floor shuddered as the engine started. "I guess the pilot knows we're aboard," she said.

"Indeed he does," came a familiar voice as Ferguson appeared from the cockpit. "As soon as I close the door, we can leave."

CeCe blinked. How had Ed arrived so quickly? Especially since he was supposed to be on vacation this week?

"I hope you don't mind," Shane said. "We're going to have a little company on our trip. There's plenty of room for them."

"You mean Ferguson?" she asked.

"Not just him," Shane said. "I thought your secretary and her daughter might enjoy a week's vacation in California, too."

O'Connell Industries maintained offices and facilities on the West Coast, so it made sense that they were going there. But how could Ed and Linzy have known they'd be heading that way in an emergency?

Unless there was no emergency. Unless Shane had orchestrated this whole scenario.

CeCe tried to make sense of what had happened. There'd been no staff in the apartment, but her husband might have asked them earlier to leave the honeymoon couple alone. As for the security guards, he'd probably never approached them in the first place.

The guards hadn't vanished. The apartment hadn't been unlocked. She'd simply taken Shane's word that there was a crisis.

From the back room, a little girl ran toward them. It was five-year-old Betsy, followed by her mother, Linzy. "Mind if we join you, Miss Carradigne?" asked the secretary. "I mean, Mrs. O'Connell?"

"Not at all," CeCe said, still preoccupied with Shane's treachery.

He'd kidnapped her. And she'd helped him.

"Better fasten your seat belts," Shane advised. A moment later, with a roar, the plane set off down the runway.

There was no turning back.

Chapter Thirteen

Shane knew he ought to be ashamed of himself. He could tell that he'd frightened CeCe, despite her self-possession. Nevertheless, he felt gleeful.

Tricking her had been the only way to snatch her from her grandfather's control. Thank goodness the Carradignes' plans for the day had dovetailed with his scheme.

Bringing Ferguson and Linzy along was partly generosity and partly in service of his plan. He figured that, with them around, CeCe was less likely to go ballistic.

"Comfortable?" he asked his wife once the Fasten Seat Belt sign clicked off.

"Oh, very comfortable," she said sarcastically.

"Is something wrong?" Linzy asked. Ed hadn't told her about the plot, since loyalty might have forced her to tip off her boss.

"I was told there was an emergency," CeCe said. "My plans called for flying to Korosol with my grandfather tomorrow."

"You didn't expect to join us?" Linzy shot a questioning look at Ferguson.

"It's going to be a fantastic trip," he said, and hurried into the kitchenette.

"I'm so sorry." The secretary looked distressed. "Miss...Mrs. O'Connell, I was thrilled at the chance to have a real vacation with Betsy. I had no idea you were being conned into it.''

''I don't begrudge you the trip. You deserve a break.'' Averting her face from Linzy, CeCe glared at Shane. She'd get over it, he thought merrily.

''Can I draw in my coloring books?'' Betsy asked.

''Certainly.'' Shane found her space on one of the desks. ''You know, this computer came with a few basic games. Would you like to try one? They're card games.''

''I'm not sure if she's ready for that,'' Linzy said. ''Although she already knows her numbers and letters.''

''Does she know clubs and spades from hearts and diamonds?'' Shane clicked on a solitaire game.

''I don't think so.''

He began showing the child how to lay out the cards for Patience. She watched with growing confusion. ''Can I try it?'' she asked before he'd completed his explanation.

''Well, sure.'' Dubiously, he handed her the mouse.

Her face alight, Betsy clicked on one card after another. At first, Shane thought she was moving them in random patterns, but then he saw that she was creating little groupings.

''There's the king and that's his son,'' the little girl said, indicating a jack. ''The king just quarreled with the queen and now the little boy's going to help them make friends again.''

''That's quite a story,'' Shane said.

''You know how children are,'' Linzy said apologetically. ''I'm sure she'll learn the rules of the game if you give her time.''

''This is a better game.'' Shane watched as Betsy surrounded the queen of clubs with cards from the diamond suit.

''She's got lots of jewelry, doesn't she?'' the little girl

asked. "See, the king bought it for her and that put her in a good mood."

"Mercenary woman." Quickly, CeCe added, "Very creative, Betsy."

Linzy came over to supervise her daughter, and Shane took CeCe aside. Instead of apologizing about his ruse, he said, "I'm surprised to learn that you'd met your secretary's daughter."

"Why?" CeCe asked.

"You don't seem like the type to socialize with the staff," he said, being deliberately provocative. If she got angry about his comment, it might defuse some of her righteous wrath about his trickery.

"Ever heard of Bring Your Daughter to Work Day?" CeCe asked. "We honor it at DeLacey Shipping."

"I see," he said.

"Doesn't O'Connell Industries?"

He vaguely recalled seeing a lot of little girls wandering around the office once. At the time, they hadn't interested him, since he'd had no idea of becoming a parent himself. "Sure we do."

She folded her arms. "Okay, enough of that topic. Let's get on to the main event. Shall we have this fight in front of your other guests, or shall we go somewhere private?"

"There isn't anywhere private," Shane lied. He knew the boom was about to be lowered and hoped to put off the reckoning as long as possible.

"There's a back room," CeCe said.

"It's haunted," he improvised.

"By Markus and his invading hordes, perhaps?"

"Okay, I pulled a fast one, but I really was worried about you," Shane said. "There's no telling what your cousin might do."

"A coup d'état in Korosol." CeCe shook her head. "I can't believe I bought that." She glanced at Linzy, and lowered her voice. "My grandfather might think I had some part in this."

"I left a message on his desk, and another one in your mother's suite," Shane said. "I took full blame for the escapade."

"You can't take the blame for my acting like an idiot," CeCe said. "I shouldn't have been so trusting."

Now he did feel guilty. She'd trusted him, and he'd burned her. "If you insist, we can leave Linzy, Betsy and Ed in California and come back as soon as the plane's refueled."

"I'm not setting foot in your plane again, thank you," she said. "The way you maneuver things, we'd end up in Hawaii."

He'd known as he planned this adventure that persuading her to spend more time with him wouldn't be easy, Shane reminded himself. "Look, a week's difference in flying to Korosol isn't going to matter. Why not stay?"

"We'd be inconveniencing a lot of people, including a head of state and his staff," CeCe said.

"You're worth it, princess." Shane grinned.

"You're outrageous!"

"Thank you," he said. "Oh, come on, CeCe. For all the ballyhoo about the royal wedding, our honeymoon was strictly low-rent. What kind of couple doesn't even get away from the homestead?"

"A couple who keep their promises," she said.

They stopped talking as Ferguson approached with a tray of Greek delicacies, including spinach-filled pastry puffs and dips for pita bread. He'd planned the menus for their trip and taken great pains with them, Shane noted approvingly.

"That looks great." He helped himself. Even CeCe unwound enough to fill a small plate.

Ed crossed to the desk and sat down with Linzy and Betsy, who was telling more tales about her card characters and their family doings. The two adults listened in amusement.

"Your assistant and my secretary seem well suited," CeCe said.

"They're not the only ones."

In her unguarded expression, he saw a flash of wistfulness. "Shane, this isn't a question of what I want or don't want."

"It's a question of duty," he finished for her.

"And promises that must be kept," she reminded him.

It was time to drop the teasing, Shane decided. "You're right. We do need to talk privately."

They carried their plates into the back room. Equipped with several convertible couches and a dining table, it was much cozier. He considered opening one of the sofas and letting nature take its course, but he owed CeCe more than to try such a diversionary tactic.

"I told you we needed to lay a foundation for our marriage," he said, sitting at the table.

She took a seat across from him. "Whatever relationship we've got isn't going to change much in the course of a single week."

"Maybe not," Shane agreed. "The issue isn't just you and me, though. It's also who you are, even when I'm not around."

"Who I am?" She regarded him as if he'd lost his mind. "Shane, I don't need your help establishing my personal identity."

"In some ways, you've been a very sheltered person," he said.

She drew herself up indignantly. "May I remind you that I overhauled a major shipping company. I also hold an MBA—"

"That's what you've done, not who you are." He knew he was venturing into none-of-your-business territory. Yet between husband and wife, those boundaries didn't exist.

"CeCe, I care about you a great deal. You're the most intriguing and contradictory person I've ever met."

"Thanks, I guess." She nibbled at a pastry puff.

"But excuse me for believing you haven't stretched your wings," Shane said. "I've watched you with your family. Those ties are still incredibly strong for a grown woman."

"I have an incredibly strong family," she answered.

"You're right about that." He leaned forward. "You've never discovered who you are apart from them. Once you get to Korosol, you never will."

"And you're an expert on the subject?" she shot back. "I'm not trying to rub in the fact that you don't have a family, but your situation isn't inherently superior to mine."

"Nobody said anything about being superior." Shane struggled to bring the discussion back on course. "CeCe, think about it. What kind of wedding did you want?"

"It doesn't matter," she said.

"Do you know?"

"What Charlotte planned was beautiful," she said. "Don't you agree?"

"Krissy Katwell certainly does," he couldn't resist saying. "Okay, here's another one. What kind of honeymoon would you like to have?"

"Shane, this is pointless!"

"Suppose your mother decided to sell DeLacey Shipping," he continued. "And for some reason you didn't become queen. What kind of work would you do?"

"There are lots of opportunities," she answered tautly.

"Name three that appeal to you."

"I can't do that off the top of my head," CeCe said. "Are you planning to hold a career seminar on our honeymoon?"

"I want to give you a chance to make your own choices free and clear," Shane said. "Not that I'm trying to discourage you from becoming queen. But I want you to be Queen Cecelia, not Queen Easton by Proxy.''

''I don't see how you're going to accomplish that in such a short time,'' CeCe said.

Frankly, neither did he. Shane only knew that since their wedding, the closer he'd come to his wife the more he'd realized how much she'd been shaped by devotion to her family, and how few decisions she made completely on her own.

''You have to get in touch with your reactions, even if you're only choosing what to eat for dinner or whether or not to buy a souvenir,'' Shane said. ''It isn't simply for the good of our marriage. It's also for the good of Korosol.''

''Grandfather doesn't want a renegade queen,'' CeCe said. ''I have to follow his guidelines.''

''Your grandfather's old,'' Shane reminded her. ''He won't always be around. What if something happens to him? What if you find yourself on the throne with no one to steer you?''

''I'll manage.'' She drew a deep breath.

''Markus isn't going to go away,'' he added. ''He'll be nipping at your heels, trying to win over the public. Your people already know him, while you're a newcomer. Unless you can stamp your own personality on the throne, you'll get swamped in a sea of politics.''

''Shane!'' she snapped. ''Are you trying to use my cousin as a bogeyman again? Twice in one day is a bit much!''

''Think about it.'' Shane stood up. ''If you don't change your mind by the time we land, which should be in about four hours, I'll put you on the next commercial flight back to New York.''

''Do you have an air phone?'' she asked. ''I want to call my family.''

''There's no point in disturbing them while they're visiting relatives,'' he reminded her. ''Come on, CeCe, think for yourself.''

He left her stewing in the back room, and hoped he hadn't permanently alienated the woman he loved.

SHANE HAD INCREDIBLE GALL, implying that she couldn't think for herself. CeCe had challenged Charlotte repeatedly since she joined DeLacey, including her insistence on forming an alliance with O'Connell Industries.

Judging by today's events, that had been the biggest mistake of her life. How dare a man who'd virtually abducted her complain that she failed to act for herself?

CeCe looked out a window. She didn't register much about the landscape passing below, however, because her mind was racing.

Shane didn't understand because he'd never had to meet anyone's expectations or standards but his own. There'd been no danger of disappointing his parents, because they hadn't been around. Even his mentor had no longer been alive when Shane made his climb to glory.

He'd succeeded alone because he had to. In a comparable situation, CeCe would have done the same. It angered her that her own husband was like the other doubters, the ones who claimed she'd never have made it without her connections.

The minutes ticked by, and her fury abated. Shane's questions came back to her.

What kind of wedding had she wanted, and what sort of honeymoon? If her mother hadn't owned DeLacey Shipping, CeCe might still have earned an MBA, but what field would have attracted her?

She didn't know.

She'd never thought beyond trying to live up to the high standards she set for herself. To fill the role vacated by her father's death.

Any instinct or emotion that didn't fit, she rejected as

a weakness. Even now, weeks after learning she was pregnant, she hadn't allowed herself to explore what it was going to mean to be a mother. She got excited just thinking about holding a tiny baby in her arms, and yet she was ready to turn her child over to a nanny.

Suddenly the prospect of getting on another plane and returning to New York, then immediately flying to Korosol, overwhelmed her. What Shane was offering sounded a lot like freedom, at least for a brief interlude.

Freedom was the one thing Cecelia Carradigne had never known, not since she was nine years old and felt the weight of responsibility settle over her. Perhaps she'd imposed that weight on herself, but it hadn't budged in twenty years.

She couldn't escape it now. Still, the prospect of a few days without any pressure seemed like sheer heaven.

It was infuriating to let Shane win, especially when he'd behaved so abominably. On the other hand, it would prove she knew how to think for herself.

Still unsure what to say, CeCe went into the front chamber. She found the great Shane O'Connell down on his knees in his slacks and polo shirt, crawling around with Betsy on his back. "Giddyap!" she shouted happily.

"It's my turn," Ferguson said.

"I buck better than you do!" Shane demonstrated by bouncing the little girl lightly a couple of times.

"My whinny is much more realistic."

"Okay, Ed, you sit over there and whinny. Betsy and I haven't finished our ride."

"Go, horsey!" said the child.

Linzy smiled at CeCe, who'd never seen her secretary look so at ease. The woman was quite pretty when she didn't have pucker lines between her eyebrows.

"I hope they have lots of oats and sugar lumps where we're going," CeCe said. "I can see your daughter's going to keep the livestock busy."

Shane peered up at her. "You're coming with us?"

"I don't even know what you've got planned," she said. "But what the heck? After all, I've come this far."

She knew she would have to make explanations to her mother and grandfather. Once she did, she planned to turn off her cell phone and keep it off for the rest of the week.

FROM THE LONG BEACH airport, a limousine carried the quintet south along a freeway. After New York's lingering chill, CeCe enjoyed the warm, clear weather and the sight of rustling palm trees.

When she took out her cell phone, Shane said, "They probably haven't even discovered our absence yet."

"That's fine." CeCe dialed Charlotte's personal line at the apartment instead of her mother's cell phone. At the beep, she said, "In case you're looking for me, Shane's whisked me off on holiday."

His mouth formed the words, "Answering machine?"

She nodded and continued. "I didn't know what he was planning, but now that we're here, I think it's in the long-term best interest of Korosol for us to have a real honeymoon. Please give my apologies to Grandfather. I'll explain everything next weekend when I get home."

She clicked off, then powered down her cell phone. Turning it off was like unhooking a leash, CeCe discovered with a surge of exhilaration. It was the first time she'd ever thumbed her nose at her family.

Lucia might pursue her own career and keep her own apartment, and Amelia might travel all over the globe incognito. They were entitled to their independence, because they weren't the eldest. CeCe had always known that. She was different.

Anxiety shafted through her. How could she abandon her responsibility? What if the king decided she wasn't fit to be queen, or Charlotte never forgave her?

It's only for a week, she reminded herself. She didn't

believe her family would reject her for such a minor and understandable transgression.

A short time later, they left the freeway. The air became touched with brine as a low bridge carried them over a stretch of water.

"Where are we?" she asked.

"Newport Beach," Shane said. "We just crossed onto the Balboa Peninsula."

Betsy, who'd been showing her doll the sights, piped up, "I want to play on the beach!"

"We'll do that another time," Linzy said. "First we're going to do something else that's fun."

So her secretary knew more about their plans than she did, CeCe mused. Well, it didn't matter, because today she wasn't playing the role of executive and she didn't have to be in charge.

The limousine halted on a narrow side street crowded with funky houses and apartments. Beach real estate must be very expensive, because despite the modest appearance of the dwellings, expensive cars lined the street.

While the chauffeur fetched their luggage, Shane led CeCe and the others down a narrow walkway between two cottages. They emerged to a wonderful view.

Before them spread a harbor filled with every sort of small boat, from tiny craft that were little more than rigged surfboards all the way to yachts. Brightly colored sails billowed in the mild breeze.

On both sides of the harbor, houses had their own piers. Docked at the one directly before them was a magnificent yacht.

On board waited a steward in a white uniform. He straightened at their approach and waved to Shane. "Welcome aboard, Mr. O'Connell!"

The name painted on the side was *Morris's Memory*. Morris had been Shane's benefactor, CeCe recalled. So that's what he'd been talking about on the phone!

"We're going for a cruise?" she asked.

"First stop, Catalina Island," said Shane, steering the little group onto the pier. "Then down to San Diego. If we've got time and we're in the mood, maybe Ensenada, Mexico."

"I've never been to a foreign country except Canada," Linzy said. "I'm glad I studied Spanish in high school."

Betsy held up her doll to face the water and told it solemnly, "You won't drown, Mary Anne. I won't let you fall in."

"We don't have a doll-size life jacket, but we've got one for you, young lady," the steward said. "What kind of soda pop would you like?"

Betsy marched ahead to inspect the choices, giving a happy skip en route. Her mother followed.

After stepping on the deck, CeCe walked along the railing, trying to get her sea legs. She'd sailed on one of DeLacey's liners for several weeks one summer to get the feel of the operation, and had spent a little time on board her family's yacht, the *Duchess*.

In the harbor, or in calm seas on a huge craft, she enjoyed the experience. Even a hint of rough water—and it didn't take much in a modest-size boat like a yacht—and she became violently seasick.

She'd been grateful that her morning sickness had abated. No way was she going to yield to this new disruption.

And yet, CeCe wanted to feel the wind in her hair and set out across the Pacific toward the fabled Catalina Island, leaving her old self behind. Including the part that got queasy.

"This place is like a hotel!" Linzy announced excitedly. "I just peeked inside. Have you seen it, Mrs. O'Connell?"

"Not yet." Going inside intensified seasickness. But not in the harbor, CeCe reminded herself.

Steeling her resolve, she joined the others for an impromptu tour of the premises. It was soon obvious that Shane hadn't stinted on anything, even though surely he couldn't spend much time on board.

The main cabin was spacious, with games tables and a large dining table. The full galley was staffed by a cook, while a female cabin steward bustled to show them the comfortable staterooms, each with its own head. On the bridge, CeCe met the captain and the pilot.

Everyone greeted her warmly and joked with Shane. Betsy and her doll became immediate favorites. It was obvious Linzy would have no shortage of baby-sitters when she wanted them.

"I presume you use the boat for employee incentives and office promotions," CeCe told Shane when they resurfaced on deck.

"Of course. I have to keep the staff motivated, don't I?" He grinned. "We sponsor monthly productivity contests, with a weekend trip to Ensenada for the winners. Sometimes I loan the yacht to major clients, as well."

"How about your New York staff?" she asked. "Do they get to use it?"

"Flying them out is no problem, since our planes are always making runs," Shane said. "Are we going to talk business much longer?"

CeCe's face grew hot, and not just from the sunshine. "I can't help it."

"Let go." Shane stood beside her at the railing, his body sheltering her from the breeze. "Trust your instincts. Indulge yourself."

"What if...?" CeCe bit her lip.

"What if what?"

"What if, once I start indulging myself, I can't stop?" she asked.

"Do you really think the barracuda is going to turn into

a goldfish?'' Shane asked. ''Because if so, I can hardly wait!''

The ship's motors rumbled to life, and crew members hurried to make preparations for departure. With a warning blast of its horn, *Morris's Memory* eased away from the dock and wove its way through the busy harbor.

CeCe had the sense of leaving everything behind. Everything except what mattered most—her husband and her future.

She still wished, though, that she knew how she was going to put all the pieces back together once this adventure ended.

Chapter Fourteen

There was one problem with the yacht, Shane mused. It was way too full of people.

He hadn't given that fact much thought when he planned this getaway. On previous yachting trips with assorted buddies and dates, he'd enjoyed socializing.

Now he didn't want to make chitchat with Ferguson, or accept a mimosa from the steward, or consult with the cook about the dinner menu. He wanted to haul CeCe off to their stateroom, rip away her clothes and make love to her. Afterward, they could stand naked on the bow and pretend they were that young couple in the movie *Titanic*, minus clothes and minus the pain-in-the-neck ending.

It wasn't going to happen. That didn't mean the two of them couldn't have fun, though.

"You're different here on the boat," CeCe said, coming to stand beside him.

"More sunburned?" Shane joked.

"Not yet!" She laughed with a freer, more heartfelt sound than before. "You look dashing, though."

"And you look exquisite," he said.

That was an understatement. CeCe had never been more beautiful, not even when she was gliding down the aisle like an angel. The California sunshine brought out the creaminess of her skin and the jade depths of her eyes.

She moved differently, too, he thought. Her step had more spring, and the fluttering sea breeze made her blouse hug her body.

Which was exactly what Shane wanted to do.

"How long do you think we have to stay above deck for courtesy's sake?" he asked.

"What do you mean?"

He couldn't believe she wasn't as eager to make love as he was. "We *are* still on our honeymoon."

"Oh, right." She sipped her lemon-lime soda. "Let's wait until we get out of the harbor and see how it goes."

"See how what goes?" From this close angle, Shane had a clear glimpse down his wife's blouse, of which the top two buttons were open. Another inch and he wouldn't have to rely on his memory for anything. "See, here's my schedule. We hit the hay right now, which means we can get cleaned up in time for dinner. Then we…"

"Here we go." CeCe stared past him toward the mouth of the harbor. Beyond lay open ocean, with Catalina faintly visible in the distance. "The sea looks rough, don't you think?"

"Not really." How could she expect him to think about anything but sex, with her delicate fragrance wafting up at him?

The movement of the yacht shifted from a slight forward roll to a distinct side-to-side bob. "I guess it is a little choppy," he admitted. "The best thing for that is to lie down. Preferably with me."

Ferguson and Linzy joined them. From here, Shane could see Betsy inside the lounge, playing a board game with the cabin steward.

"This is fantastic!" Linzy said. "I've been on the *Duchess* a few times, but it was always so filled with people, I could hardly move. This is like flying solo. Well, not entirely solo." She smiled at Ed.

The solemn lines that sometimes made him look older

than his thirty-one years had vanished. The slightly built man carried himself with more confidence than usual, too, Shane noted.

"I've always enjoyed *Morris's Memory*," Ferguson said. "It's never been this entertaining before, though. Must be the company."

"It certainly is." Shane waited for CeCe to add a similar sentiment, but she was gazing toward the blue-and-gold sunset. By its light, he noticed how pale she was. "I don't want you to get burned, but a few rays tomorrow will do you good."

"How long did you say it takes to reach Catalina?" she asked.

"A few hours," Shane said. "We'll anchor there tonight and go exploring in the morning."

"Betsy will love a trip in a glass-bottom boat," Ferguson told Linzy. "The whole place is a nature preserve. It's gorgeous."

"Do they sell postcards?" she asked. "I brought my camera, but it isn't very good, and I want lots of pictures for our scrapbook."

"They sell tons of postcards," Ed assured her. "We'll swing through the souvenir shops and see what we can find."

"Let's save the tickets from the glass-bottom boat trip," Linzy said. "Things like that add zest to the pages."

Much as he liked his assistant, Shane couldn't take much interest in a conversation about scrapbooks. He was glad when the pair of them wandered away.

"There's still over an hour left before dinner," he told CeCe.

"Oh?" she asked faintly. "Wha—what's on the menu?"

"Lobster and crab bisque," he said. "Artichoke hearts and marinated mushrooms. Followed by…"

"I don't know if mushrooms are such a good idea." Against the darkening sky, she looked even paler than before.

Shane sighed. It didn't appear that his bride was as eager as he was to explore making love at sea. "I hate to wait until we're docked tonight," he said.

"We don't eat until we dock?"

"I meant to make love." Might as well say what he meant, he decided, since CeCe wasn't taking hints. "There's something thrilling about making love while the boat is rolling. It kind of throws you together and pulls you apart."

"Do we have to talk about this?" She gripped the railing.

"I thought you'd enjoy it." Shane couldn't understand her attitude. He knew CeCe hadn't had many previous lovers, but surely a woman in the shipping business had experienced the joys of sex on the bounding main at least once.

She inhaled deeply. "That fresh air is wonderful." She hardly seemed to notice him in her fascination with the horizon.

Shane decided to back off for a while. Clearly his wife loved the sea and wanted to revel in it. They were going to have a great time on their voyage.

CeCe KNEW SHE SHOULD pay closer attention to what her husband was saying. The roiling in her stomach, however, commanded all her attention.

She wished it would go away. It was embarrassing for a woman in her profession to get seasick.

Charlotte had always declared that if CeCe put her mind to it, she could conquer this weakness. No one else in the DeLacey family suffered from this problem, and neither had Drake.

Most likely nobody in the history of Korosol had ever

endured seasickness, either, CeCe thought with a flare of annoyance. Well, when she was queen, she'd make sure she never had to go anywhere on a yacht. If people pestered her about it, she might outlaw them altogether.

For the next hour, she tried to distract herself by taking a brisk walk around the deck. She explained to the others that she'd missed her morning exercise and felt like letting off steam.

She drank another lemon-lime soda, which helped settle her stomach. The sea cooperated by remaining calm.

But as darkness descended, the chop of the water increased. Dinner was almost ready, and she knew she wouldn't be able to eat.

It was time to come clean with Shane. CeCe hated to do it, though. She wanted to enjoy the cruise. And she loved the way her husband looked, like a buccaneer with the breeze blowing his dark hair.

But she was miserable. How likely was it that she'd overcome these feelings anytime soon?

She joined her husband on the rear deck. "I'm supposed to get in touch with my feelings this week, right?"

"Sure," he said. "All of your feelings. Especially the ones that involve me."

"And you don't want me worrying about pleasing others, isn't that so?" she probed.

"You do too much of that with your family," he agreed. "Come on, CeCe, whatever's on your mind, please tell me. The sooner you get it off your chest, the sooner we can start having fun."

He was right. "What I need to tell you is…" she began.

A swell rocked the boat. CeCe hadn't seen it coming, and she wasn't prepared for the next wave, either. The yacht dipped and rolled sideways before righting itself.

"Yippee!" cried Shane, like a kid on a roller coaster.

The last shred of self-restraint vanished. CeCe grabbed

the railing, leaned over and deposited the contents of her stomach into the briny deep.

She hung there, ashamed to face Shane. She hated to reveal this kind of frailty. It made her feel like a whiny female who couldn't handle pressure.

"I guess that about says it," Shane commented close to her ear. "Why didn't you tell me?"

She gulped in some sea air. "Barracudas don't get mal de mer."

"I've got seasickness medicine on board," he said. "If you take some tonight, you'll be fine."

"It doesn't work on me." She straightened, still clutching the rail.

"You've tried it?"

"Darn right. Besides, I don't think I should take something like that while I'm pregnant."

"Hold on." Shane disappeared for a few minutes. CeCe's stomach grew calmer. Then the boat hit another swell and she repeated her performance.

When she straightened, Shane was standing a few feet away. Obviously, he'd witnessed her encore. How humiliating.

But his face reflected only tender concern. No disdain. No amusement at her predicament.

"The captain says we're closer to Catalina than to Newport," he said. "We'll continue on and dock there tonight. You and I can stay at a hotel if you prefer."

"I'll be all right in the harbor," CeCe said.

"My steward's making arrangements for us to fly back to the mainland in the morning," he said. "Ed and Linzy can take *Morris's Memory* from there. I'm sure they'll enjoy having the ship to themselves."

"I've let you down," she said unhappily.

"Are you kidding?" Shane's eyes sparkled as they caught a last gleam of the sunset. "Nothing invigorates me like a challenge. I'm already working on an alternative plan.''

''Where can we go?'' she asked. ''If we stay at a hotel, some gossip is likely to notify the newspapers.''

''Leave it to me,'' he said.

CeCe nodded and clung to the railing. In her present condition, she was more than willing to let Shane run the show.

SHANE WOULD HAVE LIKED to whisk CeCe away immediately. Finding a helicopter on such short notice and arranging a rescue at sea, however, would entail complications far beyond what was justified.

He tried, in deference to his wife, not to enjoy himself during the rest of the trip. It was hard not to, though, when the cook had prepared a fine meal and Ferguson and Linzy were in high spirits.

CeCe seemed content to stand near the bow of the ship with the wind in her face. She shooed Shane away, after thanking him for his promise to spare her the rest of the trip.

Among the other people on board, the most interesting person turned out to be Betsy. Not having much awareness of the stages of childhood development, Shane had considered five-year-olds to be bundles of squalling childishness who threw tantrums in department stores and burst into tears on Santa Claus's lap.

Betsy, however, was a distinct personality. She inhabited a vivid world in which dolls came to life, characters in books were more real than most people and ordinary routines inspired fascination.

She read *The Tale of Peter Rabbit* to Shane, picking out some of the words and repeating others from memory. Occasionally she would digress from the plot to explain how Peter was feeling or what other mischief he had in mind.

It was amazing that a helpless baby could, in five short years, turn into such a creative person. When he went to check on CeCe, Shane sneaked a peek at her midsection. It seemed to him that it bulged a tiny bit.

Was the baby already dreaming? he wondered. Did it sense his presence?

"What's wrong?" She frowned. "Do I look that wretched?"

"Not at all." He slid one arm around her waist. "I was admiring your motherly figure."

"Oh, no. Am I getting fat?"

He couldn't believe she would worry about a thing like that. "CeCe, you're pregnant. Who cares about your weight?"

"Mother always said we had no excuse for letting ourselves go, because we're tall and come from a long line of thin women," she said. "I mean, I know I have to gain weight while I'm expecting. After that, I plan to lose it right away."

"You should do what's best for your health, not worry about what your mother wants," Shane said.

"It's not just Charlotte." CeCe ran her hands down her tummy distractedly. "People like Krissy Katwell make the snidest comments about my sisters and me. Once Lucia got a weird haircut to twit my mother, and they made such a fuss in the newspaper, you'd have thought she killed someone."

"Or got pregnant out of wedlock by an upstart like me," Shane joked.

CeCe regarded him levelly. "I'm glad I did."

"Really?" he said. "Your life would be a lot simpler without me."

"Simpler, but more boring," she said.

Shane looked at his watch.

"What?" CeCe sounded hurt. "Are you late for something?"

"We've been on this boat for two and half hours," he said. "You're already talking like a different person. Somebody who knows what pleases her and isn't always bowing and scraping to her mother and grandfather."

"Shane..." She swallowed hard. "When we come back to reality, I'll still have my duty."

"There's another thing you'll still have," he told her. "Me."

"You won't be with me in Korosol," she said.

"I'll be there in spirit."

"Shane..."

"Let's not worry about it," he said. "I declare this week to be an island in time. There is no future."

"No past, either?" CeCe teased.

"The past must be selectively edited to leave only the happy parts," Shane said.

That suited her fine.

THE NEXT MORNING, they rented a Cessna at the small airport high in Catalina's hills. Shane announced that he was to be the pilot, and assured his wife that he had all the necessary qualifications.

He didn't get cocky, CeCe noted with appreciation. He followed the checklist and consulted a weather report, then made sure they were both properly strapped in.

"The main cause of small-plane problems is pilot error," he said. "I try not to take anything for granted."

She overcame the urge to grab on to her seat as the plane taxied forward. CeCe always got that urge, even though she'd often flown in small planes. Still, the layout of this airport did create a natural concern.

"The runway looks dangerous," she called as they raced along it. "If you don't pull up in time, you go right off a cliff."

"It's happened." They soared into the sky with room to spare. "But not to me."

"Do you fly a lot?" Now that they'd cleared the airport, CeCe felt lighter than a feather.

"I used to." Shane kept his attention on the instrument panel and the horizon. "In the early days, we never knew when we might need a pilot to take over a flight. It was Morris who encouraged me to get my license."

"You must be fairly advanced to handle one of those cargo jets," CeCe said.

"Morris paid for my lessons, so I got started early and put in a lot of hours," he said. "The man was always looking ahead."

Below, the plane's tiny shadow trailed them across the sparkling Pacific like a lovesick puppy. "I'm glad we're doing this, and not just because I felt lousy," CeCe said. "Much as I like Ed and Linzy, I didn't want to spend our entire honeymoon with them."

"I like being alone with you, too." Shane's smile flashed a cleft in his cheek.

A short time later, they landed at John Wayne Airport in Newport Beach. Small planes like theirs took turns on the runway with commercial jets, she saw in surprise. "This is a funny place."

"People do things differently in California," Shane said. "Especially when they don't plan ahead. This airport used to be used for general aviation—small planes—and it grew kind of hit or miss."

After they landed, he made arrangements to return the plane to Catalina, then picked up a rental car. "No limo?" CeCe teased.

"I thought you didn't want to be noticed."

"Is that possible?" Realizing how egotistical her comment sounded, she explained, "All my life, even in a big place like New York, people have pointed me out."

"You certainly won't run into anyone you know here," Shane said.

"We did get our pictures on television," CeCe reminded him. "And in the tabloids, too."

"I don't think people in Newport Beach read tabloids," Shane said. "They're a bit upscale for that. They won't be expecting you here, so I doubt they'll make the connection to whatever they've seen on TV."

CeCe wasn't convinced. Since childhood, she'd never known a place where she could move around freely. "We'll see."

Unfamiliar with the area, she didn't know where they were until they crossed the low bridge to the Balboa Peninsula. "We're staying here?"

"That house with the pier belongs to me," Shane said. "I bought it as an investment years ago. My management company rents it by the month, and right now it happens to be empty."

"Our own house." CeCe leaned back dreamily against the seat cushion. "The only time I've lived in a house were some summers as a child when my parents rented a cottage."

"I'll bet you had a good time," Shane said.

"A sinfully good time." That was how she felt now, too, like a woman breaking bounds and smashing rules.

Shane found a parking place half a block from their destination. "Sorry, no garage," he said.

A teenager on roller skates whizzed by on the sidewalk. A couple of girls skirted the car and crossed the street, walking a chihuahua.

"We'd better grab our suitcases and dash inside," CeCe said.

"Why? Is somebody chasing us?"

"Everything's so close together and there aren't any guards," she pointed out. "If someone recognizes us, we'll never get away."

"Stop worrying," Shane said.

A tantalizing image formed in her mind. The two of

them were strolling on the beach hand in hand, talking and laughing without a care in the world. And without anyone noticing.

CeCe got an idea. "I saw a drugstore on the way. Let's go out later and get a colored rinse for my hair."

"Let me guess," said her husband. "Charlotte never let you dye it."

"I'm doing this as a disguise!" she said. "Oh, all right, I do want to see how I'd look as a redhead."

"Why didn't you say so?" Shane pulled away from the curb. "This week, we act on impulse. Let's go now."

WHEN HE BOUGHT THE HOUSE five years ago, Shane had considered it a perfect bachelor retreat. The rooms, although small, were filled with light, and he'd had it decorated with tasteful subtlety.

The one thing that had been missing until now was CeCe. Full of energy, delighting in their escapade, she brought the cottage to life.

"What do you think?" she asked, toweling her hair as she emerged from the shower half an hour after they returned from the store.

"I can't see the color properly." That was probably because Shane was too busy staring at her body wrapped only in a towel.

CeCe grabbed a brush and ran it through her maroon locks. "Is this red enough for you?"

"Come closer and I'll tell you," he said.

"Better take the suitcases off the bed," she warned. Although they'd begun unpacking, she'd been eager to try out her new hair tint.

Shane put the cases on the floor. "How's that?"

CeCe checked to make sure the curtains were closed. "Just taking precautions."

"The heck with that." He grabbed his bride and pulled her on top of him. "Let's act like wild animals."

He discovered in the next few moments exactly how wild CeCe could be. Something had been unleashed in her, and in him.

With luck, it would never be stuffed back into the old mold again.

Chapter Fifteen

It must be the red hair, CeCe thought, that made her feel so wanton. Or maybe it was that lustful expression on Shane's face, the one he wore almost constantly. How did men ever get any work done?

And how did women?

After they cleaned up, she discovered there was no food in the house. The two of them threw on some clothes and walked a few blocks from the harbor side of the peninsula to the beach side. There, they bought fried clams at a kiosk next to the strand.

Despite a brisk breeze, the sunshine had brought out a scattering of surfers and sunbathers. Children dug in the sand and babies played on blankets beside their mothers.

"I never knew there were this many kids in the world," Shane said as they walked and ate.

CeCe felt her fingers and mouth getting greasy. Charlotte would never have approved. "These clams are great," she said. "And I never paid much attention to kids, either."

"You mean you weren't the type to make goo-goo eyes at babies?"

"I'm a barracuda. It's lucky I never ate any babies," she joked.

He finished another fried clam. "Maternity has changed you, I hope."

"I'll never bite another baby again," CeCe promised, straight-faced.

Shane laughed. "Have you thought about names?"

"I'd like something traditional." She dropped her empty paper wrapper into a trash container and paused at another kiosk to buy fried onion rings. She didn't recall when she'd eaten this much grease in one meal, or even in one day. It felt great.

"You mean I might have a son named Easton the Umpteenth?" Shane groaned.

"My great-grandfather's name was Cyrus," CeCe said. "I had an uncle Byrum and my dad's name was Drake. I have an uncle James, too, so there are lots of names to choose from."

"You've got an uncle still living?" Shane asked.

"He's the black sheep of the family," CeCe said.

"Worse than Markus?"

"All I know is that he wouldn't be interested in the crown even if he got a chance at it," she said. "Anyway, I don't think we'd want to name our kid after him, considering that he's in my grandfather's bad graces."

They strolled past a large public pier where people were fishing off the sides. "What about girls' names?" Shane asked.

"My grandmother was Cassandra. People say I look like her." CeCe nudged her slipping sunglasses into place with the back of her hand. "Or used to when I was blond." She halted in front of a beachwear shop. "Now, there's what I need. An old-fashioned bikini."

"You call that old fashioned?" Beside her, Shane ogled the skimpy Hawaiian-print ensembles.

"Sure." She wiped her hands on a napkin and tossed the rest of the trash in a container. "Old-fashioned in the sense that I like the styles of about thirty years ago. And

I'd better wear them now, before my tummy starts protruding.''

On the boat, Shane had given her several swimsuits that his secretary had chosen, at his request, for CeCe to wear in case she hadn't brought any. They were tasteful, dignified and boring, although no worse than the conservative one-piece suits Charlotte restricted her to at home.

Inside the boutique, a young woman wandered over. She gave no sign of recognition. ''Can I help you?''

''Just a sec.'' CeCe selected half a dozen bikinis. ''I'd like to try these on.''

''Right here.''

The dressing room consisted of a tiny alcove with a curtain that didn't hide CeCe's feet or her face. It was a far cry from Yuki Yamazaki's salon.

At the counter, the saleslady was absorbed in a well-thumbed copy of *Surfer Girl* magazine. Nobody bothered with too much service around here, CeCe thought, and realized she was glad.

''If any other men come in while you're dressing, I'll pummel them with my fists and drive them into the sea,'' Shane said.

''They couldn't really see anything.'' Then she bent to disrobe and discovered that her movements set the curtain rippling. The discovery made her glad for Shane's protective presence.

CeCe's concern about her figure faded as she regarded herself in the mirror. Although she was getting rounder thanks to the pregnancy, that fact wouldn't be obvious to anyone else because she was so lean. In fact, she liked the way she looked, less angular and more feminine.

Three of the suits pleased her, so she bought them. The girl put them on the credit card, stuck the tiny purchases into a bag and went back to reading her magazine.

''Maybe I should wear one of these now,'' CeCe said. Shane shook his head. ''Not in public.''

"Excuse me?"

"I mean—" He looked confused. "On our private pier would be all right."

"People sail by," CeCe teased.

"If they stare, I'll buy a water cannon and let them have it," growled her husband.

On the way home, CeCe added sandals and a beach cover-up to her purchases. She felt a moment's guilt as she realized that, by now, her mother and grandfather had long ago discovered her absence and were probably stalking around the apartment with scowls on their faces.

Well, she hadn't given them a moment's thought from yesterday until now. And she didn't intend to give them any further thought until the end of the week.

CECE AND SHANE FOUND no end of things to do and places to visit. Small cafés with live music. Unusual shops. Long walks during which they mingled with tourists and offbeat beach types.

No one shouted their names or flashed cameras in their faces. A few men gave CeCe the eye, and a couple of women nearly keeled over when they spotted Shane, who got even handsomer as his skin bronzed. Their interest was casual, however, not frenzied as in New York.

For once in her life, she was free to observe others. What she noticed most were the children. Babies in strollers, toddlers riding in backpacks, preschoolers holding their mothers' hands. Sometimes the parents looked frazzled, but many radiated pure joy.

It thrilled CeCe to know that a baby was growing within her. Day by day, she imagined the little features taking shape, the tiny toes wiggling, the vague dreams forming in its tiny brain.

Now that she wasn't preoccupied with the wedding, she had time to relish the fact of being pregnant. The flow of hours, the leisurely passage of the days was a gift from Shane that she would treasure always.

She'd heard older people say that the childhood years passed quickly and kids grew up before you knew it. She must find a way, she resolved, to cherish the special daily moments so they didn't slip away unremarked.

"I've decided I don't care for the name Cassandra," Shane said one afternoon as they sat reading in sling chairs on his cozy front porch.

"Why not?"

"Too classical for a little kid." A shock of dark hair fell across his forehead, and his nose had turned slightly pink from the sunshine, she noticed.

"We could call her Sandra," CeCe suggested. "Or Sandy."

"She deserves her own name, not a secondhand one," Shane said. "What girls' and boys' names do you like, other than the ones in your family?"

She started to say that she'd never thought about it, but stopped. This week they were exploring their own tastes. "I like Beth. Short for Elizabeth, and it's the name of my doctor. And Bertrand."

"Bertrand?"

"Don't you think Bertie's a cute nickname?" she teased.

"No son of mine is going to be called Bertie!" Shane whipped off his sunglasses. "If we're going for oddball names, I vote for Morris."

"No offense, but…"

"King Morris," he said. "That has a nice ring to it."

"We could name him Kong," CeCe said, and they both laughed.

"Elizabeth gets my vote," Shane said. "But if it's a boy…"

"What was your father's name?"

"Rory," he said.

"Rory Drake Carradigne," CeCe murmured. "Named after both his grandfathers."

"I like it."

"Done!" she said, as if they'd just concluded negotiations. Which, in a sense, they had.

Down the block a motorist strained to fit an RV into a tiny space by the curb. CeCe watched, amused, as the driver climbed out and measured his vehicle with a tape, then checked the size of the opening. From where she sat, it looked as if the space was only a few inches longer than the vehicle.

The man tried one more time to back in, as if the laws of physics might rearrange themselves in the face of his frustration. Finally he drove off, and almost at once a small car zipped into the space.

Out climbed a mother, father and three kids. One boy carried a remote-controlled car, while the girl had a kite.

The family conferred briefly, then headed down the block. The father swung the younger boy onto his shoulders and the girl's hand slipped into her mother's. Their closeness and happiness were obvious even to a casual observer.

Would her own children experience that kind of casual intimacy? CeCe wondered. She didn't see how that would be possible, with their father living far away.

They'd never know the utter freedom that she was enjoying this week, either, because they would grow up under even more scrutiny than had the New York princesses. After all, CeCe and her sisters hadn't been considered heirs to the throne.

Well, there would be compensations, she told herself. The satisfaction of serving one's country. Visits with Shane when he came from New York and, as the children matured, trips to America. And of course they'd grow up sheltered by their grandfather's love.

He won't always be around.

Shane's words of a few days ago came back with frightening force. CeCe couldn't imagine not having her grandfather to guide and support her. What if she really did have to run the kingdom alone, with Markus scheming to turn the people against her?

Worrying solved nothing, she reminded herself. She was going to be queen of Korosol, and that was that.

SHANE'S EYELIDS POPPED OPEN and he found himself staring into darkness. It took a moment to realize he was lying in bed, that the bedside clock read 4:30 a.m. and that someone was shaking him.

"What's wrong?" he mumbled.

"Nothing." CeCe sounded disgustingly wide awake. "We're going to take our breakfast to the beach and watch the sun rise."

"Whose idea was that?" He barely avoided attaching the adjective "dumb" to "idea," since he already knew whose idea it must be.

"Come on, sleepyhead." She yanked the covers off him, admitting the early-morning chill. It was the most blatantly aggressive act anyone had perpetrated against Shane since adolescence. What a lucky break for CeCe that he couldn't move yet, because otherwise she'd have been toast.

He searched for a biting remark. "Go away" was the best he could manage. Getting up early had been fine in New York when there was work to do. Something about that sea air, though, made him want to snooze late.

"Let's make breakfast sandwiches," CeCe cooed in his ear. "How about eggs and cheese on an English muffin?"

Shane's stomach rumbled. He'd never known he possessed such a traitorous organ.

"Don't expect me to do all the work myself," she added. "You can eat plain bread if you're going to be a lazybones." He heard her rustling around, and then she added, "Also, I plan to take a fifteen-minute shower and use all the hot water, so you'd better join me."

Since the puny size of the hot-water heater had been the only drawback to their love nest this week, Shane didn't take the threat lightly. Besides, it was cold without covers.

He sat up grumpily. "Who invited you along on this vacation, anyway?"

"No one," CeCe said. "You kidnapped me." A moment later, the bathroom door closed behind her.

Cursing himself as a moron for not leaving her in New York, Shane scurried barefoot across the tile floor. He found the bathroom steamy, and the hot water, along with a shoulder massage, went a long way toward allaying his crabbiness toward his wife.

By the time they reached the sand with their bag of food, the world was coming awake. A couple of grizzled fishermen huddled with their poles on the public pier under the lazy scrutiny of a pelican. Beyond the surf line, diehard surfers in wet suits caught the waves.

CeCe stopped on the sand. "How's this spot?"

"Compared to what?" Shane still refused to concede that this outing might be a good idea.

"You're so crabby in the morning." Grinning, she reached to rumple his hair. "But cute."

"I hate being cute." Shane spread the blanket and deposited the sack of food atop it. "Can we eat now?"

"You're transitioning from grumpy to churlish," CeCe warned. "Lighten up, buster."

It was cold and damp and by now their food was probably cold and damp, too, but suddenly he didn't care. This crazy woman made him feel warm all over. She'd nipped at his heels for the past hour like a sheepdog, and Shane had to admit he kind of enjoyed being with a woman as strong as he was.

That was why none of his prior relationships had

worked out, he conceded. No matter what good qualities the women had, sooner or later, without intending to, he ran roughshod over them. He could never do that with his wife because she wouldn't let him. In fact, if he weren't careful, he'd find her shoeprints on his face.

He dropped onto the blanket and pulled her down beside him. "See that stray dog over there?" he said.

CeCe followed his gaze to a mongrel with floppy ears and a dark patch over one eye. It was nosing around the side of an unopened hamburger kiosk. "Yes?"

"It's going to eat our food if we don't hurry," he said. "Okay with you?"

"Sure. Let's eat."

"By the way," Shane said, "there's nobody in the world I'd rather be eating breakfast with. And nowhere else I'd rather be eating it, either."

CeCe didn't let him off the hook that easily. "What about the time? Is there any other time of day you'd rather be eating?"

"You drive a hard bargain." Shane swallowed his pride. "No, you were right. Breakfast at dawn is perfect."

She leaned across the picnic basket and kissed him. Before he could snatch more kisses, however, she thrust a sandwich into his hand and settled back to enjoy her own.

While they ate, the world brightened around them. Sunrise proved to be not a splashy show of nature's beauty but a slow shift from darkness into morning. The increasing volume of voices, seagull cries and distant traffic played like a CD, and soon Shane caught a whiff of bacon frying at a nearby restaurant.

"It's a symphony for the senses," he said. "Pure pleasure."

"To top it off, I think that dog just found a home." CeCe indicated an older woman crouched near the mongrel, making friends with it.

Even the dog was having a good day, and so, despite his early rousting, was Shane. Happiness swelled inside him. He hadn't known this much contentment in his entire adult life, and he owed it to CeCe.

I don't ever want to give her back.

The longing to keep her was so intense that for a moment he was afraid he'd spoken aloud. CeCe went on nibbling her food unperturbed, however, so he knew he hadn't.

Shane had thought a few weeks together would be enough to tide him over until the next time they met, close to the baby's due date. Now he wanted to be there to touch CeCe's abdomen every morning and feel the baby's increasing size. He wanted to join his wife at natural childbirth classes and practice that ridiculous breathing he'd seen on television.

Of all the women in the world, he'd fallen in love with the wrong one. The right one in a way, but the wrong one if he planned to wake up beside her every day, because he couldn't.

He'd made a promise. And he knew CeCe too well to believe that she would back out of her duty for his sake.

A shadow falling over his spirits warned Shane that he had better start preparing to let her go. In his thirty-two years, he'd lost every person he loved, from his parents to Morris. This time, he needed to draw back before it hurt too much.

He reminded himself that he'd had a life before CeCe and would have one afterward. A life that centered on his rapidly expanding business.

It was still there waiting for him. In the meantime, Shane intended to squeeze as much happiness as possible out of the few days left with his wife.

ALTHOUGH THEY WERE on their honeymoon, there was no reason to be annoyed just because Shane called his office for messages on Friday morning. CeCe would have liked to do the same thing, except that with Linzy rollicking around the Pacific, she had no secretary to call.

Besides, she was going to be giving up her work at DeLacey Shipping. To whom, she didn't know. The executive VP position hadn't existed until CeCe reorganized the company.

Before her arrival with MBA in hand, her mother had done a good job, considering that she'd taken over the business without preparation. Still, long-range planning had fallen between the cracks and the chain of command had been like a vine that branched and turned back on itself. There hadn't been enough audits, and some of the executives had become unacceptably sloppy.

For the last few years, as she fixed those problems, CeCe had enjoyed the sense of building a future for herself and her family. She'd had something special to contribute, and even if her mother was slow to acknowledge it, the company prospered as a result.

Well, that wasn't her concern anymore. She'd have her hands full running a kingdom, CeCe mused while she took out her phone to order pizza for lunch. She made it pepperoni, with a salad on the side.

That afternoon, she and Shane browsed through the Lido Village shops. The artwork and offbeat clothing intrigued her, although she had no use for any of it. In Korosol, she'd be expected to stick to products made by her own people.

Her own people. They'd be Europeans who spoke French, a language in which CeCe was fluent but not letter-perfect. It was important for her to improve, however, because she wasn't going to be an American anymore.

The thought distressed her, even though she'd been planning for weeks to succeed her grandfather. Her family's roots lay in Korosol. Her soul was filled with the stories her father had told of growing up in the palace.

But CeCe had been raised in New York. When she read the newspaper, she identified with the American point of view. The prospect of taking the throne as queen of Korosol made her feel like a fraud.

If she didn't give her whole heart to her father's country, Markus would notice. For the past year, since Prince Byrum's death, her cousin had believed he was almost the king already. Once again, the prospect of standing against him if anything happened to her grandfather sent a chill down CeCe's spine.

What if she didn't go to Korosol after all? Would that be so terrible?

Standing in a handicrafts shop before a display of Native American pottery, CeCe began to tremble. It shocked her that she was considering turning down her grandfather. Rebellion went against everything she knew about herself. Yet what had she really known about Cecelia Carradigne before this week?

With Shane's encouragement, she'd learned to be spontaneous and playful. She'd also begun to listen to her heart instead of her head.

Yet she'd never failed her family. To let them down now was unthinkable.

But to spend the rest of her life being miserable was unthinkable, too.

SHANE COULD FEEL CECE pulling away from him. All afternoon, her gaze remained distant even while they were shopping together. When she examined the Native American pottery, he suspected she was really thinking about her upcoming move to Korosol.

Although it hurt, he had to let her go. Not only had he made a promise, but Shane would never stand in the way of CeCe's dreams. He hadn't married a strong, independent woman so he could try to treat her like a lapdog.

It was time to cut his losses and protect himself. He'd

suffered blows before and risen above them. The key was hard work.

And it was certainly needed. According to this morning's news, dramatic increases in California fuel prices were predicted for the coming summer. According to the executives he'd consulted in his Long Beach office, he urgently needed to strategize in order to keep his company profitable. O'Connell Industries stood to lose money on long-term contracts for which the customers' fees were fixed.

Shane received several more business-related calls while they were shopping. He was both disturbed and relieved to find CeCe too absorbed in her thoughts to notice.

He'd promised to fly her home tomorrow, so today was bringing their idyll to a close. The sad part was that they weren't spending the day interacting, and when another call came in, he knew he couldn't avoid disappointing her further.

"I'M TIRED OF FINDING sand in my food and grease on my hands," CeCe said. "Tonight we're going out for the best food in Newport Beach."

She didn't want to give one more thought to Korosol or the future. They'd be in her face soon enough.

"That sounds great." Shane lay stretched along the wicker couch in the cottage's front room. "Unfortunately, I won't be able to make it."

"What do you mean, you can't make it?" CeCe demanded. "I didn't realize your social secretary had provided you with a list of alternative activities."

His smile took on a strained edge. "I won't be socializing. The governor's in Los Angeles tonight. He's meeting with industry leaders to talk about energy policy, and it's important that I be there."

She wanted to argue, not like a shipping company executive but like a woman whose husband was slipping away. This was their last night alone for months. Still, she'd heard the fuel price forecast and understood the urgency of the situation. "I'll come, too."

"I'd appreciate your insights," Shane said. "But I'm afraid you're a little too famous these days."

"And you're not?"

"Most of the people present will be men. They're not going to get excited about seeing me. You're a different story, my dear."

CeCe glowered. "That's what people have been telling me all my life. No one takes a blonde seriously, including a strawberry-blonde." Her reddish tint had faded to that color. "Or a princess, or whatever. I'm not window dressing, you know."

"The governor will try to impress you, and he'll want to pose for pictures with you," Shane said. "I hate to discourage you, but your presence tonight would distract from the issues."

She was tempted to argue. What stopped her was the realization that, since her agreement to go to Korosol, she could no longer be considered a businesswoman. Besides, DeLacey Shipping was only marginally affected by California fuel prices, while Shane's profits were directly on the line.

"All right." They'd have tomorrow morning together and the flight home. And maybe another night in her suite before she and her grandfather left for Korosol, CeCe reflected. "When do you have to leave for the meeting?"

Reluctantly, Shane stood. "As soon as I clean up. Believe me, I'd much rather be spending the evening with you."

As he dressed, CeCe played the role of little wife, knotting his tie for him, making sure his hair lay flat and smoothing a wrinkle from the shoulder of his jacket. She liked the excuse for touching him.

Then, with a kiss, he was gone. CeCe didn't like being

left behind, out of the mainstream of events, and she particularly didn't like being away from Shane.

She read for a while but lost interest. After tossing the novel aside, she went to buy take-out Chinese food.

Back at the cottage, she turned on the TV and watched a game show while she dined out of little white boxes. Hardly the sort of thing Krissy Katwell would picture Princess Cecelia doing on her honeymoon.

She missed Shane. It didn't help to know he was with a bunch of high-powered industry leaders, voicing their concerns to the governor, debating his responses. Making a difference.

In Korosol, she'd be like the governor, she reminded herself as a TV contestant bought an *E* and still couldn't figure out the puzzle. Once she was queen, people would expect her to solve their problems. If she failed, they'd target her with the same scorn that Americans heaped on politicians.

She wouldn't be on the hot seat for a mere four or eight years. She'd be there forever. And unlike the governor, she'd never possessed an ounce of political ambition.

CeCe halted with a forkful of Mongolian beef halfway to her mouth. If she became her grandfather's successor, she'd be condemning herself to a role she wasn't cut out to play and that she would undoubtedly come to hate.

That was no favor to the people of Korosol. Or to King Easton, either.

It wasn't enough to have an MBA or to know one's duty. To rule a country, a person needed an aptitude for the job. CeCe couldn't be a proper queen of Korosol any more than Lucia would make a good executive at De-Lacey Shipping.

Her grandfather had said he was evaluating her suitability, CeCe recalled. Maybe this was what he'd meant, that she needed to dig deep inside herself before they made a public announcement.

She didn't have to go. In fact, it would be wrong for her to accept the throne, now that she understood her shortcomings. The king would get over it, although she wasn't so sure about her mother.

Maybe he'd choose Amelia instead, CeCe mused. Her sister had done fine work with the children's organization. Becoming queen might suit her better than anyone expected.

A wave of relief washed away the guilt. She could stay in New York with Shane and continue expanding De-Lacey Shipping. The prospect was almost too wonderful to bear.

Sure, they were both busy people and their marriage wasn't going to be a picnic on the beach. But they'd truly be husband and wife, and their children would grow up in a loving, two-parent family.

Such a simple, normal dream. Yet to a princess like CeCe, it was magic.

She couldn't wait for tomorrow morning. Shane was going to love this.

Chapter Sixteen

Shane arrived in Newport about midnight, irritable and snappish. He still felt that way the next morning when he awoke.

There'd been more executives present than he'd expected, and several of the younger ones had kidded him nonstop about his marriage to a princess. They'd called him "Your Majesty" and acted as if he were only playing at being CEO of a corporation.

That was annoying enough. Worse, he'd soon concluded that the governor was making decisions for political rather than common-sense reasons. The man's "solutions" might provide temporary relief, but in the long run the underlying problems would only worsen.

Yet when Shane objected, few voices had supported him. What was wrong with the other executives? Why couldn't they see the future as clearly as he could?

Or did they really believe, as one envious industrialist had hinted, that Shane himself had political aspirations? The sly references to his popular appeal might have put off some people, including the governor.

Shane spent all night stewing about the meeting, with only brief periods of sleep. By Saturday morning, he knew he couldn't let the situation ride.

He needed to meet with those executives who'd agreed

with him. Together, they would line up support and approach business-friendly members of the legislature to fight for long-term answers to the state's fuel problems.

The job didn't have to be done today, he supposed. But if he took a break to fly to New York with CeCe, he'd be chomping at the bit.

If only she could stay here and help him plan his strategy. The woman had a sharp mind and excellent financial instincts. He needed her beside him now more than ever.

Shane gazed at his sleeping wife, haloed by reddish-blond hair. Who was he kidding? He didn't just want CeCe here because he valued her input.

Despite his cautions, he'd fallen in love with her. Hopelessly, heartbreakingly in love. He wanted to kidnap her all over again, and this time take her so far away that no one would ever find them.

He wanted to hear her laughter and see curiosity light up her face day after day. He wanted to feel her mouth moving against his and lose himself inside her whenever the mood seized them.

Going back to New York and pretending that everything was fine would tear him apart. Better to stay in California. Better to make a clean break.

CeCe awoke to the sound of the shower running. Her first reaction was to be glad that Shane had returned as promised, since she'd fallen asleep before he got home.

Her second reaction was disappointment. She'd expected to make love with him first thing this morning.

When he emerged from the bathroom, he was wearing a business suit. Except for the slightly damp hair, there was little of the playmate she'd come to cherish.

"What's going on?" CeCe asked.

"The situation's pretty bad," he said. "I have to do some organizing, starting immediately."

She wanted to tell Shane her good news in an intimate,

leisurely conversaton, not to fling it at him in a rush. "It's not so urgent you can't spare me an hour or so." Distressed to realize she was nagging, she added, "Unless you'd rather we talked on the plane."

"I'm not flying back with you." He sat on the edge of the bed. "I'm sorry, CeCe, but it's best this way."

"No, it isn't." She sat up, eager to touch him yet put off by his distant manner. "Look, I did some serious thinking last night. That's what I want to discuss."

"Unless it concerns the state's energy policy, I'm in no mood to hear it." He got to his feet. "You'll have to talk to me while we eat."

The man was infuriating! Still, preferring to avoid a fight on their last morning, she accompanied him to the kitchen.

He dumped cereal into a bowl and added a splash of milk. "Would you mind making coffee? Or is that too much to ask of a queen?"

"There's no need to be sarcastic." CeCe measured ground coffee into the coffeemaker.

"The guys were giving me a hard time last night." In a shaft of sunlight, she could see how tense Shane looked.

"About me?"

"There were a few references to the bridegroom as the Prince of Swords," Shane said. "People asked if they have to bow when I come into the room. Things like that."

"Is that why you're running away from me?" CeCe demanded.

"I'm not running away." Shane glanced around as if looking to focus his attention on anything but her.

She'd never seen him this tight and withdrawn before, his dark eyes averted and his mouth drawn into a thin line. Those jokes last night must have really bothered him, or maybe it was the rising fuel prices, although she didn't see why he was taking the matter so personally.

When the coffee was ready, CeCe poured them each a cup. She hoped Shane would calm down once he drank his.

She sat opposite him. "Can we talk now?"

"Go ahead." Before she could start, however, Shane's cell phone rang. She was tempted to yank it out of his hand and stomp on it.

He clamped it to his ear. "Bill? I'm glad you called. I was thinking the same thing. Sure, let's have lunch...."

CeCe tried to bottle her temper. In the same situation, she'd be eager to meet with her colleagues and swing into action, too.

But darn it, Shane seemed so glad to be rid of her. As if this week, which had changed her life, had been only a temporary diversion for him.

She was about to take a huge risk in order to spend the rest of her life with him. Was it possible he didn't want that?

CeCe dismissed the negative thought. Obviously, Shane was concerned about the fuel situation. When he heard what she had to say, he'd be as excited as she was.

After he hung up, Shane dialed another number. She heard him instruct his West Coast secretary to arrange meetings with a number of other people for later in the day.

By now, CeCe was steaming. It was Saturday, for heaven's sake. Nobody was going to keel over, go broke or get stuck with a fleet of empty gas tanks if he waited until Monday.

After he hung up, Shane checked his watch. "Is it that late already?"

"It's nine o'clock," said CeCe, who could see the wall clock.

"Nine-fifteen." He cleared his throat. "Your pilot's expecting to depart about noon. I've arranged for my driver to pick you up at eleven."

"You're not even coming to the airport?" As he rose, CeCe reached across the table and grabbed his wrist. "Don't you dare walk off!"

Startled, Shane sank into his chair. "Look, I know you want to chat. CeCe, this week has been terrific. I've enjoyed the long walks, the picnics, all that stuff. But we both knew it was temporary."

A knot formed in her chest. "Our marriage isn't temporary."

"Of course not." Shane met her gaze at last, yet there was something absent from his expression. It struck her that he'd deliberately composed his features to look friendly, as if for a press interview or a meeting with a tax auditor.

Where was the love she'd seen shining there? Where was the mischief and the tenderness?

"I know we agreed on a marriage of convenience," CeCe said. "But after what we've shared, I want more than that."

"I'll be there when the baby's born, I promise you." Beneath her hand, Shane's wrist muscles tightened. The man was so eager to flee, he could hardly contain himself, she thought in dismay.

"I need more time with you," she said.

"No."

"What?"

"I can't do it." For a fleeting second, she thought she glimpsed pain in his eyes, or something beyond pain. But it vanished so fast that CeCe figured she'd fantasized it.

"You don't understand what I'm proposing." Maybe he thought she expected him to dance attendance on her. "At the start of this week, you told me that I needed to get in touch with my feelings, to be spontaneous."

"I don't want to sound like a hard-hearted stereotypical male," Shane said. "But CeCe, this isn't the time for a feel-good discussion. We're going our own ways, so why drag this out?''

''Because I care about you!''

''I care about you, too,'' he said. ''That doesn't change anything.''

She stared at him in shock. Apparently he could turn his emotions on and off like a spigot. The honeymoon was over, so no more warm, fuzzy closeness. Kick out the wife and get back to work. ''Shane, I don't understand you. You aren't interested in trying to work things out with me?''

''I've taken off more than enough time already,'' he said. ''I can't afford to play any longer.''

''Is that what you think I'm doing—playing?'' CeCe demanded.

''If you insist on an answer, then, yes.'' His shoulders had gone rigid beneath the designer jacket. ''You expect to have it all, because you always have. I guess you consider me part of the package now, but unfortunately, I don't have someone like Lady Charlotte to take over my responsibilities for me. I can't fly across the country or the ocean every time you snap your fingers. That wasn't part of the deal.''

''Stop being so stubborn!'' To her frustration, CeCe discovered she was close to tears. ''Why don't you shut up for a minute and listen!''

''I hate to say this, but you're acting like a spoiled princess.'' Shane got to his feet. ''I don't want to part this way, honestly I don't. But if I stick around any longer, we'll both say things we'll regret.''

He walked out of the kitchen. A moment later, CeCe heard the front door close behind him.

She sat there, stunned. The man to whom she'd surrendered her heart considered her a spoiled brat who was playing at being a wife.

He didn't want to work out their relationship so they

could be together. As soon as his business needed him, he'd put her on the back burner. Permanently, it seemed.

Her hands fisted in her lap. The man who'd just left wasn't the man with whom she'd spent her honeymoon. Or at least, he wasn't the man she'd believed him to be. He'd said he cared for her, but obviously he didn't love her the way she loved him.

How could she have made herself so vulnerable to a man who cared so little? For once in her life, she'd dared expose her true feelings, and Shane had thrown them in her face.

Grateful that there was no one around, CeCe dissolved into tears.

SHANE'S GUT TWISTED as he remembered calling his wife a spoiled princess. He hadn't meant to say that. Yet why had she ragged at him so mercilessly when he was already close to the breaking point?

Although there was no reason to get to his office this early, his torment had driven him to leave as quickly as possible. He could barely stand to be in the same room with CeCe, knowing how much it was going to hurt to live without her.

Obviously, she wanted to continue their closeness to a greater extent than they'd agreed. Shane supposed he should be pleased. The terms, however, weren't acceptable.

His pride still smarted from some of the digs he'd endured last night. *"I'd sleep my way into a royal family, too, if I could figure out how to do it." "Hey, everybody listen up, his lordship is speaking."*

Most of the execs, of course, hadn't stooped to such pettiness. Nevertheless, Shane was proud of his rise from poverty and sensitive about his lack of family background. He hated for anyone to perceive him as a parasite who'd married for prestige.

It hadn't been right to take out his ill humor on his wife, he conceded. The outcome, however, would be the same no matter how he soft-pedaled it.

He refused to become CeCe's pet poodle, running to her side whenever she got a spare moment. Granted, she might occasionally deign to fly to his side, but that wasn't the point.

A husband and wife belonged together, building a home, giving their children a solid foundation as his parents had once tried to do for him. To come so close, to find a woman who inspired his passion and to know he could never have a real marriage with her, cut Shane through the heart.

He knew he'd been rude. For his own sanity, however, he'd had to leave, and he wasn't going back.

As SHE TOOK THE ELEVATOR to her family's apartment, CeCe wondered if she was walking into a minefield.

Her mother must be furious. As for her grandfather, she didn't even know whether he'd stayed in New York or returned to Korosol. By now, he might have rethought his opposition to Markus. Maybe her cousin was going to get his wish, after all.

In a way, she'd been almost surprised when the guards recognized her a few moments earlier. Not that tan skin and strawberry hair had changed her appearance beyond recognition. Rather, she didn't feel like the same woman who'd left a week ago.

The events of her honeymoon played like TV reruns through her brain. Shane's pride as he showed off his yacht. Her trying on bikinis in a tiny shop while he glowered at passersby. The two of them watching the sunrise from the beach.

CeCe didn't need a scrapbook to preserve those memories. Despite the turmoil of her emotions, she would treasure them always. And share them with her baby, even if Shane wasn't around.

She'd mulled over their last conversation repeatedly, with growing discouragement. How ironic that she'd finally gained insight into her own soul, only to be denied what she needed most.

Her husband thought she was spoiled. How little he knew her!

She stepped into the foyer on the apartment's first floor. There was no welcoming committee this evening, although she'd called from the airport to say she was arriving.

From the gallery peered Hester, who had a stack of towels in her arms. "CeCe!" she cried. "Everyone, she's home!"

The housekeeper hurried forward to kiss her cheek. Quincy, arriving a moment later, took CeCe's suitcase. Behind him came Amelia and, at a more measured pace, Charlotte.

Her mother's first comment had nothing to do with errant bridal couples or shirked duties. It was, "What on earth have you done to your hair?"

"You should have seen it a week ago," CeCe said. "It was dark red."

"That does wash out, doesn't it?" her mother asked.

"It looks great," said Amelia.

CeCe gave them both hugs. "Where's Grandfather?"

"In the office," Charlotte said. "I hope you plan to apologize. You've put everyone to a great deal of trouble."

"I'm sorry."

"Don't be," responded her sister. "That was ridiculous, expecting you and Shane to honeymoon in your rooms."

"I suppose it was," said her mother in a rare concession. "Well, go and talk to His Majesty. I have no idea what he plans to say to you."

And I have no idea what I plan to say to him. "I'll go straight up," said CeCe.

EASTON HAD FALLEN ASLEEP in his chair while sorting through his correspondence. He dozed off more and more frequently these days, although he hadn't weakened significantly during his trip, much to his relief.

When he opened his eyes, Cassandra stood in the doorway of the office. Had he died in his sleep? Had she come for him?

He wasn't ready to go. *"Pas encore,"* he said.

"I can come back later." She spoke English, not French. And he found it hard to believe that angels dyed their hair.

"Ah, Cecelia." The king blinked off the last traces of sleep. "Please sit down."

She obeyed. The girl had browned like a berry this past week and there was a new maturity to her movements, he observed. "I'm sorry for inconveniencing you," she said.

He shrugged. "I have made good use of my time. A few weeks isn't very long to catch up on a family I've neglected for twenty years. Is your husband with you?"

"No." In that single word, he noticed an unexpected tension.

What had gone wrong? Easton had recognized the love growing between the couple. As a result, he hadn't been surprised when they ran off.

It was a good sign that Cecelia had returned. He didn't like to think that he'd chosen a successor who lacked the courage to face him. That didn't mean he took it for granted that she still meant to go through with their plans.

He wasn't sure whether he hoped she did. This young couple had the same deep devotion to each other that he'd known with Cassandra. It would grieve the king to tear them apart.

Yet Shane O'Connell hadn't returned with Cecelia. That development puzzled him.

"I never meant to place too heavy a burden on your shoulders," Easton said. "You've borne more than your share of responsibility since your father died, I've learned. Now that you've had time to reflect, have you decided what you want to do with your life?"

His granddaughter's eyes filled with tears. "Oh, Grandfather! I'm not fit to be queen. I'm too confused."

"Tell me what's happened," said the king.

Her green eyes glimmered as she struggled to contain her emotions. "I love my husband but he doesn't love me. Not the way I need him to."

"A lover's quarrel?" Easton suggested.

"It goes way beyond that." She stared down at her hands. "I've concluded that the most important thing is for me and my husband to raise our child together."

"Mr. O'Connell doesn't agree?"

She shook her head. "He's content to stick our marriage into a corner of his life. After a few weeks, he couldn't wait to get back to work. He didn't even fly home with me."

"I expected better of him," the king said thoughtfully. What kind of man could fail to adore a woman so much like his Cassandra? "Well, my dear, what sort of future do you want now? Does the throne still interest you?"

"I was afraid by now you'd have changed your mind," CeCe said. "I thought you might decide Markus isn't such a bad choice after all."

The king suppressed a shudder. If only he could believe that his beloved grandson was innocent of any wrongdoing in the death of his parents! Yet the innuendo was too strong.

"I haven't changed my mind," he said. "As for you,

my dear, you consented to my offer without having a chance to consider the implications. I grew up with the people of Korosol, I know their history and their hopes and fears, but to you they're strangers. Tell me honestly whether you want to be their queen.''

He could see the answer in her face before she spoke. ''If I had the aptitude, I'd be eager to get started, the way I was with my job at DeLacey Shipping. These past few weeks, I should have been studying Korosol on the Internet and working up a list of goals and objectives. Instead, I've been falling in love.''

''If your husband asked you to, you'd give up the throne in an instant, wouldn't you?'' the king said.

''Yes.''

There it was, an honest, shining answer. ''I don't find you unfit, and I'm not taking it away from you,'' he said. ''But my dear granddaughter, if you would give up the throne for Shane, you are equally entitled to give it up for yourself.''

''Not just for myself,'' CeCe said. ''For my child, too. I'm going to cut back my work hours and spend time with her, or him. Even if Shane and I don't live together, our baby will have more time with him if we're both in New York.''

Easton smiled at the energy in her response. She came alive when she talked about her child and the man she loved. That young O'Connell would be a fool to keep her at arm's length. ''This marriage may turn out better than you expect.''

''I hope you're right.''

''Cecelia, I have one request of you,'' the king said.

''Shoot. I mean, of course.''

''Be selfish,'' he advised. ''Relish every moment of this time with your child. Youngsters who are loved grow up fine whether their mothers are there all the time or not.'' Except for Markus, he thought sadly. ''In my observation, it's the mothers who look back years later and ache for the moments they missed. Don't bring that on yourself.''

''You've been so busy with affairs of state, how could you notice something like that?'' CeCe asked.

''I listen to people,'' Easton said.

''I hope as I grow older that I learn to listen as well,'' she said.

''You would have made an outstanding queen.'' The king reached for her hands and held them across the table, taking pride in this fine young woman. ''I wish you very well indeed.''

What he didn't mention was that it wasn't only mothers who looked back over their lives and wished they'd spent more time with their families. It was grandfathers, too.

Chapter Seventeen

Shane was pleased to find that the executives who agreed with him were willing to call on their influential friends. Several legislators, upon learning the extent of opposition to the governor's plans, promised to fall in line.

Not a bad day's work, Shane mused as he drove home in light Saturday traffic. It was six o'clock and he was in much improved spirits by the time he returned to the cottage to retrieve his clothes.

When he opened the door, he caught a whiff of CeCe's perfume. For one heart-lifting moment, he thought she'd stayed.

Then he noticed the emptiness. The silence was so profound he could have sworn he actually heard atoms knocking together disconsolately.

Shane trailed into the kitchen and found Chinese food in the refrigerator. Mongolian beef, one of his favorites, and orange-flavored chicken. Steamed rice, too.

As he put the cartons in the microwave oven, he decided to stay overnight and eat breakfast here rather than move to his apartment in Long Beach. Ferguson and Linzy were due to arrive tomorrow, and they would all fly back to New York. Then things could return to normal.

Normal. Shane tried to remember what that meant. He recalled that Ed cooked breakfast for him, and that he enjoyed walking into O'Connell Industries each morning and hearing the phones ring.

What was he, some kind of idiot? That wasn't a life. Life meant waking up with his legs tangled around CeCe's. It meant going out for croissants together and sharing the newspaper, both of them trying to snatch the business section first.

They should buy two subscriptions to the *Wall Street Journal,* he thought, and then remembered that he and CeCe wouldn't be fighting over any more papers. Or tangling their legs together in bed.

She must be in New York by now. She'd be taking the heat from her family. Would King Easton still give her the throne? Surely he wouldn't punish her for such a small transgression.

Tomorrow she might fly with him to Korosol. Once on native soil, no doubt the king would announce her as his successor. There'd be no turning back after that.

The timer rang on the microwave. As he carried his food to the table, Shane thought about CeCe sitting here eating breakfast with him this past week. And the time they'd played impromptu volleyball on the beach, when she'd won cheers from her team for returning a difficult serve.

His throat constricted. If only he could turn the clock back. If he could only relive this week forever.

But that would mean never seeing the birth of their child. Also, never seeing CeCe in her royal robes, or whatever the monarch of Korosol wore on state occasions. Surely she wouldn't wear them into the delivery room, though, he mused, and grinned at the notion.

He'd have to tell his wife. She'd get a kick out of it.

He could pick up the phone. Sure, great idea. After insulting CeCe and abandoning her on their last morning together, he'd call and expect her to laugh with him over the stupid image of her wearing fur-trimmed purple robes into a maternity ward.

Longing squeezed Shane. Without CeCe, his world lacked color and spark. Six months without her? Might as well make it eternity.

The alternative was almost as bleak. Jetting to Korosol whenever her schedule permitted, living from phone call to phone call, dancing like a puppet on her string. Shane's strong, independent nature rebelled.

He had to come up with a better solution.

ONE DOWN, ONE TO GO. She'd made peace with her grandfather. Her mother was going to be harder.

CeCe hesitated outside the bedroom door. Charlotte, who had retired early, was not going to like the news that her daughter had turned down the chance to be queen.

Only a few weeks before, CeCe's main worry had been revealing her pregnancy. How long ago that seemed!

At her tap, her mother called "Come in!" CeCe opened the door.

"Well?" Charlotte lounged in bed, wearing a lavender silk nightgown and reading *New York* magazine. "Please tell me you and your grandfather have made up."

"He's absolutely wonderful." CeCe pulled a cushioned velvet chair alongside the bed.

"Not angry?"

"Not at all."

"So you're leaving tomorrow." Her mother laid her magazine aside. "Not that I'm eager to be rid of you, but what a great honor!"

"I'm not going to be queen," CeCe said.

Warring emotions flitted across her mother's strong, still-beautiful face. "You said he wasn't angry."

"He offered me the opportunity if I wanted it, but it's wrong for me," CeCe said. "And I'm wrong for Korosol."

"What kind of nonsense is this?" Charlotte appeared almost relieved to settle on a single emotion: outrage. "This is your father's heritage. Now it's your heritage!"

"That's why I was willing to go in the first place." CeCe kept her tone level. "Unfortunately, my heart isn't in it."

"Don't tell me your heart belongs to Shane O'Connell and there isn't room for anything else!" snapped Charlotte. "If your husband's so madly in love with you, why didn't he face the king himself?"

To CeCe's humiliation, tears pricked her eyes. "He doesn't love me. That isn't the point."

Contritely, Charlotte touched her daughter's cheek. "What do you mean, he doesn't love you? I'll break his head open!"

Through her tears, CeCe started to laugh. "You're like a tigress, defending your child. A minute ago, you were ready to tear me apart yourself."

"I still am," her mother said. "You can't turn down an honor like this. It isn't in your nature, and believe me, I know you."

"How can you, when until this week I didn't know myself?"

"Don't be ridiculous," Charlotte said. "I've watched you all your life. You're never happier than when you're running the show. In a lot of ways, you're like me, only tougher."

"No one's tougher than you," CeCe protested.

"They don't call you the barracuda for nothing," said her mother proudly. "You went in there and kicked those 'old boy' executives in the tail. I'd been struggling with them for years."

"You never told me that," CeCe said. "I thought you were happy with things before I came."

"No, but I figured it wasn't a good idea to say so,"

Charlotte admitted. "I didn't want to give you too much power. You'd have wiped up the floor with me."

"I wouldn't!" CeCe paused. "Well, maybe. I had so much to prove to myself and to everyone else."

"That's why I know you'll regret turning your back on a chance to be queen," Charlotte said. "Think of it! Ruler of Korosol—it's the opportunity of a lifetime."

"Yes, but not my lifetime." CeCe wondered how to explain the voyage of discovery she'd taken. "I've changed in so many ways."

"It's a temporary aberration," her mother said.

"All these years, I thought I was listening to my inner voice," CeCe said. "It told me to be strong, to fill Dad's shoes. You needed someone to help you and that someone was me."

"You did help me." Her mother's expression softened. "Tremendously."

"The voice I was listening to—well, it was mine, but only in a way." CeCe spoke her thoughts as they came to her. "It was the voice of a nine-year-old girl who'd lost her father and was trying to make everything turn out right. I'm not that child anymore. I'm going to be a mother myself."

Charlotte hugged her knees beneath the hand-stitched quilt. "What is it you want?"

"To stay in New York and spend time with my child. With Shane, too, if he feels the same way, although I don't think so," CeCe said. "I'd like to remain at De-Lacey Shipping part-time, if that's okay with you."

"Of course it is." Charlotte frowned. "I must say, I'm surprised."

"I'm sorry to let you down."

Her mother shook her head. "You haven't. You see, you're the most like me of my three daughters. I suppose I'm hardest on you because I expect the most from you."

"You're tough on Lucia," CeCe pointed out.

"That's because she asks for it," Charlotte said matter-of-factly. "Not you—you always try to live up to my expectations and beyond. But you're like a part of myself, and I never let myself get away with anything, so I put the pressure on you."

"We'll have to relate to each other differently now," CeCe warned. "I'm not simply your daughter anymore."

"Wife and mother," Charlotte said. "I respect that."

"You're not angry about Korosol?"

"I suppose not, since your grandfather's taking it well." Her mother brightened. "It's a great opportunity for Amelia."

"If she wants it."

"She could do lots and lots of good for her orphans," Charlotte said. "She'll love the idea once she gives it a little thought."

Although CeCe's sympathies went to her sister, she decided not to argue. Amelia had to speak for herself.

ON SUNDAY, SHANE FLEW to New York. Ferguson, Linzy and Betsy chattered for nearly the entire flight about the fun they'd had. The San Diego Zoo had been a favorite, and, in Ensenada, the three of them had bought enough sombreros, serapes and piñatas to nearly fill the rear cabin.

They accepted without question his explanation that CeCe had gone home a day early to talk to her family. Clearly, Ed and Linzy were too absorbed in each other to spare much thought for anyone else's romance.

Shane felt at loose ends. When he'd wished for Ferguson to develop more of a private life, he hadn't counted on being so completely left out. Still, he was pleased for his friend.

En route, he called the Carradigne apartment and asked to speak to Hester Vanderling. "Before I talk to my wife, I need to confer with her grandfather in person," he said. "Is he going to be there about, say, four o'clock?"

"No, he's attending a tea at the United Nations from two to four," replied the housekeeper. "Then he said he's going to review some paperwork at the embassy."

That was good news. Meeting him at the Carradigne place without alerting anyone else in the family wouldn't have been easy, even had he been able to secure Hester's help.

"Thanks. I'll get in touch with him there," Shane said. "I can't tell you how much I appreciate this."

"I trust you have good intentions toward my CeCe." Steel underlay her polite tone.

"Absolutely," he said.

The plane landed shortly after three o'clock. Concerned that the king might not stay at the embassy long, Shane snared a ride on one of his company's delivery trucks. It dropped him off right at First Avenue and Forty-fourth Street.

On a Sunday, the embassy wasn't open to the public, but a staffer who answered Shane's insistent knocking recognized him and opened the door. The man summoned the acting ambassador, the Duke of Raleigh, who listened to Shane's brief statement of purpose and ushered him upstairs.

He found the king seated at a desk in a luxurious office. His Royal Highness fixed Shane with a knowing gaze when he entered.

"Ah," said Easton. "I was expecting you. Thank you, Cade."

"Happy to be of service, Your Majesty." The ambassador withdrew.

"Did Mrs. Vanderling call?" Shane asked.

"No one called. I knew you would come." After rising to shake hands, the monarch gestured him to a chair.

There was something imposing about King Easton, despite his courtesy. The man sat ramrod straight, and his eyes seemed to probe beyond the surface right to a person's heart.

"I'll speak plainly," Shane said.

"Please do."

"The first time we met, you questioned my motives." He hadn't forgotten a word of that conversation. "You implied I was trying to climb the social ladder by marrying royalty."

"Not very tactful of me, was it?" the king said.

Surprised at the mild response, Shane nearly lost his train of thought. He quickly found it again. "I assured you then and I assure you now that I have no ambition to advance myself through my marriage."

"I accept your assurance."

"However," Shane said, "your country's going to have to accept me as its Prince Consort, or whatever you call the husband of the queen, because I'm not giving up my wife and I want to be there to watch my child grow up."

"I see." It was impossible to read a reaction in the king's bland expression.

"I already have offices in California and New York, and I'll be moving my corporate headquarters to Korosol." To his embarrassment, Shane couldn't remember the name of the capital city, so he avoided being specific. "I've been intending to expand in Europe, anyway, and having my company based there should be good for your country's economy."

"It sounds like an excellent plan," said CeCe's grandfather. "It's too bad your wife has turned down the chance to be queen, although I'd still encourage you to make Korosol the base of your European operations."

Shane had opened his mouth to continue his argument when the king's meaning hit him. "She said no?"

"She wants to spend time with her child," the man said. "And, I presume, with her husband."

After the way he'd treated her, Shane couldn't believe

his beloved barracuda wanted anything to do with him. "She told you this?"

"She did."

He stood up. "Sir, I don't know how to thank you."

"I haven't done anything," the king said. "Except enjoy watching a good love story unfold."

"I'm sorry I messed up your plans," Shane added. "Not terribly sorry, though."

"Do me a favor," the king said.

"Of course. What is it?"

"Be happy."

"Yes, sir!"

LINZY CALLED CECE AT HOME to rave about the trip and ask if it was all right to take a day of sick leave on Monday, as Betsy was coming down with a cold. "I know I'm not the one who's sick, but…"

"You almost never use your sick leave, and you're entitled to it. Of course you should take off." Hesitantly, CeCe asked, "Did Shane fly back with you?"

"He sure did." Linzy went into a rapturous description of their flight and how intently the great Mr. O'Connell had listened to every detail of her cruise.

Sure he had, CeCe thought. He'd been lost in his own reflections and pretending to listen. She wondered what he'd really been thinking about. Probably California fuel prices.

He was here in New York. Was he going to call? Why hadn't he phoned already?

She didn't intend to sit around waiting. The man owed her…he had a duty to…

She stood in her bedroom and inhaled the essence of him, which had permeated the place during their week here. She missed him with every cell of her body.

What she needed was his arms around her. If she had

to storm his apartment to get it, that's what she was going to do.

I'M SORRY I ACTED like an idiot, Shane rehearsed during his cab ride to Central Park West. *I shouldn't have let you leave.*

That sounded too wimpy. CeCe Carradigne was not a woman to give the advantage to, even if she did care for him.

I hear you deep-sixed the throne. If I had anything to do with it, all I can say is, hurray!

Too flippant. She might be agonizing over her decision and get seriously ticked off.

It wasn't easy being in love with a strong-willed woman. Still, Shane conceded, it would never be boring, either.

As it turned out, his preparations came to naught. CeCe wasn't at her apartment and the guards didn't know where she'd gone.

Disappointed, Shane headed for home.

When he reached it, he wasn't surprised to find the door unlocked. It was typical of Ferguson to unpack Shane's suitcase immediately.

"Hey, why don't you take off the rest of the..." he began as he stepped inside. The rest of the sentence vanished from his mind.

CeCe Carradigne was moving the furniture.

Reddish-blond hair falling across her face and a smoke-green dress hiked up to reveal an intriguing amount of leg, she was shoving a heavy chair from its corner into the center of the room. A sectional couch had already been shifted into a new alignment.

"Stop that!" Shane said. "You're pregnant. You shouldn't be lifting things."

"I'm not lifting them, I'm pushing them." His wife shook a hank of hair off her forehead. "Doesn't anyone ever sit down in this room? I don't see how they could talk across those vast spaces.''

"I sit in this room," he said.

"Just you?"

"Ed has been known to read a magazine in here."

"No wonder it looks unused! You treat it like a hotel lobby." Straightening, CeCe dusted off her hands. "We've got a few things to talk about."

"I just met with your grandfather," Shane said.

"You did?" She frowned. "How'd it go?"

"Oh, we talked business." Shane closed the door behind him. "We didn't mention you at all."

"Sure you didn't!"

"Except for the fact that I love you and want to spend the rest of my life with you," he amended.

She went absolutely still. It was the quietest he had ever seen CeCe.

"Are you joking?" she asked at last.

"Not even a little bit," Shane said. "I was willing to move to Korosol for your sake. Thank goodness I don't have to."

"You shouldn't assume I'm going to fall into your arms," warned his wife.

"You aren't?"

"I didn't say I wasn't going to do it. I said you shouldn't take it for granted."

"If there's one thing I will never do," Shane said, "it's take you for granted."

CeCe regarded him with mingled joy and disbelief. "What about those things you accused me of in California? You told me I was asking too much."

"I didn't...did I?" he protested.

"You called me a spoiled brat." Her voice quavered.

"I called you a spoiled princess."

"That's no better!"

"You were tearing me apart," Shane said. "I wasn't in my right mind."

"Are you sure you're in your right mind now?" It was obvious CeCe couldn't quite bring herself to believe the truth.

"More or less sure," he joked. "How about you? The last thing I expected was to find you moving my furniture."

"I wanted this place to feel like home." She planted her hands on her hips. "Did you really offer to move to Korosol just to be with me?"

"Yes." Shane could hardly stand to leave so much space between them, yet he knew his wife needed to absorb this momentous change in their lives. "I heard you gave up the chance to be queen. Are you sure you won't regret it?"

"I've never been more sure of anything," CeCe said.

"I was hoping you were even more sure that you loved me." Shane waited, still uncertain exactly what her response would be.

"For me, loving you is like breathing and dreaming and growing. It's so much a part of me that I can't imagine life without it," she said. "Even when I thought you didn't want me—"

"I never said that!" He was dismayed. "CeCe, I was trying to keep my bargain, to give you the freedom to go your own way."

"I am going my own way," she said. "Being with you gives me all the freedom I need."

"Me, too." Shane felt light-headed with joy. His dream was coming true. He was going to wake up every morning with CeCe in his arms and together they would watch their child grow, every step of the way.

"Good." Her eyes sparkled. "So we agree. Now, will you help me rearrange the furniture so we can sit on it properly?"

"I'm sure we can find a better use for it," Shane said. "Particularly this sofa. It's oversize, you'll notice. I've always suspected it would be perfect for...is Ferguson here?"

"He left."

"Then let me say that if we remove some of these clothes, I'll show you what I mean."

"I get a personal demonstration?"

"Very personal," he said, and reached for her.

CeCe made it clear, as she caught his hands and pulled him down onto the couch, that she'd already figured out what he had in mind. And she thoroughly agreed with him.

Epilogue

It was Monday morning by the time they came up for air. As she entered the bedroom after showering, CeCe heard Shane put in a call to his office and inform his secretary that he'd be late.

"I still intend to conquer the world," he said after hanging up. "I'm just not in as much of a hurry as I used to be."

Appreciatively, CeCe studied her half-dressed husband. "It's amazing how love can change your perspective." She stretched, and enjoyed the way his gaze glued itself to her body.

"Did I mention I like that green outfit?" he said, watching her slip it on. "I liked it even better when it was on the floor, though."

"We need to go tell my mother and grandfather that we've worked things out," CeCe said. "We'll have lots of time together after I move in here. I am moving in, aren't I?"

"Sure. Or we can buy someplace bigger," he said. "We'll need an extra office for you and another bedroom for the baby. Maybe two extra bedrooms."

"Two?" CeCe asked. "I thought you didn't like children."

"I changed my mind." He gave her a rueful grin. "Of course, if you don't want more..."

"I'd love them!" She hugged him. "And yes, I think we need someplace bigger. I'll enjoy looking as soon as I cut back my hours."

"When will that be?" he asked.

"Soon. I want to enjoy this pregnancy." CeCe reflected for a moment. "Still, I don't want to let the execs think they can slip back into their sloppy old habits. I discovered my mother was grateful for the way I whipped them into line."

"We're a team now." Shane's expression grew serious as he buckled his belt. "We're going to be working together more closely than ever, and if Charlotte needs any help when you're not available, she can count on me."

"I'll tell her." A team. CeCe relished the idea that, from now on, she could share her responsibilities. And her joys.

She was still floating on a cloud when they reached the Carradigne apartment. As she and Shane exited the elevator, she heard agitated voices from the kitchen.

"I have no idea!" Charlotte was saying. "She won't talk to me."

"This Katwell woman likes to sensationalize," came King Easton's response. "I'm sure Amelia has a reasonable explanation."

"Oh, no." CeCe exchanged glances with Shane. "I wonder what's happened now."

"I knew we should have read the newspapers before we came," he said. "Let's hope it works out as well as the last bombshell that newspaper dropped on your family."

CeCe hurried to the kitchen with her husband. Before she could speak, an agitated Charlotte thrust the *Chronicle* into her hand, folded open to Krissy Katwell's column.

"Princess in Marriage Tangle!" screamed the headline.

"Barely have the shock waves abated from Princess Cecelia Carradigne's surprise pregnancy than this reporter has uncovered another scandal in the family. Her sister Amelia is secretly married!" read the opening paragraph.

"Details are not immediately available, but we learned the news from an unimpeachable source," it went on. *"We'll have more juicy facts soon. Much more!"*

Lucia set down her coffee cup. "Can you believe this? m sure it's not true." Still, Lucia must have been curi- or why else had she come here for breakfast this ng? CeCe noted.

phone rang and, in another room, Hester answered. minutes later, when the housekeeper arrived in the chen, Charlotte demanded to know who had called.

"A man, asking for Miss Amelia," Hester said. "She took the call."

"Did he give a name?" asked the king.

"I'm sorry, Your Majesty, he did not. Your granddaughter didn't seem surprised to hear from him, by the way," Hester said.

"The plot thickens," murmured Shane.

Charlotte blinked at him. "Oh! So CeCe did spend last night with you. My father-in-law thought so."

"I'm sorry I didn't let you know," CeCe said. "We were busy…" She stopped. "Anyway, I'm going to see if Amelia needs anything. I remember how stunned I was when Krissy the Kat did a number on me."

Without waiting for reactions, she hurried upstairs and along the gallery toward her sister's suite. The phone conversation must have ended, since she didn't hear Amelia speaking, so she rapped on the door.

"It's me, CeCe," she called. "Are you all right?"

"Don't ask," came her sister's voice.

"I don't mean to be nosy," she said, "but everyone wants to know who was on the phone. Would you mind…"

"Tell them it's my husband!" wailed Amelia. "And that's all I have to say right now!"

Her sister was married? To whom? CeCe wondered on her way downstairs. Good heavens, her grandfather was going to think they were all crazy.

In the kitchen, she repeated what Amelia had said. No one, not even Lucia, could guess at the groom's identity.

Shane alone wasn't fazed. "I'm sure he's a terrific guy," he said. "The Carradigne women have great taste."

"We do, don't we?" CeCe slipped an arm around his waist.

"She's going to ruin everything!" Charlotte moaned. "How could she behave so badly?"

"You ought to trust your daughters," said Lucia. "We're more sensible than you think."

"I hate to ask it," said the king, "but do you have any secrets we should know about, my dear?"

"I'm afraid not," Lucia said. "My life isn't that interesting."

"The important thing is Amelia's happiness," CeCe said. "I hope this works out for her. We each deserve a happy ending."

"I'm going to have a nervous breakdown," said Charlotte. "No, cancel that. I'd rather give some of my executives a nervous breakdown."

"That sounds like fun," said CeCe. "When do we start?"

To her surprise, her mother laughed. It must have been contagious, because soon they were all laughing, even the king.

CeCe understood why. It was because, even if fate

didn't make things easy for them, the Carradignes couldn't help having fun along the way.

She rested her cheek on Shane's shoulder and yielded to a sense of pure delight.

*   *   *   *   *

Who is Amelia's husband?
Find out in the next installment of

THE CARRADIGNES:
AMERICAN ROYALTY

#917
THE UNLAWFULLY WEDDED PRINCESS

by Kara Lennox
Available April 2002
at a store near you.

A royal monarch's search for an heir leads
him to three American princesses in

The Carradignes: American Royalty

from

HARLEQUIN®

AMERICAN Romance®

King Easton's second choice for the crown is
Princess Amelia Carradigne, the peacekeeper of
the family. But Amelia has a little secret of her own…her
clandestine marriage to a mercenary—
under an assumed name. Now news of her unlawful
has been leaked to the press and her
"husband" has returned for some answers!

Don't miss:

THE UNLAWFULLY WEDDED PRINCESS
by Kara Lennox   April 2002

And check out these other titles in the series:

THE IMPROPERLY PREGNANT PRINCESS
by Jacqueline Diamond   March 2002

THE SIMPLY SCANDALOUS PRINCESS
by Michele Dunaway   May 2002

And a tie-in title from
HARLEQUIN®
INTRIGUE®

THE DUKE'S COVERT MISSION
by Julie Miller   June 2002

Available at your favorite retail outlet.

HARLEQUIN®
Makes any time special ®

Visit us at www.eHarlequin.com

HARAR2